SCYTHE
DEVIL DADDIES MC
BOOK 2

PEPPER NORTH

PHOTOGRAPHY BY
JW PHOTOGRAPHY

COVER MODEL
JOEL ROS

Pepper North
With a Wink Publishing, LLC

Text copyright© 2025 Pepper North®
All Rights Reserved

Pepper North® is a registered trademark.
All rights reserved.

NO AI TRAINING: Without in any way limiting the author's [and publisher's] exclusive rights under copyright, any use of this publication to "train" generative artificial intelligence (AI) technologies to generate text is expressly prohibited. The author reserves all rights to license uses of this work for generative AI training and development of machine learning language models.

CHAPTER 1

Please let this work. Please don't let me run into anyone I know. Winnie slid out of her eleven-year-old sedan and smoothed down her borrowed dress. The evening air whisked through the gaps between the straps, making her shiver. She rolled her eyes. Of course Belinda would consider this to be a complete outfit. Winnie forced herself to walk away from the safety her car offered.

"You can do this!" she told herself sternly.

"Baby, in that dress, you can do anything," a male voice assured her.

Winnie turned to see a man leaning against his motorcycle, smoking a cigarette. He could snap her in half with one arm tied behind his back. She waved a hand nervously and skittered past, almost rolling her ankle as she tried to balance on the borrowed, sky-high stilettos.

A line had already formed at the entrance of Inferno. Joining it, she restrained herself from correcting those who jumped ahead of her to join their friends. *These are not second graders you need to teach, Winnie.*

She struggled to keep from touching the itchy makeup Belinda had piled on her face as she slowly advanced to the door. *Please don't let that giant man turn me away again!*

Crap! He's there. The doorman stopped checking IDs to kiss his girlfriend. Maybe Winnie could scoot around him while he was distracted. She ran into his powerful arm as he blocked her. *Crap!* Now he'd never let her in.

"ID," a rough voice demanded.

Winnie glanced up to see another Devil Daddies MC member had stepped in to screen people. Gathering her courage and donning the bored expression Winnie saw often on her stepsister's face, Winnie extended her license. He gripped the small card in his hand and looked back and forth between her picture and her person.

"Not cool," the regular doorman growled after ending his kiss and turning toward the door. He held out his hand to take her ID from the other biker.

"Wraith," his girlfriend said as she patted his massive thigh.

He scanned her image and her face several times as well. When he opened his mouth, Winnie could tell he was going to send her away.

Her already fast heart rate skyrocketed. She had to get to Lucien. He was the only one who could help her.

Suddenly, the burly doorman looked at the curvy woman at his side. She nodded, and after a slight hesitation, he handed back her ID.

"Welcome to Inferno. Don't cause trouble."

"No, sir. Thank you." Winnie clutched her ID and ran as fast as her high heels would allow her into the crowd. A sign caught her eye near the door, and she raced to the women's restroom and escaped into a stall to recover. Collapsing on the toilet, she forced herself to slow her breathing. She'd made it inside. Getting to Lucien was the next challenge.

After carefully patting the panic sweat from her face so she didn't screw up her makeup, Winnie emerged from the stall and washed her hands. The other women in the bathroom chatted and added fresh layers of lipstick over their already red lips.

They greeted her as if she were a regular, complimenting her on her dress and shoes. Winnie appreciated their kindness. It helped her restore her bravery.

Winnie emerged determined and in control. Staring at the interior of Inferno for the first time, she paused to take in the vast space and the crowd. No wonder they had no problem turning people away. It was packed. The dimmed lighting filled most of the area but there were two main bar areas lit by spotlights and glowing neon signs. One area held tables where a lot of people ate. A dance floor extended from one side with an elevated DJ booth. Immediately, Winnie wished she had come to enjoy herself.

That thought reminded Winnie of her mission. Tugging at her short dress, she forced herself to focus and walked forward into the crowd. She ignored her wobbly step in the heels. *I can do this.*

She scanned the dimly lit interior of Inferno. Male and female bartenders put together drinks behind a huge winding bar. No flashy tossing of bottles or smoking cocktails in this place. Inferno seemed to specialize in beer and frozen drinks with whiskies and other hard liquors.

When a server walked by with a huge tray, she asked, "Where can I find Lucien?"

The woman shook her head. "You don't."

What did that mean? Winnie stared after her as the server adeptly wove through the boisterous partiers. Winnie lifted the scant fraction of an inch more she could rise onto her toes and scanned the crowd. If she were the boss of all this, where would she hide?

"Why do you want to see Lucien?"

The barked question made her jump. Winnie came down on the heels and wobbled. She reached out to grab something to stabilize herself and regain her balance. She met the man's accusing eyes and blurted, "You scared me. You should talk nicely to others."

"I should talk nicely to others? I'll get right on that." He looked down at her hand wrapped around his forearm.

"Oh! Sorry." Winnie snatched her hand from him, trying not to dwell on how hard his muscles were.

"Why are you looking for Lucien?" he repeated. His tone had not improved.

It was the man who'd scanned her ID at the door. Now that the stress of getting inside had faded slightly, Winnie realized how drool-worthy this biker was. Even in the dim light, she could see his shiny chestnut-brown hair and handsome face. She wanted to lean forward to check if his eyes were blue or green, but controlled herself. His chest and arms bulged with strength. When he cleared his throat, she realized she was staring.

"Sorry. I'd like to show him a collection I think he'll find interesting." She told him the truth.

"He won't. Enjoy yourself at Inferno or go home. Lucien doesn't meet with anyone."

The massive biker turned and stalked away. *Jerk!* Winnie noted the name written on his leather vest. Scythe. An image of the grim reaper popped into her head. The representation of death carried a scythe, right? That was a terrifying thought.

Pulling herself together, Winnie promised herself she would collapse into a melting ball of anxiety when she got to her car—maybe better, at home. Someone might still see her in the parking lot. She glanced around the bar, searching for any familiar faces. Not spotting any, she found the courage to continue.

Scythe was a handsome, leather-clad, muscular bad boy. Winnie surreptitiously wiped the corners of her mouth in case she was actually drooling. Of course she wasn't. She shook off her anxiety and vowed to show him.

Winnie returned to scanning the bar. She shook her hand when she realized she was rubbing her fingers together as if she were caressing his arm. Forcing herself to concentrate, she zeroed in on a staircase with another biker standing at the bottom. That had to be the way to Lucien.

Striding as purposefully as she could on those precarious heels, Winnie made a beeline for the biker. Winnie cursed her former middle school teacher's withering assessment of her acting skills that always rebounded into her mind at a time like this and gathered her bravado. She shook the self-doubt from her mind and stopped in front of the guard in what she hoped was a vampish pose.

"Hi, there, tall, dark, and handsome."

The man bristled, and Winnie realized she towered over him in the four-inch heels. "I have an appointment with Lucien."

"No, you don't," he said, staring her down with even more vehemence now.

She was the worst liar ever. Winnie floundered for something to say before admitting, "You're right. I don't, but I need to talk to him. I don't suppose I could sneak past you for a couple of minutes?"

Winnie bit her lip as she exuded positive vibes to get him to agree. He had to let her see Lucien.

"Not happening."

"You didn't even think about it," she protested. Maybe he wanted a bribe. She fumbled with her phone wallet, opening section after section to find her money.

"You are really bad at this," he growled.

She darted a glance at his face, hoping his attitude was softening at her incompetence. Nope. Winnie tried the truth. "I am. Look. I have a collection of rare guns I need to unload, and everyone says Lucien is the one who would buy them."

"Give me names," a familiar voice demanded behind her, making Winnie whirl around to face the biker she'd talked to previously.

Crap! Him again? Winnie swallowed hard.

"I'll take care of this, Gamble."

"Thanks, Scythe." Gamble looked past her to monitor the crowd.

"Hi, Scythe. Thanks for coming to help." Winnie tried to be positive.

Scythe wrapped his fingers around her biceps and headed for the door, towing her with him.

"Wait, I can't walk that fast," Winnie protested, teetering desperately on the stilettos.

"Why are you wearing those things?" Scythe demanded before sweeping her off her feet and carrying her.

"Ooh!" While embarrassed by the crowd who watched their progress toward the door with interest, Winnie couldn't help but enjoy being in his powerful arms. Heaven knew no one had ever carried her books, much less her! She sniffed his chest, savoring his manly cologne. Were bikers supposed to smell this good?

"Stop that," Scythe growled.

To distract him from noticing her heated cheeks, Winnie fumbled with her wallet again.

"If you try to bribe me...."

"Oh, no. I wouldn't do that. Here, look!"

Winnie lifted her phone into his line of sight, displaying one of the photos she'd taken of her stepfather's collection. Scythe stopped in his tracks. "That's just the first picture. I have hundreds to show Lucien," she assured him.

Scythe pivoted 180 degrees and headed for the staircase. Gamble stepped out of the way without a word.

Feeling like a princess, Winnie noticed his breathing didn't change as he climbed the steps, carrying her easily in his arms. He really was in great shape. "You're not a fireman, are you?"

Scythe shook his head, making her wonder.

"Does that mean no, you're not a firefighter?"

"Fuck, woman. You are exasperating!"

Winnie blinked away the tears that filled her eyes at his harsh assessment and whispered, "Sorry." She didn't expect a response from him. Inferno was so loud, he'd never hear her apology, but she needed to tell him. Somehow, she rubbed people wrong, despite her best intentions.

She forced herself to stay quiet as he opened the door and carried her through into a dark office lit only by the bank of windows, providing a bird's eye view of the bustling bar floor. A heavily tattooed man looked up from a pile of papers on his desk to stare at them. Thankfully, Winnie was relieved of having to talk as Scythe set her down on the troublesome shoes.

"Yes?" Lucien asked.

His voice made Winnie shiver. He sounded like a man who could rip off her ears and eat them in front of her. Maybe this was a bad idea. She forced herself to stand straight and tugged the borrowed dress into place. Unfortunately, one of the straps had hooked on the metal buckle at the bottom of Scythe's leather jacket.

Winnie tried to help, but Scythe lifted her hands away with the instruction, "Let me do it." She stood, patiently waiting for long seconds before he freed himself.

"Thank you, Winnifred," Scythe said quietly, meeting her eyes without the angry glare that had shone from his eyes all night.

"Winnie," she corrected him.

"I don't want to interrupt this sweet moment, but this is my office. Scythe, is this your Little…."

Scythe jumped in to stop him with a shake of his head. "This is Winnifred, Winnie, Bradley." He recited her address and added, "She came to see you after someone recommended that you would buy a collection of firearms."

"You have an excellent memory," Winnie commended him. "You saw my ID for thirty seconds and you remember all that?"

"Who?" Lucien barked.

"She hasn't told me yet."

Both men studied Winnie. She swallowed hard. This was worse than the meeting with the principal and the angry father last week. Time for Super Winnie. She pulled on her professional personality and smiled. "Who?"

"Who recommended you come to see me about guns?" Lucien asked, before looking at Scythe to demand, "Did you check her for wires?"

"That outfit would make wires hard to hide," Scythe pointed out before confiscating her small phone wallet and flipping through it.

"Hey. You can't do that," Winnie protested.

"Better him than me," Lucien said with a searing glare. "Who gave you my name?"

"Pull up the photo you showed me," Scythe directed, removing the phone from the wallet. He knelt at her feet to unfasten her shoes. A secret part of Winnie loved having him taking care of her. A sudden flash of a scene from one of those naughty books she devoured like candy popped into her mind.

"Well?" Lucien drew her attention back to him.

"My uncle, Stanley, suggested you. He said you're an arms dealer who's been buying up everyone's guns." Winnie threw her relative under the bus.

"Stanley Bradley?" Lucien asked, making a note.

"Underhall. Stanley Underhall. He's dead now." She stopped and sniffed sadly before pulling herself together to continue. "He died with my stepfather in a tragic barbecue grill explosion. It might sound like a joke, but it wasn't."

"The photo," Scythe reminded her as he lifted one foot and then the other to remove her shoes.

Winnie whispered, "Thank you," before sighing with relief as her toes curled into the thick carpet. He might try to be a meanie, but she suspected Scythe concealed a very sweet side from the world.

When he rose to loom over her staring, Winnie remembered what he'd asked her to do. She opened her phone and located the picture as Scythe stood. He tossed her shoes onto one of the chairs in front of Lucien's desk before stripping the phone out of her hand and passing it to Lucien.

"A flamethrower?" Lucien asked in disbelief.

"That's not the photo she showed me. Scroll," Scythe suggested as he threaded his fingers through Winnie's hair.

"Hey! It took a lot of hair spray to create this look!" Winnie protested, whacking at his hands. He didn't even pause.

"She's clean, boss."

"Where is this collection?" Lucien asked.

"That's for me to know and you to find out if you're interested," Winnie told him pertly. She second-guessed her refusal to answer when Lucien drew his eyebrows together in a glower that could have made one of the dominant heroes from her spicy romances shake in their boots.

"Oh, I'm interested," Lucien confirmed.

Lucien glanced toward Scythe. Winnie wished she could read either man's expressions. She suspected that pointed look exchanged a lot of information.

"It's at my mother's house. I'd just give it to you, but...."

"How many trucks do we need?" Lucien asked.

"Trucks?" she repeated, not following him.

"To retrieve the guns. How many truckloads will it take?"

"A big truck like a semi or a small truck like a pickup?" Winnie asked.

"Think a delivery van," Scythe said.

"One. There are only five big boxes. They're heavy. I can't move them." Winnie didn't want anyone to hurt themselves.

"We'll manage," Scythe assured her.

Winnie considered his muscles and nodded. "You're more ripped than me." She made a fist and curled her forearm to reveal a miniscule biceps.

Again, with the exchange of glances between the men.

"That's not very nice," she muttered.

"What's not nice?" Scythe asked.

"You're talking about me. And not nicely." She reused that word deliberately to make her point.

"Let's go get those guns, Winnifred," Scythe said, sounding weary.

"Take Street, Hellcat, and Vex," Lucien directed. "I'll have them meet you at the back door."

"And you'll pay me?" Winnie made herself ask.

"Yes, Winnie. I'll make sure you get paid," Scythe told her.

"Thank you!" She hurried to pick up her shoes as Scythe steered her toward the door. Peering over her shoulder, she called, "Nice meeting you, Mr. Lucien."

"It has been a novelty for me, Winnifred," Lucien told her gently.

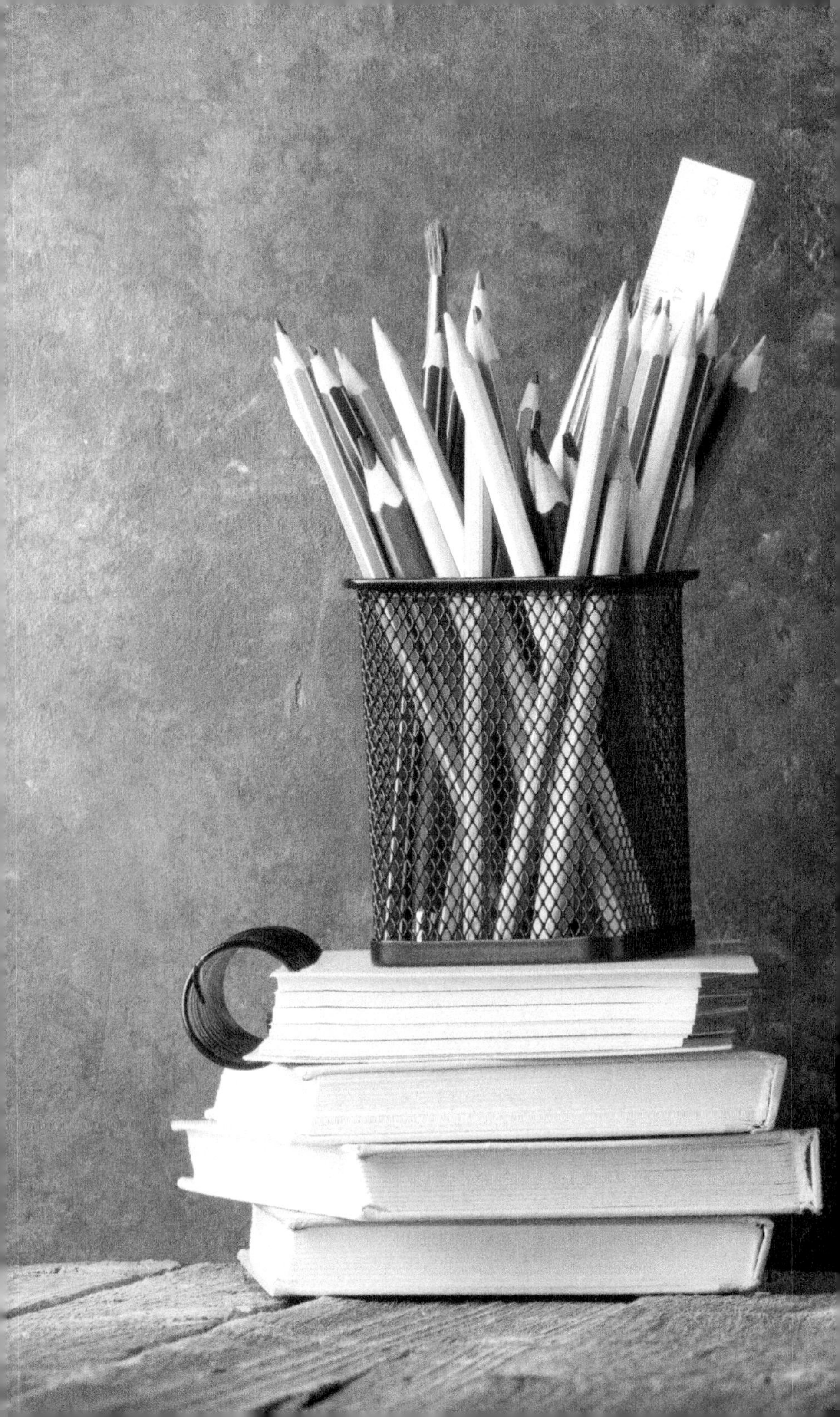

CHAPTER 2

The music swirled around them as Scythe and Winnie walked through the door. They made it down three steps before Winnie stopped in her tracks as she stared down at the crowd.

"That can't be. Oh, no! Hide me!" Winnie dove under Scythe's leather cut and hid her face against his chest.

For once in his life, Scythe had no idea what to do. Dealing with the most pressing problem, he pulled the talon heels away from where they dug dangerously close to his privates after she'd trapped them between their bodies. He awkwardly wrapped his arms around her shoulders and leaned down to ask, "Winnifred? Can you walk or do you need me to carry you out?"

"Is he still staring?"

"Who?"

"That guy down there in the brown suit, blue shirt, and green tie."

Scythe shook his head at that description. Nobody dressed like that at Inferno. He scanned the crowd and found him. "He looks like an insurance salesman. Who let him in?"

"He's the superintendent of my school district. He'll fire me if he catches me here—dressed like this!" She could hear his complaint against her already, declaring her someone with low morals in close contact with impressionable kids. Adam Young had taught social studies and coached for three years before applying for an administrative position. When he received his doctorate, he moved up the ladder at central office.

"Let's get you out of here. Keep your face hidden." Scythe reached around Winnie and hoisted the barely dressed woman off the ground. She was as stiff as a log.

Scythe couldn't believe the amount of trust she'd placed in him, a virtual stranger, and one who'd not treated her with kid gloves. He'd battled his admiration of her pluck and quirkiness during the whole interaction. Scythe bet her students loved her.

"Everything okay, Scythe?" Gamble asked as he reached the end of the stairs.

"Fine."

"Better have her move so the audience watching you doesn't think you are carrying a dead body out of Lucien's office," Gamble suggested.

Winnie's head reared back. His hands full of Winnifred, Scythe leaned his face close to hers to block everyone's view. "Hide, Chipmunk."

She nodded and extended her neck to press a kiss to his cheek. Inwardly, Scythe growled at that offense. He wasn't a golden retriever. Out of the corner of his eye, Scythe watched the man's head turn to focus on them. His hands full, Scythe did the only thing he could to hide her. He pressed his mouth to hers and froze when her lips moved hungrily under his. Surprised by her passion, he took a fraction of a second to respond as intensely as she did.

Scythe tightened one arm around her torso and slid the other hand up to press her forehead to his chest as he raised his head. With her features hidden once again, he strode for the rear entrance, weaving his way through the crowd. He passed the man in the suit, avoiding his gaze.

Once outside the back door, he carried her past the smokers and vapers to a shadowy patch. Setting her bare feet on the concrete, Scythe said, "He didn't see your face. Sorry about the kiss. I had to act fast there."

"It was a solid C+. I'm sure with practice you can get better. Maybe you have a friend who could help you fine-tune your skills?"

"What are you talking about?" he asked, completely baffled.

"Oh, sorry. I always rate kisses. You got a C+. That's good...." Her voice trailed away.

"You think I need to practice kissing?"

"Well, only if you want to get better," she suggested.

Scythe shook his head and chose to abandon this line of conversation. "Let's go get the supplies you've promised."

He unlocked the gate into the warehouse area behind Inferno and escorted her into the area. Mud from that day's workmen covered the pathway. When she paused, unwilling to step into the muck, Scythe lifted her to drape over his shoulder. As she sputtered with indignation, he relocked the gate.

"Settle down. I'll have you in the truck soon. Next time, wear shoes you can walk in."

"I can walk in those heels!"

"Hey, Scythe. I hear we're going with you," a rough voice said from in front of them.

Winnie pushed against his waist as she scrambled to lever herself up to see the man waiting for them.

"Whoa!" Scythe warned. To protect himself from her flailing feet, which got way too close to his privates in her quest, he sighed and tugged her into his arms in front of him.

"Better?"

"Thank you," she answered pertly and waved at the three men waiting for them.

"Right. This is Street, Hellcat, and Vex. This is Winnifred Bradley." He introduced her to the crew.

"Winnie," she interrupted.

"Winnie," he corrected himself and tried to ignore the grins on his MC brothers' faces. "Vex, you drive. Get one of the delivery vans."

As his MC brother jogged away, Scythe waited quietly with the others at the entrance of the warehouse. That silence lasted exactly sixty-seven seconds. He knew because he'd started counting immediately.

"So, what do you do in there? Does the business have anything to do with guns? Are you all illegal gun runners?" Winnie pelted them with inquiries.

"What the hell?" Street asked, staring incredulously at the woman in Scythe's arms.

"She's okay. I must have dangled her upside down too long," Scythe created an excuse for the woman who didn't seem to have a filter.

"Am I not supposed to ask those questions?" Winnie checked with Scythe in a too loud whisper that reached everyone's ears.

"No, Chipmunk. Never ask questions like that."

"Because they're true or false?" she persisted.

"Oh, look! Vex is pulling the truck up." Scythe didn't answer her. This woman had less self-awareness than the baby goats he'd raised on his parents' farm years ago. And talked more too.

Street and Hellcat let themselves into the back of the delivery vehicle as Scythe lifted Winnie into the cab and crowded in after her. He grabbed the middle seatbelt and tugged it around her before securing his own. When she scooted closer to him, Scythe pretended not to celebrate that she preferred sitting plastered against him instead of Vex. He lifted his arm from between them and wrapped it around her shoulders, allowing her to shift over a bit more.

"Where to, Scythe?"

"Winnifred, can you tell him your address?"

"Winnie. Of course." She recited it slowly and clearly, as if speaking to a child.

When Vex looked at Scythe in disbelief, Scythe shook his head and asked Winnie, "What grade do you teach?"

"Second. It's my favorite. The kids love to learn."

Vex exchanged a glance with Scythe before nodding thoughtfully. "My elementary teachers didn't dress like that."

"Keep your eyes to yourself, Vex. She wore this to make it into Inferno."

"Can you believe they turned me away twice? I overheard something that sounded like 'too churchy', so I borrowed this dress," Winnie explained as they merged into traffic.

"And got in," Vex said. "She made it upstairs to talk to Lucien?"

"Winnifred is extremely determined," Scythe said.

"A problem solver," Winnie corrected. "And it's Winnie. Should I add that to the notes I'm going to write out for you?"

"Notes?" Vex asked, obviously amused by the situation.

"Scythe wishes to improve his kissing technique. I promised to jot down some notes for him," Winnie shared.

"His... kissing technique?" Vex choked, repeating that phrase.

"You tell anyone else this, and I'll slash your tires for the next year. Every. Single. Day," Scythe assured him, meeting his gaze directly.

"That's not nice. Vex isn't the reason you can't kiss," Winnie chirped before she turned to stare at Scythe with her mouth open in shock. "Or is he? You're gay, aren't you? That's why you didn't kiss a girl well."

While Vex practically hyperventilated with laughter, Scythe corrected her false assumption. "No, Chipmunk. I'm not gay."

"Okay...," she answered, drawing out her response as if she weren't too positive he was telling the truth.

"Two years." Scythe corrected himself, glaring pointedly at Vex.

His phone buzzed with a message. Since he only had the

MC's chat notify him of updates, Scythe pulled out his device to see what had happened. "You're a dead man, Street."

"At least I'm a good kisser." The answer came from the back. Of course, Street and Hellcat were listening through the vent into the storage area of the vehicle.

"Have you had that confirmed?" Winnie asked. Silence followed that question, making Scythe grin.

The rest of the trip was quiet as they entered a middle-class, suburban neighborhood. Vex stopped in front of a house surrounded by the proverbial white picket fence.

"Is this it?" he asked.

"Yep. This is my mom's house. Let me go inside and tell her what's happening." She pushed at Scythe's torso, and he unfastened their seat belts before he slid from the truck.

Scythe lifted her out and set her on the smooth driveway. He followed her as she rushed to the front door and opened the obviously unlocked door. As he stood in the doorway, Winnie darted forward to turn on a small lamp. A hospital bed became visible in the middle of what had been a living room previously. The couch and chairs hugged the walls.

"Winnie?" a weak voice sounded from the bed.

"Hi, Mom. I did it. The guys are here to collect Niles's collection. Now we can get you that next treatment," Winnie said softly as she brushed the frail woman's hair from her face.

"You are such an angel. Were they nice?" The whisper-soft voice clued Scythe in more than the hospital bed alone that Winnie's mother was seriously ill.

He swallowed hard as flashes of standing in the hospital beside his father after the accident filled his mind. That awful day had taken his dad and eventually forced his mother to sell the family farm. Even from a short distance away, Scythe could sense that Winnie's mother was not long for this world. He forced himself to pay attention.

"Of course, Mom. The men will make some noise for a while. Try to go back to sleep if you can."

Those tired eyes closed once again. When Winnie rejoined him, he wrapped an arm around her waist in comfort and leaned down to whisper, "I'll tell the guys to be quiet."

She nodded as tears coursed over her cheeks, creating tracks in the thick makeup. "Thanks."

Before walking out the door, he glanced over his shoulder. Winnie wrapped her arms around herself. Damn, this wasn't a good situation. He could connect all the dots easily.

Back at the truck, he gathered his brothers. "Winnie's mother is seriously ill in the living room. Let's get this accomplished as quickly and quietly as possible."

The guys took one look at his face and sobered.

"Got it, Scythe," Street answered for them.

They followed him silently to the front door. Winnie held a handful of tissues in her hand and had wiped away the tears. Scythe didn't have the heart to tell her one of her false eyelashes had fallen off.

"Let me show you where the boxes are." She led them downstairs to the basement. "I'm afraid you'll have to move some of this stuff to get to them. It's those black boxes back there, as well as this one I opened to take the photos."

Vex whistled low. "Is that a flamethrower?"

"I thought they were guns. Are you still interested in them? Lucien seemed to be," Winnie said, sounding nervous.

"Some are guns, Chipmunk. Others are equally collectible. Lucien will buy what you have," Scythe assured her.

"Oh, good. Can I just leave it to you?"

"We've got this," Scythe assured her. He understood why she needed the money now. Scythe would make sure Lucien treated her fairly.

He waited until she disappeared up the stairs before warning the others. "I don't know what else we're going to find, but none of this should be in the basement of a house that the residents don't lock. We'll take everything and take an inventory of everything in the warehouse."

When the others nodded their agreement, Scythe instructed. "Let's clear the way to get these out without creating chaos for Winnie. I think she has enough to deal with now."

In a short time, they'd shifted all the boxes to the side, isolating those that Winnie had pointed out. Scythe checked each box and grew more concerned with the contents. This "collection" exceeded what any casual gun enthusiast would have. The weaponry could equip a small army bent on destruction. What in the world had Winnie's stepfather been involved with?

As quietly as possible, they carried the bins up the stairs and to the truck. Each time, they rotated a biker to stay behind to guard the items already loaded. The others muscled the heavy containers and held the door.

When they finished, Scythe turned out the lights downstairs and returned to the living room alone as the others guarded the truck. The neighborhood would wake up soon. They needed to get out of there.

"Chipmunk?" he whispered, seeing Winnie slumped, her forehead down on the hospital bed.

She rubbed her eyes and stood to stretch. Winnie wore pajamas and had wet hair. She had showered with them in the house. The exhausted woman had no self-preservation instincts.

"Did you finish?" she whispered.

"Yes. We've loaded everything. How do you want your money?"

"Can I give you a canceled check, and you can deposit it?" she asked.

"I only need your phone."

Winnie searched her pockets and then glanced back at the bed. She breathed a sigh of relief when she spotted it. When she retrieved it, Scythe put his cell phone number into her device and called himself.

"I'll be in touch soon, Little girl." He looked past her to her mother. "What does she need?"

"Hope," Winnie said without hesitating. A tear rolled down her cheek, and she dashed it away.

Scythe drew her forward into his arms. He cupped the back of her head and leaned forward to kiss her tenderly. "Let me know if you need anything," he told her in a gruff voice.

She nodded and whispered, "That was a definite B+. Maybe an A-."

Scythe shook his head, chuckling as he released her and walked to the door. He couldn't believe how much his world had spun on its axis in one evening. "Go get your car keys for me, Winnie. I'll have your car brought here."

"Thank you, Scythe. I was worried how I'd get to work tomorrow."

She was back to hand him a sequined chipmunk keychain in seconds. "Don't stay up. I'll have them put your keys in your mailbox." He headed to the door. She needed her sleep.

With one last glance at the woman behind him, he saw Winnie kiss a brown, fuzzy stuffed animal. Lucien was right. He always was. Scythe had found his Little girl. He locked the door behind him and headed to the truck.

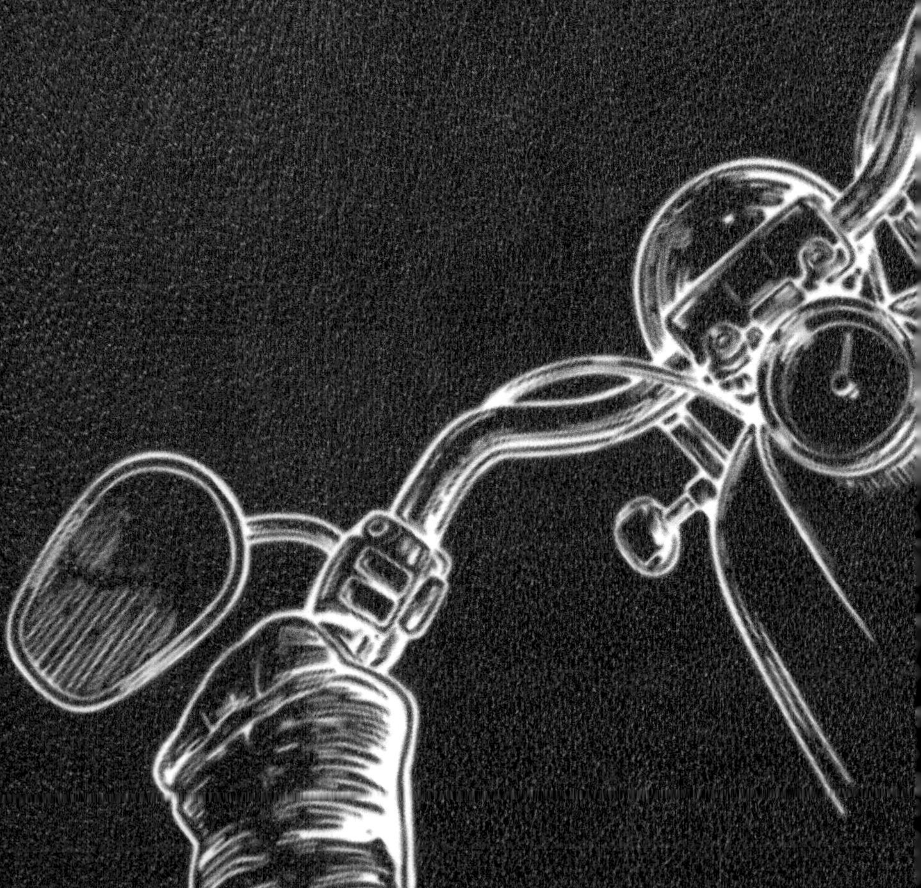

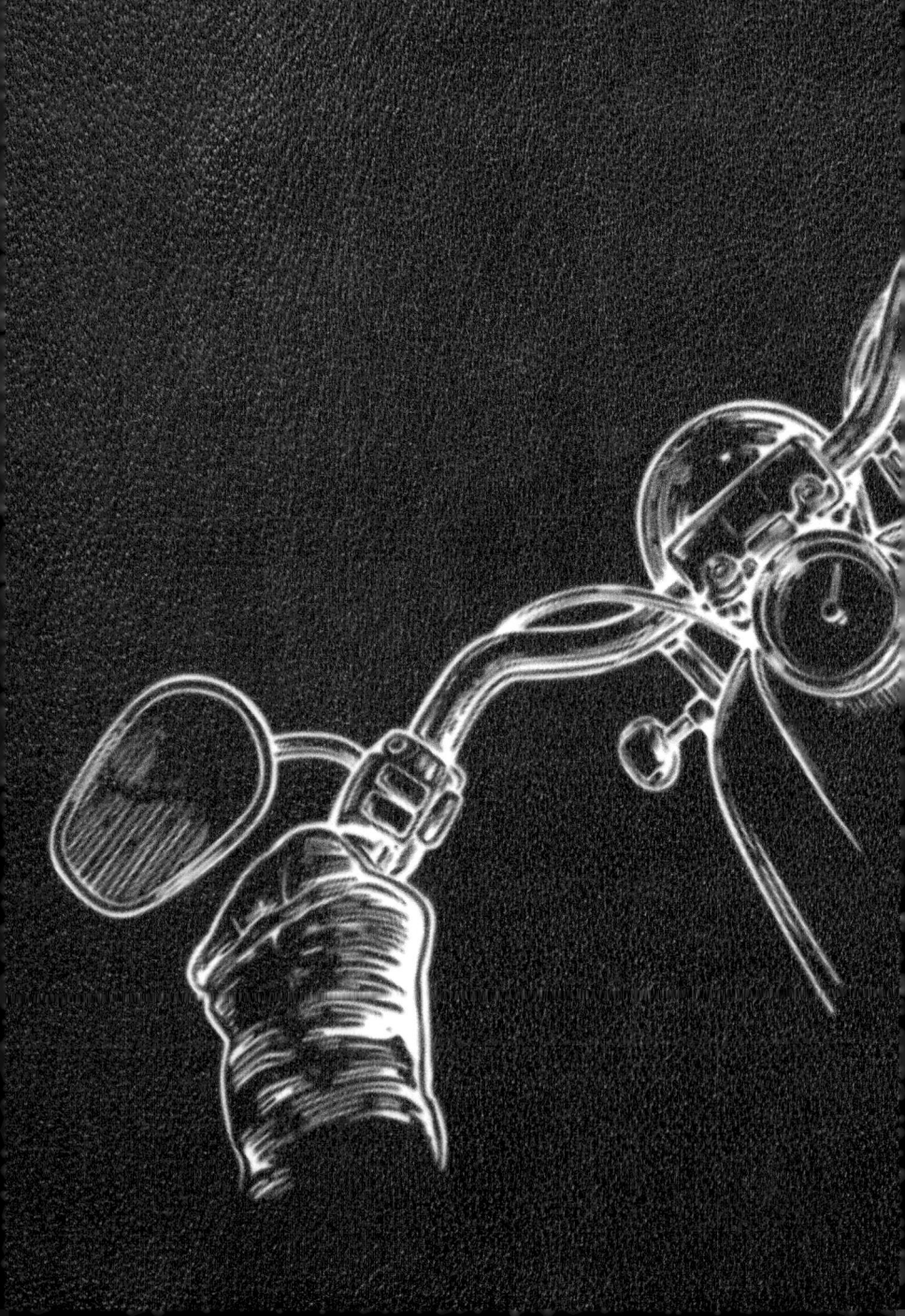

CHAPTER 3

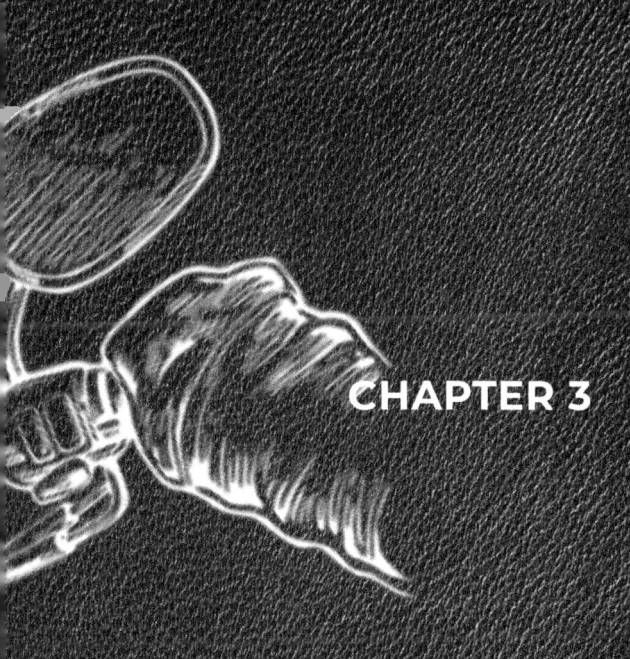

A dozen Devil Daddies stood around the open containers, shaking their heads in disbelief. They'd pulled everything out as soon as the delivery truck had made it back to the warehouse. The weapons inside would have to go into disguised storage areas until they decided what to do with them.

"What would have happened if these had gotten into the Ravagers' hands?" Wraith asked the next morning.

"I bet they'd have shown up on our doorstep quickly," Vex pointed out.

"No doubt," Razor agreed and leaned down to pick up an oversized shell casing that was longer than his hands. "I appreciate you all preventing me from having to dig bullets this size out of your hides."

"Like the Ravagers can hit anything," Fury said, smirking.

A scrape of a boot on the concrete floor made the group turn to see who approached. At the sight of Lucien accompanied by Pirate, the circle opened, allowing him to join them.

"She had this?" Lucien said and shook his head.

"We should get her some money quickly," Scythe urged.

"She needs funds?" Lucien asked, studying Scythe's face.

"Her mom's dying," Hellcat said.

"Undergoing cancer treatment," Scythe corrected.

"She's past that, Scythe. The mom knows that. She waved me over to talk while Winnie took a shower. Our conversation delayed me in coming back in to secure the load on one trip," Hellcat shared. "The doctor already broke the news to the family. Mom wanted the guns gone so her daughters wouldn't have to deal with them and possibly get into legal trouble."

"And you didn't think to tell the rest of us?" Scythe demanded. His protective instincts flared. His Little girl knew of her mother's impending death and couldn't or wouldn't stop trying to make everything okay. She would be crushed when her mother passed away.

Hellcat shook his head. "I liked her mom. She shouldn't be dealing with this. I thought Pirate could work his magic on the computer and gather some information for us. Maybe there's a specialist somewhere."

"I'll need some details," Pirate told them.

"Scythe, send him everything you've got tomorrow," Lucien said.

"I saw a hospital bill on the entryway table," Vex shared. "I'd bet the mom's name is Evelyn Morgan."

"So, money?" Scythe reminded everyone as Pirate made a note in his phone.

"The street value of this is high. We'll keep everything," Lucien decreed. "Pirate, while you're researching tomorrow, give us a used regular retail price. We'll pay in installments to avoid questions. Scythe, you'll see her tomorrow?"

"Yes."

"Stop by my office after two. I'll have the first amount ready for you."

"Thanks, Lucien." Scythe felt some of the worry lift from his shoulders. If they were right that the mother was beyond hope, her daughters could make her comfortable with enough money to pay for the expenses.

"Pirate, send me her medical files when you locate them. I'll check over everything to see if any resources could possibly help outside the normal treatments," Razor offered.

"Got anything to share with the group, Scythe?" Lucien asked with one side of his mouth quirked up in amusement.

"I probably need to tell someone else first." Scythe would share the news about finding his Little with the MC after talking to Winnie. He might admit that Lucien guessed immediately.

"Then, let's get these boxes moved into storage areas C, T, and W. Ammo in one section, guns in another, and miscellaneous items in the third. Bring me the details and the keys," Lucien directed.

"I'm going to grab a couple of guys to take Winnie's car home from the parking lot first. I'll be right there," Scythe told the group.

"Of course," Lucian agreed with a uncharacteristic smile.

Scythe didn't react but walked away, tossing the cute keychain in his hand.

That afternoon, Scythe climbed the steps to the elevated office. Lucien stood up from behind his desk as he entered. He grabbed a thick envelope from his desk and walked to meet Scythe. "Installment one. There's five thousand in fifties in that packet. Those should be easy enough to spend. Tell her not to drop the entire amount in the bank. It's best if she uses the cash for groceries, medicine, etc."

"How much more is coming?" Scythe asked.

"I'm not sure. Pirate will give us an estimate soon. She can count on at least two more payments like that one."

"I'm sure this will help." Scythe slid the envelope inside his shirt. It would be safe there under his cut.

He got almost to the door before turning around to meet

Lucien's gaze. Scythe decided to go ahead and share the news. "You were right. She's mine."

"Of course I was," Lucien smirked. "Congratulations. I'll look forward to meeting her in second-grade teacher mode."

"How did you know that?" Scythe asked. He wasn't surprised Lucien knew things about her. He checked out everyone on his radar.

"The other guys. They like her—think you're a good match. Plan a ride on Sunday. Midnight."

"Sure. How many can be gone?"

"Let's take twenty bikes."

"Old ladies allowed?" Scythe checked.

"Not this time. Leave from the warehouse at midnight. We'll be back before dawn."

"Destination?"

"I'll reveal that on Sunday," Lucien stated firmly.

"Many of the Devils will be interested in that," Scythe pointed out.

"Choose our best riders. No newbies on this one. Loyal members. Move Street up to that level."

"Will do." Scythe patted his vest. "Thank you for helping Winnie." He never regretted joining the Devil Daddies MC, but times like this reinforced his confidence in Lucien's leadership.

"She's going to keep you on your toes."

"I'm counting on that." Scythe couldn't imagine Winnie any other way than she was.

Scythe closed the door behind him and descended to the main floor of Inferno. He returned the greeting of the other MC members as he walked to the side door. His bike waited outside in the lot.

Scythe took a seat and pulled out his phone. Choosing several riders, he sent a message: "Next Sunday, midnight ride." He'd select more as he thought of them.

A bike rolled up beside him and parked. Street checked his phone and read the message. "No way! Really?"

"Lucien says you go," Scythe told him.

Street's face revealed the power of that statement. He nodded and didn't comment, as if he needed to sit with that information before he could react to it. Lucien had made the right call. Street was ready.

He grabbed his helmet and strapped it on without saying another word. The Devil Daddies connected on many levels. Lucien had handpicked his officers to create a rock-solid MC they were all proud to support.

Heading out of the parking lot, he focused on his next stop. He would go find his Little. She needed his support.

Thirty minutes later, he turned into the school parking lot. At the front entrance, school buses were already lined up to whisk the kids home. Scythe chose a spot in the faculty parking lot and removed his helmet to enjoy the beautiful weather.

A bunch of impish kids appeared in one of the windows. A hand shooed them back to their seats before Winnie's beautiful face appeared. Her mouth rounded in a silent O. Scythe waved and grinned, and she automatically returned the gesture before catching herself and rushing away from the glass.

Scythe counted the windows leading to that room and memorized it. The chubby chipmunk decoration posted in the window would jog his memory. He bet it wasn't the only one in the classroom.

He'd timed his arrival well. Under ten minutes later, professionally dressed adults streamed out with clipboards. They roamed between the busses. Several stopped and stared pointedly at him. Scythe knew he'd have a visitor soon when a starched-looking female lifted her walkie-talkie to her lips.

The police car approached exactly two minutes later and stopped in front of him, blocking Scythe into the parking spot. Well, trying to pin him into place. Scythe had driven a bike for years. He wouldn't have a bit of trouble threading the handlebars through the gaps in the cars.

The police officer stepped out of his car and walked forward, stopping a safe distance away. The fit man's expression was guarded as he looked at Scythe. "Hello, there. I'm Officer Riley, the school resource officer. Could you tell me your business here?"

"Officer Riley." Scythe greeted him with a nod. "I'm waiting for a staff member to finish her day."

"For what purpose?" the officer asked.

"She's a friend. I'm not here to cause trouble. Just to give a her a ride home if she needs one."

"Who's that?"

"Is that principal going to cause her trouble for having an acquaintance who rides a bike?" Scythe nodded at the principal who stood on the edge of the sidewalk, staring intently at him.

"Of course not. Devil Daddies MC. Is that the MC that runs the bar? Inferno?"

"Inferno is owned by the founder of the motorcycle club."

"I think he's an ex-con...." The cop let his voice trail away as if he were hoping Scythe would comment.

"A lawful resident and successful businessman."

"Some might not agree with that."

"I'm sure you deal with a lot of bad people. It must be hard to guard yourself from making instant judgements about someone's character based on their appearance or that they're riding a motorcycle. I'm going to grab my ID from my pocket. You can run my license."

At the cop's nod, Scythe reached carefully into his pocket and withdrew a slim wallet containing nothing but his license and his health and vehicle insurance cards. He was careful not to make any other moves.

The officer returned to his squad car and maintained his view of Scythe while running his information. In the meantime, the front sidewalk exploded with elementary-aged children. The chaotic mass of kids organized themselves into lines with encouragement from the adults. Staff members walked each group to the correct vehicle in a well-practiced routine.

"Here you go, sir." The officer handed him back his cards. "Nothing on your record would endanger the kids. I always have to check. Thank you for your cooperation."

"I understand you have a job to do."

The resource officer left to park his car before resuming his school duties with dismissal. Both he and the principal kept their eyes on Scythe.

"Crap," Scythe swore under his breath. He pulled out his phone and called Winnie. He wasn't concerned about their bias against him, but he didn't want anything to harm Winnie.

"Scythe? Is something wrong? I had the worst day. Don't tell me something else happened."

"I'm sorry, Chipmunk. Unfortunately, I may have screwed things up for you. I'm in the parking lot, but I can get out of here."

"Why would you leave?"

"The resource officer and your principal are way too interested in who I know here. I didn't give them your name. If I head out now, they'll never know I came to see you."

"Don't move an inch."

He smiled at the steel in her voice. "You okay, Chipmunk?"

"I could use a hug…. And a ride home if you wouldn't mind?"

"I'm on my bike, Chipmunk."

"Even better. I'd like to blow this day out of my hair. I'll be out in fifteen minutes. Teachers can't leave before then," Winnie shared.

"Take your time. I'll be here."

Disconnecting the call, Scythe sat back on his bike. He couldn't care less about others' reactions to his presence. As long as Winnie was okay with him staying, he'd stay as long as she needed him.

As the last bus departed, the female principal headed directly to him. "Sir, who are you waiting for?"

"Good afternoon," Scythe said without a trace of sarcasm in his voice.

"Good afternoon. Who are you waiting for? This is the faculty parking lot."

"I'm Scythe. You're the principal here?" Out of the corner of his eye, he saw the side door open, and a small figure emerged.

"Yes. Lorraine Oberson. Who are you waiting for?"

"He's waiting for me, Ms. Oberson. Is that a problem?" Winnie spoke.

"Ms. Bradley? Are you acquainted with this… gentleman?" the principal asked after a deliberate pause. Winnie's administrator chose to call everyone Ms. instead of learning what title her staff members preferred to use.

"Yes. This is Scythe. He came to my rescue and will give me a ride home. Remember? You wrote me up this morning for being late when my car broke down on the way to school?" Winnie said in a pleasant tone.

"Of course, I remember. Very well. I'm glad you had someone to help. Too bad he wasn't available earlier to get you to work on time," Ms. Oberson said snidely.

Scythe bristled at her attitude toward Winnie. Automatically, he knew she put in a lot of personal time into her job. He forced himself not to snarl at the bitchy woman. "Had she thought of phoning me, I would have been happy to help her. These things happen to everyone at some point. I bet this was her first time in," he paused and looked at Winnie. "How many years have you taught here?"

"Six years," Winnie provided.

"Her first time in six years. Sounds like an extremely conscientious teacher," he said deliberately before continuing, "Good job, Winnie. Are you ready to go?"

"Not yet. I didn't want you to get in trouble." Winnie glanced at her principal as if to see if everything would be okay.

"I'm sure Ms. Oberson won't write me up. Go grab what you need, Winnie," Scythe urged.

"Rules are rules," Ms. Oberson snapped.

"Thanks, Scythe," Winnie said. "I'll be just a few more minutes!"

Winnie scurried back to the building like the cute chipmunk stuffie he'd spotted last night. She was adorable. Dismissing the administrator from his thoughts, Scythe pulled out his phone and sent the name Lorraine Oberson to Pirate along with the word "dirt".

Out of the corner of his eye, the unpleasant woman smacked her walkie-talkie against her palm to grab his attention. "Since Ms. Bradley has vouched for you," Ms. Oberson said and turned sharply on her heels.

"No problem, ma'am," Scythe answered as he swung his leg over the seat to dismount on the opposite side of the bike. He turned his attention to retrieving his extra helmet and jacket to protect his Little girl. Scythe pushed the thought of that awful woman away to make plans to turn Winnie's day around. It sounded like she needed to have some fun.

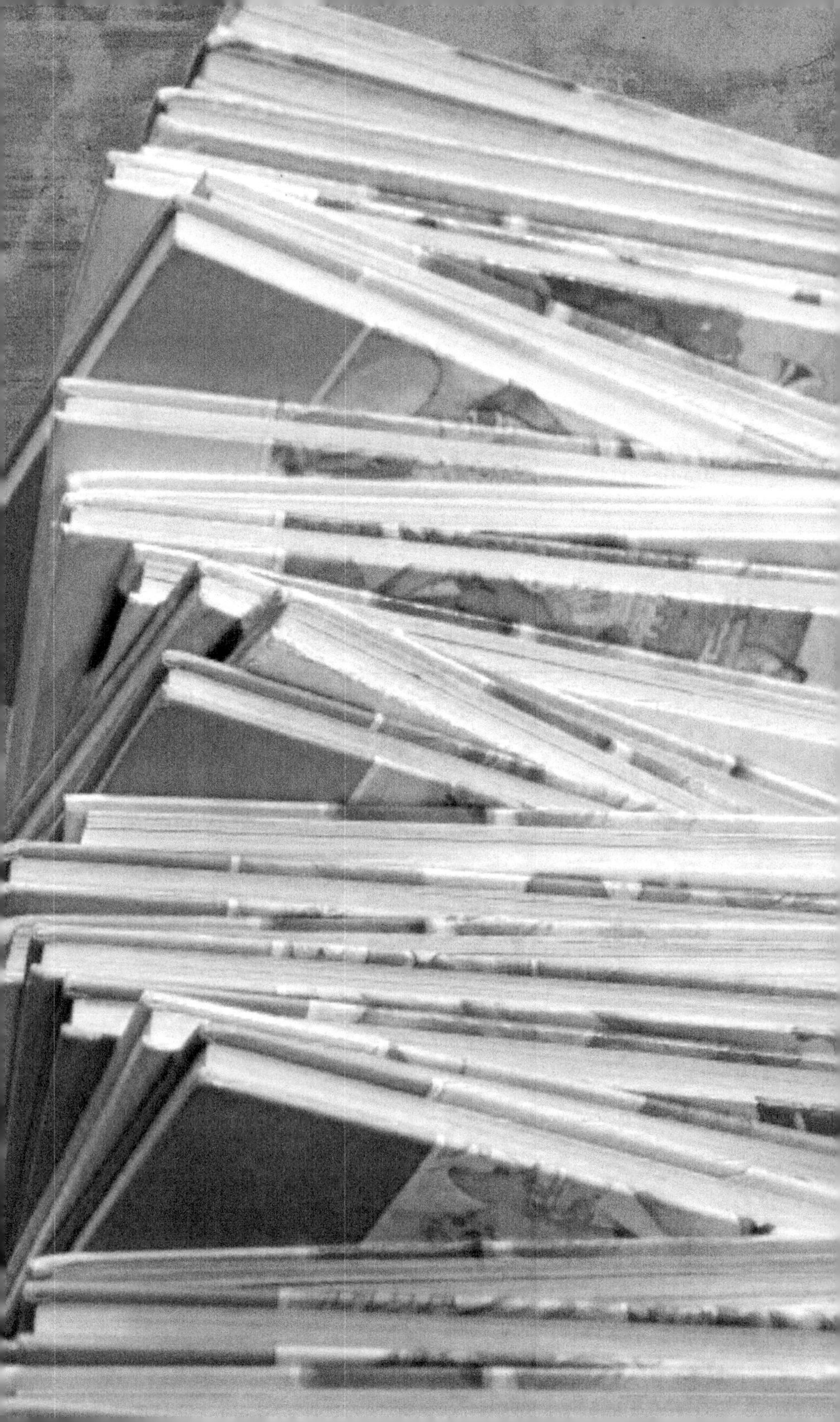

CHAPTER 4

"That biker is waiting on you?" Abby Fairchild asked.

Winnie nodded at the third-grade teacher who'd become her bestie in the school. She loved everyone she taught with except Lorraine Oberson. The entire building had groaned collectively when the superintendent had chosen the fifth-grade teacher to fill the suddenly available principal's position. Winnie didn't blame their former educational leader for moving with his family when his wife took a prestigious law partnership in New York City, but everyone missed him.

"He's sexy," Abby said, waggling her eyebrows. "You haven't told me anything!"

"Sorry. I met him last night at Inferno," Winnie shared as she gathered papers to grade at home.

"You went to Inferno? Without me?"

"Or us!" chimed in three more teachers clustered inside the door. Those closest to her classroom had gathered magically to get the scoop. Handsome men on motorcycles didn't show up frequently. Or at all.

"You guys! Was everyone watching?" Winnie asked.

"You bet. You have nose prints all over your windows. Julie

stopped to see what would happen. She was super interested," Becky, the other third-grade staff member, said, chuckling.

Julie, their custodian, joining those monitoring the encounter in the parking lot meant everyone in the building would know—soon. Winnie shook her head. *Here it goes.*

"What's his name?" Abby asked.

"Scythe."

"Like the big blade thing Death carries?" Becky asked.

"That's his biker name," Winnie explained.

"I'd hope so. That would be a fun name to find on your roster at the beginning of the year. Three Michaels, two Johns, and a Scythe," Susan said.

Winnie stared at the other second-grade teacher and considered that discovery. "You'd guess his parents were unique?" she suggested.

"So much better than a hellion named Precious," Becky said. "They're never precious. But Scythe is a grown man. And hot."

"At nine months pregnant, nothing should be hot," Susan reminded Becky.

"I'm not dead." Becky laughed and rubbed her baby bump.

"I don't want to make him wait," Winnie said, lifting her bag. "Run interference for me? Tell everyone he's a friend of the family." That was true. He'd definitely helped her deal with her stepfather's collection.

"We've got you," Abby assured her. "But you have to share all the details at lunch tomorrow."

Rolling her eyes, Winnie agreed. "See you ladies on Tuesday." Winnie was surprised to find herself smiling as she walked down the hallway to the parking lot with her evening stack to grade. She felt more energetic than she had in forever, even after getting a letter in her file for the first time.

Maybe she should fight that. Pushing open the door, Winnie smiled at Scythe. Four young teachers dawdled in the parking lot. She bet they were trying to figure out how to start a conversation with the powerful biker. He only had eyes for her. Winnie liked that a lot as she crossed the asphalt.

Scythe took her bookbag and slid it into a storage pouch on the side of his bike. "I thought the kids had homework, not the teacher."

"You don't know a lot of people in the education field, do you?"

"I know one now. Let's get you protected for the trip home." He held out a huge jacket.

"Um, it's not cold. I'll be fine."

"You don't ride without something made to protect your skin."

She stared at him, wavering in her decision that she could ride a motorcycle. "Do you crash a lot?"

"No, Chipmunk. But people are crazy out there. Better prepared than hurt. Think of this like a rubber. You like bareback but don't want the complications of something bad happening."

"A rubber?" she repeated, feeling confused.

"Protection." He suggested another word.

Rubber? Protection? What was he talking about? The knowing smile on his face helped Winnie make the connection.

"Scythe!" she said and had to laugh. She leaned closer and whispered, "Who else would compare a motorcycle coat and a condom?"

"In you go," he prompted, shaking the jacket.

In a few minutes, he released the zipper pull when she stood swallowed up by the volume of material around her. Winnie flapped her arms, feeling ridiculous. Scythe shook his head at her silliness and rolled up her sleeves so she could use her hands.

"Scythe, I'm going to act like a parachute to slow you," she warned.

"I won't be going racing speed with you onboard," he told her, picking up the helmet and setting it on her head. He carefully brushed the escaping wisps of hair from her face and fastened the chin strap before tucking the length of her ponytail inside the borrowed coat. "Now, you won't have to battle tangles when you get home."

"Thanks. Do I need to know anything about riding?"

"Keep your feet on the pegs," he said, flipping down metal supports. "Don't get your leg close to the tailpipes. They get hot, and you'll have a nasty burn." He tapped the area on the bike to avoid.

When she nodded, he added, "Rest your body against my back. Lean the way I do, even if you think you'll tip over. I promise you that won't happen."

"Okay." Winnie hoped she'd remember all of this when they started.

"Let me get on first. I'll wave you to my side when I'm ready. You'll swing your leg over, and we can go on an adventure. Do you have to get to your mom's quickly?"

"By five. My stepsister leaves for work at fifteen after."

"She stays with your mom during the day?"

"Yes. She sleeps after the late shift but is there if Mom needs her and I'm at school," Winnie shared.

"Okay, I'll make sure you're home before five. That gives us time for an adventure and maybe ice cream to make up for your lousy day."

"That would be incredible. You're sure you have time?"

"I'd make time for you, Chipmunk."

As she digested that statement, he got onto the bike and started it up. Scythe lifted the bike from the kickstand and held it steady after dealing with the metal support.

"When you're ready, Winnie."

She moved closer and considered her options. Winnie hadn't planned on riding a motorcycle this morning when she chose her outfit for the day. The full skirt was comfortable but would make straddling the bike a challenge.

Remembering something she'd seen in a movie, Winnie reached between her legs to grab the hem on the back of her skirt. She pulled it to the front and up to tuck the material into her waistband, creating a divided garment much like harem pants. Winnie looked up at Scythe triumphantly. "Ta-da!"

"So creative! Jump on, fashionista."

Grinning for the first time that day, Winnie swung her leg over the seat. She tried not to wiggle around too much, afraid to topple the bike over. Scythe reached one powerful arm behind him and pulled her firmly against him.

"Wrap your arms around me, Winnie."

When she tentatively held on to his waist, trying to scoot back a bit, Scythe tugged her wrists forward and tugged her arms around him. She couldn't believe how hard his belly was. Did he have an ounce of fat on him? She sucked in her slight tummy, hoping he couldn't feel that.

"Relax, Chipmunk. Stay close to me. It helps us move together. Hold on." With that warning, Scythe turned the handle of the bike and eased them forward.

Winnie squealed and grabbed him tighter. They moved through the parking lot, which suddenly seemed like an obstacle course. Scythe handled the bike like a dream.

When they reached the road, Winnie relaxed. She loved the wind blowing past them. It seemed to blast all her worries away. Instantly she understood why people rode motorcycles. Very little in her life felt like freedom anymore—a crappy boss, her mother desperately ill, and a demanding job she loved but left her emotionally and physically drained. Her well of inner resiliency was drained to the last droplets of water.

"You okay, Chipmunk?" Scythe asked.

"Oh, I'm sorry!" she shouted over the wind and relaxed her grip on his waist.

Scythe rubbed her forearm before easing the bike into the far parking lot of a park. When he had the bike secured, he turned to lift her around his bulk. Sitting her in his lap, he scanned her face.

"You look like you just lost your best friend," he said gently.

That bit of kindness was all it took. Tears cascaded down her cheeks, and Winnie threw herself forward into his arms. Scythe hugged her to his chest and let her cry until her sobs diminished. He kissed her temple and asked, "Can you talk to me now, Little girl?"

"What a mess I am!" Winnie wiped her hands over her face. "I cried on your leather vest. It won't ever be the same. Can— Can I have it cleaned for you?"

"Little girl, eyes on me."

Unable to refuse, Winnie met his gaze. She'd seen his blue-green eyes look angry at Inferno when he suspected the worst of her. Now that beautiful gaze radiated concern and caring. She almost started tearing up again.

"Crying's over for a few minutes, Chipmunk," he said, tapping her nose like he knew thoughts were whirling in her mind. "Did you hurt yourself?"

"No," she answered, struggling to keep her voice steady.

"Are you scared?"

She shook her head. "This is fun. It made me realize how little I get to escape from the real world."

"And that made you sad?"

She nodded.

"I'm sorry, Little girl. I'm going to ensure you get to enjoy life, starting right now." He pulled a bandana from inside his vest and wiped her cheeks and eyes.

"Blow," he told her firmly, holding the material to her nose.

When she attempted to take it from him, he tilted his head in a silent warning. Winnie knew he wouldn't hurt her. She decided to be brave and followed his instructions.

"Good girl. That deserves ice cream, don't you think?"

Winnie nodded eagerly.

"Up you go, Chipmunk." He boosted her off his lap to stand next to the bike before swinging his leg over the seat. In minutes, he had their helmets off and held her hand.

Scythe pointed to an industrial vehicle parked across the field. "I noticed a new food truck had started showing up here last week. Let's go try it."

Winnie took two steps and remembered to unfasten her skirt so she could walk easier. With her clothing restored into place, she slid her hand into Scythe's. They crossed the grassy area and stopped a short distance away to decide on a flavor. When they had their cones, Scythe led her to a bench where they sat to eat.

Licking happily on her ice cream cone, Winnie refused to think of anything other than the beautiful day, the delicious treat, and the handsome man next to her. "How's the chocolate crunch? That was my second choice."

"Try it." Scythe held out his cone.

She eyed the decadent ball on the cone. It seemed intimate to taste it after him.

"I'm healthy and got tested after my old lady decided she was tired of MC life," Scythe told her.

"Tested?" she echoed.

"For any communicable diseases, Chipmunk. That means I can't give you anything."

"Oh!" As she processed that statement, Winnie decided to live dangerously and mentally thumbed her nose at the germs. Yielding to temptation, she leaned forward to lick the stream of chocolate that dripped over the side. "Yum! That's really good. I like mine too, but yours is better."

Scythe plucked her cone from her hand and replaced her flavor with his.

"Wait! You don't have to do that," she protested.

"I wanted to try this one too." He devoured a bite of her ice cream. "Ooo! That caramel is good."

"I'm not sick either. I mean, I got tested after my last boyfriend for some weird reason.... I mean, he wasn't really my boyfriend. Just the brother of a classmate that needed help with his essays." Her voice trailed off, and she concentrated on her cone.

Winnie hated that she was awkward. She liked Scythe a lot. He'd soon figure out she was a hot mess and avoid her.

"Do you still miss him?"

She met his gaze in shock. "Heavens, no! He's a total goofball. Frankie got a job in New Jersey, and I came here to teach. We weren't *involved* involved, if you know what I mean."

"He moved after college?"

"Yes. Then mom started getting sick. It took a while for them to figure out what was wrong," Winnie said. She shook her head.

"I'm sorry, Chipmunk."

"Why do you call me that?" she asked, swirling her tongue around the edge of the cone to catch the melting bits.

"Because you dived into me like a chipmunk into his den when your superintendent almost caught you."

"I'm such a klutz," she said, rolling her eyes at her stupidity.

"I will not allow you to talk badly about yourself, Little girl," Scythe reprimanded her sternly. "The fact I'm calling you an adorable creature should clue you in that I quite enjoy having you make me your safe place."

"Oh!" Winnie repeated his statement in her mind. He thought she was adorable, and it sounded like he liked having her around. Winnie sat straighter and met his gaze directly. Maybe she should check that she hadn't misunderstood. "That's a good thing, right?"

"It's an extremely good thing, Winnie. Do you promise to tell me if you ever stop feeling safe with me?" Scythe asked.

"Are you a good guy? I mean, is your gang okay? They don't hurt people?"

"First of all, the Devil Daddies is a MC. That stands for motorcycle club. We ride together. Think of it like a social club."

"Oh, that's fun. You like, go for ice cream?"

"I won't ever lie to you, Chipmunk. We all stand together for what is right for the club. I can promise you we will never hurt you or yours. You're under my protection now."

"I don't really need protection," she pointed out. "I'm only a second-grade teacher. Nothing too exciting there."

"Everyone needs someone in their corner—even beautiful teachers."

Her cheeks heated, and Winnie knew she was blushing. "You don't have to make up compliments. I don't usually dress like I did last night. That was my stepsister's. I couldn't even get into Inferno the first couple of times."

"You'll have no trouble getting into Inferno now."

"Because I'm with you?" she asked.

"Because you're mine."

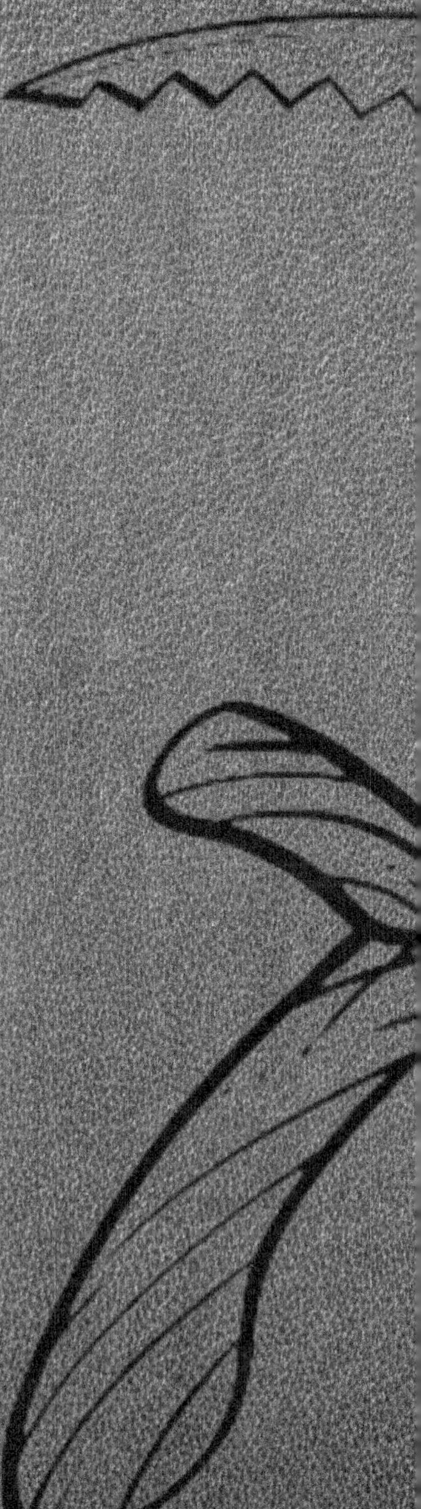

CHAPTER 5

Now that sounded like something from a romance novel. She must have heard that wrong. "Yours?" Winnie repeated.

"Mine."

A thrill went through her at his possessiveness. No one had ever claimed her before. Winnie stared at him, trying to figure out if he was punking her like others had in the past. She decided she should protest, so he didn't laugh at her for believing him later. "Don't I get any say in this?"

"Of course, as long as you say you belong to me."

"Scythe. This isn't funny." She crossed her fingers on her free hand. *Please let him be different from the other guys.*

"Do I look like I'm making a joke?"

Winnie stared at him, dumbfounded. "You can't just decide I'm yours after twenty-four hours. I could be a mass murderer. *You* could be a mass murderer."

"It's probably more likely that I'm a mass murderer." When her mouth fell open in shock, he added, "I'm not. Remember, you're always safe with me."

His biker appearance suddenly struck her as something a bad guy would wear. In the movies, the bad guys frequently wore black. She trusted Scythe and had felt comfortable with the other Devil Daddies. Her mom had talked about how nice they were. Had she misjudged everyone?

"Others not so much?" she asked.

"Exactly." That statement didn't reassure her.

A trickle of chocolate ran down her hand. Scythe pulled her cone to his mouth and licked the sticky liquid away. His tongue swiped over her skin sensually. Winnie shivered from the erotic sensation. Instantly she wanted more.

"Mmm. You taste sweet, Chipmunk."

She swayed toward him. She couldn't think rationally with him licking her. "What are you doing with me, Scythe? Please don't be mean." Winnie would be crushed to have him betray her.

"I'm sorry people have treated you badly so often that you anticipate someone is messing with you. I promise I will do everything in my power to keep from hurting you. Can you trust me?"

Winnie studied his face. He meant what he said. She swallowed hard and decided to risk it all. "A promise is like a contract. You have to do what you say."

"Okay," Scythe agreed easily as if it were a complete no-brainer. "You've got a bit at the corner of your mouth."

He threaded his fingers through her hair to draw her forward. He kissed the corner of her mouth and swept his tongue lightly over the dab, making her shiver.

Heat built inside her. Not like the mild attraction she'd experienced with her college boyfriend. She squeezed her legs together and felt herself becoming wet. Winnie turned slightly to press her mouth against his fully, and Scythe deepened the kiss.

Drawn to him like a moth to a flame, Winnie clung to the connection between them. It didn't matter that their lives were so different. Whatever linked them together assured her he was the one.

He drew his tongue across the seam of her lips, and she opened her mouth to welcome him in. Scythe tasted like caramel, rich and exotic. But his own yummy flavor drew her in the most.

She stared at him when he lifted his head. Why was he stopping?

"We've got to get rid of these, Chipmunk, before we're covered."

Winnie glanced down at her hand still clutching the cone. She'd crushed one side, and the melted chocolate had streamed from the hole. The sticky mixture covered her fingers.

"I'm such a klutz! Did I get it on you?" she asked, holding the cone far from her borrowed jacket.

"You are not a klutz, Chipmunk. No calling yourself names. Come on. Let's drop these in the trash."

Scythe tightened his arm around her waist to lift Winnie to her feet. He guided her to the trashcan and plucked the cone from her hand. After tossing the ice cream in the bin, he took her sticky hand in his, holding it a safe distance from her.

"I think we've already made a mess. I didn't realize," she said and then blushed again. Ugh! He was going to run far away from her now. To her surprise, he smiled. Maybe he was different?

"Chipmunk, you would tempt a saint. Come on. Let's visit that water fountain over there. We can rinse the stickiness off."

In a few minutes, Scythe cleaned their skin and dried her hands on his shirt, despite her protests. "Get a drink, Chipmunk. It's important to stay hydrated."

"Every doctor I have tells me I need to drink more," she blurted.

"We'll work on that then," he said as she sipped the arching water.

"Oh, you don't have to worry about me. I'm all grown-up."

That statement hung in the air as Scythe got a drink. When he stood up, he said sternly, "Little girls need help from their

Daddies to take care of themselves. Many times, they're too busy tending to everyone else and put themselves last."

"Daddies?" she repeated, and everything seemed to click into place. That was why he was so patient with her. "That's why you call me Little girl. You're a Daddy Dom?" She'd read all those books but figured men like that didn't really exist. In her mind, she'd told herself that term referred to her smaller size compared to him.

"Yes, Winnie. Better than that, I'm completely convinced that I'm *your* Daddy Dom."

"Oh!"

"Unfortunately, it's time for me to get you home. Will you promise me not to panic until we talk everything over?"

She hesitated. "I'm a bit of a worrier." Alone in her room tonight, she'd turn this conversation over and over in her mind.

"You could call me tonight when your mother is asleep if you have a question or need to talk. I'd love for you to tell me when you're tucked into bed so I can wish you good night or read you a story." He steered her back toward the motorcycle.

"You'd read me a story?" she asked.

"Of course. What kind of stories do you like? Fairy tales? Wizards and Magic? Animals?" Scythe picked up her helmet and fastened the strap.

"Chippy loves animals!" Winnie blurted and then slapped her hand over her mouth. She watched his face to judge his reaction. Her shoulders settled back into place when he smiled.

"Chippy, huh? Would that be your stuffed chipmunk?" He tugged to make sure the protective headgear was secure.

Her eyes widened. She tried to figure out what to say.

"I'll have to get you one if you don't already have a stuffed chipmunk."

She shook her head and lowered her hand to whisper, "There could only be one Chippy."

"Of course. Will you introduce me to Chippy soon? I'd like to meet him."

"Okay."

"I'll find an animal story for Chippy and for you."

"Thank you."

In a few minutes, they were on their way. This time, Winnie rested comfortably against his back with her arms locked around his waist. Riding wrapped around Scythe had become her favorite activity. Nothing could feel better than this. Making love with Scythe jumped into her mind. She nodded to herself. Winnie knew that would eclipse even this.

When they'd arrived at her home, Winnie had celebrated with an adorable happy dance upon seeing her car was in the driveway. A parent of an amazing former student had his own automotive repair shop. Winnie had called him in a tizzy. Thankfully, the mechanic remembered her fondly and had towed her car that morning. He'd even driven it to her house after repairing her vehicle. The keys were in front of the right rear tire.

"What's the repair shop's name?" Scythe asked.

"Woodson's. It's on Main Street."

"Got it." Scythe focused on Winnie. He'd check out the shop later.

"Chipmunk, I put an envelope in your bag. It's the first installment of money from the collection we carted away last night. Don't deposit it in your account in a lump sum. Buy groceries, gas, tip the pizza delivery guy. Banks ask questions if you drop a chunk of money in cash into an account."

"Is it counterfeit?" she whispered.

"No. It's real money, Winnie. I would never endanger you. You can always share the truth that your mom is selling off some of your stepfather's possessions. Just be vague. People get weird when they think about guns changing hands."

"Got it. I can be vague," she promised, hoping she could actually do that.

Scythe cupped her chin and studied the sweet face that had come to mean so much to him in such a short time. "Go to bed early, Little girl. I can tell you need more rest. I'd give you a bedtime of eight, but I know you watch over your mother. Aim to get under the covers as soon as possible, okay?"

She didn't argue. Winnie nodded and licked her lips as if she hoped he'd kiss her. Scythe didn't need convincing. He leaned down to capture her mouth and nibbled at her lips softly at first but then thoroughly devoured her mouth when her cute sounds urged him on. Winnie sneaked her arms around his neck, and she held onto him as she swayed closer.

The door flew open, grabbing his attention. The woman in the front entrance was gorgeous—all toned angles and big, blond hair. Her face, while stunning, appeared hard.

"For God's sake. Stop canoodling on the front step. What are you, twelve, Winnie?"

"I bet you need to leave, Belinda. I'll come take care of Mom," Winnie said, stepping away from Scythe. She squeezed his biceps as if signaling she didn't want to go.

"Who's this?" Belinda asked, checking out Scythe from head to toe. "I think I need to hang out with the motorcycle club. Did she catch you by wearing my dress? I look better in it."

"The woman inside it overshadowed the dress," Scythe answered smoothly, keeping his eyes on Winnie. Belinda didn't interest him at all. "Call me." He pulled her close and kissed her one more time.

Scythe lifted his head. "Call me," he repeated. She nodded and pressed two fingers to her lips.

"Wait...," Belinda said quickly.

"I'll get my bike out of your stepsister's way." Scythe turned and walked down the driveway to where his motorcycle waited, listening to Belinda sputter behind him.

"What a jerk! He didn't even look at me. So rude."

"He's incredible when you get to know him." Winnie

defended him. Scythe smiled as he moved away when she didn't let her sister speak poorly of him.

Thanks, Little girl. He listened to Winnie change the conversation as he pulled on his helmet.

"Let's go on in so you can grab your stuff for work. How's Mom done today?"

"Devil Daddies? Is that what his leather vest says?" Belinda asked Winnie before yelling toward Scythe, who had reached his bike, "Hey, Daddy! I bet you're a devil!"

"Come on, Belinda. The neighbors' blinds are twitching. Ellen is watching," Winnie said.

Scythe didn't react. He fastened his helmet in place and stowed the one she'd borrowed. He'd get a different size to fit her better tonight at the warehouse. And another jacket. He backed into the street. When Winnie looked back over her shoulder as they walked inside, Scythe lifted a hand and waved before holding it up to his ear like a phone. Her answering nod warmed his heart.

Checking his rearview mirror when he reached the stop sign at the corner, he saw Belinda rush out. When she discovered he had left, she angrily threw her purse and lunchbox to the driveway.

That wasn't the reaction he expected from a stepsister. She would have fucked him in her bedroom with the door open to spite Winnie. He hadn't picked up the same animosity from Winnie. She could probably find something good in everyone—except maybe that principal. He'd have Pirate investigate Belinda as soon as he knew her last name. Anyone that antagonistic who stayed in close contact with Winnie would be on his watch list. Thank goodness the right sister had come to meet with Lucien.

DEVIL DADDIES

CHAPTER 6

Scythe stopped in a parking lot two blocks from Winnie's school to check in with the computer wizard. Just as he anticipated, Pirate had sent him a file of information about Lorraine Oberson. He had the basic facts about her: age, education, arrests, and charges.

Nothing too remarkable at first glance. Lorraine was older than he would have guessed. Something about her degree made him stop. Scythe studied the next document in the file. Pirate had included an investigation of Amberly College. It didn't exist except as an empty shell on the internet. There was no record of the institution on any higher education listing or on tax records.

"You dog, you." She'd created her own university, given herself a higher education certification, and gone to work as a teacher.

He shook his head as he scrolled to the next items. A court document legally changing her name from Lori Young to Lorriane Oberson. A rap sheet for Lori Young followed that was years long, listing theft, assault, and extortion. She'd earned one solicitation charge at twenty-five. This was obviously not the type of person school districts usually employed. How had the district gotten bamboozled by this con artist?

Two more files sat in the folder Pirate had created. A distinguished man in a well-tailored suit stared up at him. Why did he look familiar? The silver hair and approachable expression made this the perfect headshot for several professions. Scythe checked to see who he was. Dr. Adam Young, the superintendent of Winnie's district. A flash of the previous evening popped into his brain. That was the man who Winnie had panicked at seeing.

Dr. Adam Young. Lori Young. That couldn't be a coincidence. Opening the next page, Scythe confirmed his suspicion. In the father space, Adam Joseph Young's name stared up at him from Lori Young's birth certificate. The bastard had hired his daughter without a teaching degree and promoted her to the principal's job. They hadn't covered their tracks well.

Scythe debated. Did he continue to Winnie's school and take care of the principal? He didn't want to subject Winnie to any negative actions they might levy against her before the information could be used effectively. He needed to protect her first and to plot how to use those reports in the most effective way.

Pulling back into traffic, he drove toward Inferno. The interstate was packed with rush hour traffic. Scythe maneuvered easily through the crush of stressed and tired drivers at the end of the day. When he hit Inferno, the parking lot was already half full.

Lucien had built Inferno's reputation for great food at a good price. Many stopped here on their way home to grab a generous meal and have a beer or two before the dancing and heavier drinking crowd showed up after nine. Controlling the number inside was essential in the late-night hours, but the extra revenue the early birds created supported the business.

Lucien was a shrewd businessman. Crossing him was a ginormous mistake. Lucien didn't forget anything and had a dark side. Scythe battled with his own demons. He understood the Devil Daddies MC leader. Well, as much as Lucien allowed. No one was that close to their leader.

Scythe would never have imagined his life here in the city.

Working the family farm was hard, but he'd always felt like a part of the land. When his plans had crumbled to dust with the loss of his father and all the acres, Scythe had helped move his mother to live close to her sister. She was happy there and enjoyed filling the free time she had now without demanding jobs like canning and cooking for a hungry harvesting crew.

A fight had introduced him to Lucien and the Devil Daddies. What had seemed like the worst day of his life had led to this new world. When he had taken a chance and showed up battered and bruised at Inferno asking to see Lucien, the shrewd business owner had invited him up to his office. It turned out Lucien needed someone unafraid of hard work and willing to tell him the truth regardless of what Lucien wanted to hear.

Scythe waved a hand to acknowledge the greetings of MC brothers and customers as he drove through the lot. He backed into the reserved strip of parking places where all the Devil Daddies left their bikes and went inside. Rocking music greeted him as he walked through the side door. Scythe headed for the entrance to see if Wraith needed his help.

"Hey," Wraith greeted him.

The bulky biker was a force to be reckoned with in any skirmish. He also had amazing instincts when it came to working the door. Scythe answered him with a nod before greeting the curvy woman at his side. "Hi, Caroline."

"Hi, Scythe. You're less frowny today," she observed with a smile.

"I'll try to cultivate a meaner persona." He scowled fiercely at Caroline, making her giggle and two men at the door take a step back.

Wraith waved them forward. "No worries about Scythe. He's already met his quota today. You're safe unless you cause problems."

"We just want a beer and some nachos," one customer assured Wraith as he kept his eyes on Scythe like he would strike at any moment.

"Enjoy!" Caroline urged, and the men hurried by, giving Scythe a wide berth.

"You know by the end of the night the rumor of me slaughtering all the members of a frat house will be everywhere," Scythe said.

"Way to maintain the mystique of the Devils," Wraith said.

Scythe shook his head. "Need me here?"

Wraith patted Caroline's thigh. "My trainee and I have this under control. Want to come give us a dinner break at seven?" Wraith asked.

"You got it."

"They needed some help at the back bar if you're looking for a place to jump in."

"I'll head that way. See you at seven."

Customers slammed the smaller bar. Scythe slid behind the counter and started putting together the servers' orders. Thankfully, beer and margaritas filled the vast majority of the requests. Those were easy to dispense into a glass to send the customers on their way. He could make fancy drinks, but they took more time.

"Scythe? We're running out of stock. Could you take those muscles and grab some liquor for us?" Sherry asked. The cheerful bartender was a staple at Inferno. She'd been there from the very beginning.

"You got it, Sherry. I'll hurry."

"You're a gem. Here." She tossed him the keys to the storage room.

Scythe ducked under the counter to head for the backroom. He quickly gathered all the bottles Sherry needed and loaded two buckets with the booze. He stepped out into the hallway, set the containers down, and locked the door.

"Hey, young man. I've been looking for you."

Scythe turned to see a man dressed in a suit that had to cost as much as a bachelorette party's bar bill. A lawyer. Automatically, he scowled.

"It's been a long time since someone called me a young man," he answered. "If you'll excuse me, I need to get this stock to the bar."

The man stepped in front of him. "This will take five minutes." He held out a card.

"Sorry. I'm on the clock," Scythe told him.

"Better five minutes here than ten years in jail. Take my card." He dropped it into one bucket. "You'll want my contact information. You are to stay away from East Elementary School."

"Ten years in jail, huh? For what?"

"Endangering children and trespassing on private property," the man answered.

"I see. You're working for Adam Young?" Scythe asked. Inwardly, he saluted the superintendent. He had acted immediately and had paid enough to get a lawyer to Inferno in the course of a couple of hours—after the office closed. On someone else, this attempt to intimidate might be effective.

"That is privileged information," the lawyer said.

"Gotcha. Currently, you're on private property. Allow me to walk you to the front door," Scythe said evenly. He would never allow this man to guess this crappy move bothered him.

Scythe lugged the two heavy buckets with ease through the crowd, making sure the lawyer followed him. When he reached Wraith, Scythe set down one container and pointed to a spot above the entrance. "Could you read that notice there?"

Automatically, the man glanced up. When he saw the device and the sign stating, *You are on camera*, he looked immediately down. Too late, they had a clear picture of him. Scythe checked his watch for the time before addressing Wraith.

"This guy is threatening to put me in jail for ten years. Can you add him to the banned list?"

"Sir, you are no longer welcome at Inferno. Please leave," Wraith informed him loudly.

The man scanned the crowd, noting the attention the

encounter drew and nodded. "Of course. I've accomplished my mission."

Scythe leaned forward to share, "Oh, and by the way, we have footage not only of you today but of Adam Young interacting with a bachelorette party last night. Those would be interesting pictures to have appear in the paper before the next school board meeting."

"Or on the district website. That would be better," Wraith said.

The man looked back and forth between them. "I would not suggest blackmail to a lawyer."

"No one mentioned blackmail," Scythe pointed out. "Have a nice evening, sir. Thanks for your office's address. I hope your car is okay in the parking lot."

The man opened and closed his mouth like a fish before rushing out of Inferno. He obviously liked his car. Scythe smirked at his back.

"Something I need to know?" Wraith asked.

"Not now. I'm going to take off after I get the bar restocked."

"Of course," Wraith answered.

As he walked away, he heard Caroline ask, "What's going on with Scythe?"

"I have a hunch Scythe has found…." Wraith's answer faded as Scythe retraced his steps through the customers.

CHAPTER 7

He'd forced himself to stay away on Tuesday when she hadn't called for a bedtime story. Maybe she wasn't that into him. Scythe dismissed that worry quickly. She wasn't skilled in concealing her emotions. Winnie was attracted to him. Just as he was to her.

Scythe had, of course, texted to make sure she had transportation to and from work. Her polite response had arrived within seconds. Had she been waiting to hear from him?

By Tuesday at seven p.m., he couldn't focus at Inferno anymore. He alerted the other Devil Daddies and headed out. After pulling into her driveway, Scythe cut off his engine and parked his bike. He studied the dark windows before checking the time. Eight fifteen. His Little girl wouldn't have gone to sleep that early. He had a feeling the stack of papers in her bag wasn't a onetime occurrence. Tonight's pile would have taken her several hours to correct.

A vibration rumbled inside his cut. Scythe grabbed his phone to check the screen. Winnie. He quickly accepted the call. "Chipmunk. You're not asleep."

"I heard a motorcycle and thought of you. Can you read me a

story now? I didn't want to bother you last night." Winnie spoke in a hushed whisper.

"I can. That motorcycle was mine. I'm in your driveway."

"Really?" Her voice squeaked with excitement, "Where's your room, Little girl?"

"On the backside of the house."

"I'll see you in five minutes. Open the window for me," Scythe instructed as he got off the bike.

"I'm on the second floor. I'd let you in the back door, but I don't want to wake Mom," she said quickly.

"Trust me, Chipmunk. I'll make it to you. I'm coming around the house." He disconnected the call and stowed his phone in his vest.

Reaching the backyard, he spotted a massive oak tree. *Nice.* That would help him get to the second floor. One set of windows glowed with light. A limb extended within three feet of the sill. *Easy.*

Scythe jumped to grab the lowest branch and swung his legs up to wrap around it. In seconds, he navigated to a higher branch and then over to the branch that led to the illuminated window now filled with a familiar face. She hurriedly slid the lower pane open.

"You are going break your neck," she whispered furiously. "I'll just open the door for you and you can tiptoe inside."

"I'm good. I climbed a few trees in my youth. Step back, Winnie. I don't want to hurt you."

She scrambled back as Scythe moved down the limb to the spot closest to the opening. Balancing himself with the branch above him, Scythe paused and considered the best move. He could dive in, but that was a head injury waiting to happen. Glancing up at the branch above him, he made a new plan.

His motorcycle boots were a bit of a liability, but he managed to stand, using smaller branches to steady himself. He sidestepped to a spot where the thick branch dropped slightly. Launching himself upward, Scythe grabbed that limb, holding his breath. Would it support him? When it only creaked a bit, he maneuvered hand over hand until he dangled close enough to the window to swing his legs inside and drop to sit on the windowsill.

Arms wrapped around his torso. "Gotcha!"

Holding onto the window frame, Scythe slid his hips inside and lowered himself to the floor. Winnie climbed onto his lap, scattering kisses all over his face. She wore fuzzy slipper socks and an oversized nightshirt decorated with what he suspected were chipmunks.

"That was crazy. You aren't ever to do that again," she scolded between pecks as he enjoyed her greeting.

"We'll get a fire ladder, and you can let me climb up to you," he suggested, rubbing her spine to reassure her.

She stopped and leaned back to meet his gaze. "That's a good idea. Wait! Are you planning to visit often?"

"Yes."

Winnie tilted her head as she considered his short answer. "To read me a bedtime story?"

"I needed to hold you, Chipmunk." Scythe cupped her jaw and drew her forward. He kissed her lightly before deepening the exchange. She responded eagerly, wiggling closer and wrapping her arms around his neck. Her eagerness fueled his desire.

When he lifted his head a few minutes later, she kept her eyes closed and licked her lips. His cock twitched against his fly, already on alert.

"Little girl, you're killing me," he groaned.

Her eyes fluttered open to stare at him with passion-clouded eyes. "That was a solid A. I don't think you need the notes I wrote down for you."

Unable to resist, he grinned at her. "Oh, yeah. I need to see those notes. My goal is an A+."

"An A+ doesn't exist, Scythe. An A is the top."

"We'll see," he teased. "You might invent a new level for me." When she appeared skeptical, he laughed quietly.

"Kiss me, Little girl." To his delight, she initiated the next round. He shifted his hands to her ribcage, brushing his fingers along the swell of her breasts. When she wiggled to both sides, he glided his hands to her back, concerned he was moving too quickly for her.

Winnie lifted her mouth from his to beg, "Please. Will you touch me?"

"Where, Chipmunk?"

"My tatas," she whispered and then added, "You can say no. It's okay."

"I'm never going to refuse to caress you, Little girl," he promised. "Let's get you comfortable on my lap."

He lifted her and resettled her with her thighs spread and wrapped on either side of his body. Scythe caught a quick glimpse of her silky curls and strangled a groan in the back of his throat. She quickly pushed down her nightshirt, not aware she'd already tempted him.

"Perfect. Could these be chipmunks?" he asked, trailing a fingertip over the cotton material.

Winnie nodded before shivering as his fingers slid over her. Scythe detoured to brush the sensitive side of her breast. Her nipples pressed against the fabric, luring him on. He drew a spiral around her before flicking his thumb across the taut peak. Her breath came in a shaky exhale.

"Can you tell me what you like?" he whispered.

She shook her head desperately.

He cupped her other side in his hand and caressed both nipples through the soft fabric. Her eyes closed, and she bit her lower lip. Scythe lifted his hand from her to run his fingers over her mouth.

"I need to hear your sounds, Chipmunk."

Her eyes flashed open, and she nodded.

"Yes, Daddy," he suggested.

"Yes, Daddy," she repeated obediently.

"That's my good girl. That deserves a treat, right?"

"Yes, Daddy."

"Oh, another reward," he promised. Leaning forward, he trailed kisses down the cord of her neck to the hollow of her throat. Scythe nipped and caressed his way to her nipple and paused, letting his hot breath sink through the thin material. She inhaled sharply, lifting her beaded bud to his lips.

Of course, he closed his mouth around her offering and pulled it gently into the heat of his mouth. Winnie arched her back, presenting herself to him. Scythe brushed his tongue over her nipple, wetting the material as he teased her sensitive flesh.

Before moving to repeat the special treatment to her other side, he rolled her nipple between his teeth. Scythe listened carefully to her breath for that quick inhale he'd already learned signaled a spike of arousal for her. When she pushed her pussy to his pelvis and gyrated against him, Scythe's hands tightened on the treasures he held.

Damn, she was temptation incarnate. All sweet innocence and sensual moves. If she was as inexperienced as he believed, she was naturally responsive and eager.

He dropped a hand to her bare flesh above her knee and glided his hand under her nightshirt. She stilled and then wiggled as if straining to get closer to his touch. Scythe gripped her thigh, tethering her in place. He waited to speak until her gaze met his.

"Little girl…."

"I'll give you an A+! I have gold stars!" she blurted, interrupting him.

His automatic smile at the reminder of her grading system evaporated at the panic on her face. "Winnie…."

She shivered like an abandoned colt. "Please don't tell me you're not interested in me. You climbed all the way up here to break up with me?"

"I'm not breaking up with you, Chipmunk. Let's get that straight. Okay?"

When she nodded, still breathing way too fast, he added,

"Let me help you. Inhale deeply with me, Little girl." He inhaled audibly and watched Winnie follow his instructions.

"Hold it for three seconds. One, two, three." He counted slowly before adding, "Exhale everything out of your lungs."

Her breath whooshed out, and she sucked air back in.

"Keep trying to slow down. Everything is okay. Exhale and then let's count to five as we inhale."

He led her through the cycle of slow breaths in and slow exhales until the tension in her body visibly faded. Her shoulders settled into place, and the rigidity of her muscles softened.

"That's my Little girl."

"I'm sorry. Panic attack, I guess."

"How about if we talk next time if you feel like you are going to panic?"

"I don't get them often. Never at school. In my classroom, I'm totally in control and relaxed. It happens around men. I—I haven't had much success dating."

"Have people been mean to you?"

"College was a nightmare. I dated a frat guy, and he dumped me when I started liking him too much."

"That sucks." There had to be more to the story. Scythe paused to see if she would tell him the rest.

"Then another one asked me out and ghosted me. Then another. And another and so on. Turns out, I became the frat target. How many of them could date and drop me before I caught on?"

"Give me their names," he growled.

"It was two states away and a few years ago, Scythe. You can't hunt them down for stupid games they played in college."

"I can."

"I'm not going to give you that information."

He looked at her sternly. "Tell me they stopped when you found out."

"Oh, no. They got another frat house involved, so I couldn't trust anyone on campus. I didn't date after that. Well, except for helping Frankie in the library, if you'd count that as a date. Pretending our meetings were romantic made me feel better. You know, less of a loser."

Scythe pulled her close and hugged her tight. "You could never be a loser, Winnie. They were, Little girl. I hope you realize you didn't do anything wrong. They did. Assholes."

She nodded against his shoulder, hiding her face.

"I'm not an immature college guy. I've never deliberately treated anyone poorly like that."

She pressed a kiss to his throat. "Thank you. If you get tired of me, just tell me nicely. I'll understand."

"That's not going to happen, Winnie. I've searched for my Little girl for many years. The Devil Daddies told me when I found her, I'd recognize her. After spending a few minutes with you, I knew they were right. You are my Little girl." He didn't want to scare her with the truth. To his delight, she looked at him like he'd just hung the sun for her.

He leaned down to kiss Winnie. This time, their exchange was sweet. Scythe lifted his head to meet her gaze. "What about you, Chipmunk? Can you see me as your Daddy?"

Winnie nodded. "I've read a bunch of books. The Daddies are always so handsome, and they care so much about their Littles. I never thought they existed, much less that I'd find someone who wanted to be my Daddy."

A sudden yawn opened her jaw. Winnie slapped her hand over her lips to hide it. "Sorry," she whispered a second later.

"You need to be asleep, Winnie. I came to read you a bedtime story. Let's get you tucked under the covers."

"You're not going to touch my tatas anymore?" she blurted.

Her face immediately flamed red with embarrassment. He loved that her mouth shared information before she could stop it. That would be very handy as her Daddy. "I am definitely going to caress your sweet body, but I want you to remember it, not be half asleep."

Winnie paused as if considering his statement and then nodded. "That makes sense."

"I'm glad, Little girl. I want to rip your clothes off and have my way with you," Scythe told her, holding her gaze.

"I'd like that too."

"You're going to more than like it when we make love for the first time, Winnie."

"I wouldn't grade that," she rushed to reassure him.

"Oh, you're going to give me that elusive A+."

"If it kills me?" she teased.

"I'll make sure you survive," he promised. He wasn't surprised when she changed the subject.

"You could stretch out with me and leave through the front door tomorrow when my mom is awake," Winnie suggested and then glanced away as if she were sure he would refuse.

Scythe stood, lifting her with him. He balanced his precious armful with one hand and tossed back the covers with the other. Placing her under the covers, he said, "Scooch over, Chipmunk," as he stripped off his cut and belt and threw them over a chair.

Her answering grin went right to his heart. Winnie moved to the far edge of the bed and laid down. She reached out to nab her stuffed chipmunk and pulled it to her chest as she studied him.

Back on the farm, his chores had built muscle naturally. These days, he maintained his strength in the gym with his MC brothers. He appreciated every crunch and lift as she scanned his body.

Scythe untied his boots and stepped out of those. He stretched out beside her. Winnie immediately snuggled next to him, resting her head on his shoulder. Scythe drew the covers up to her chin, taking care not to smother the precious item in her arms. Tapping the stuffie's nose, he said, "I bet this is Chippy."

"Yes. He thinks you're wonderful. And handsome too."

"Thank you, Chippy. You're a lucky stuffie to have Winnie love you. Now, we need a story. How about I tell you the one about when Chippy explored the house while you were at school last week?"

"I did find him in Mom's room one day!"

"He's very adventurous," Scythe agreed and launched into an imaginary adventure for an energetic chipmunk like Chippy. Winnie's eyes drifted shut after a few minutes, and her breath evened out. He studied her relaxed face for a long time before closing his eyes and allowing himself to sleep.

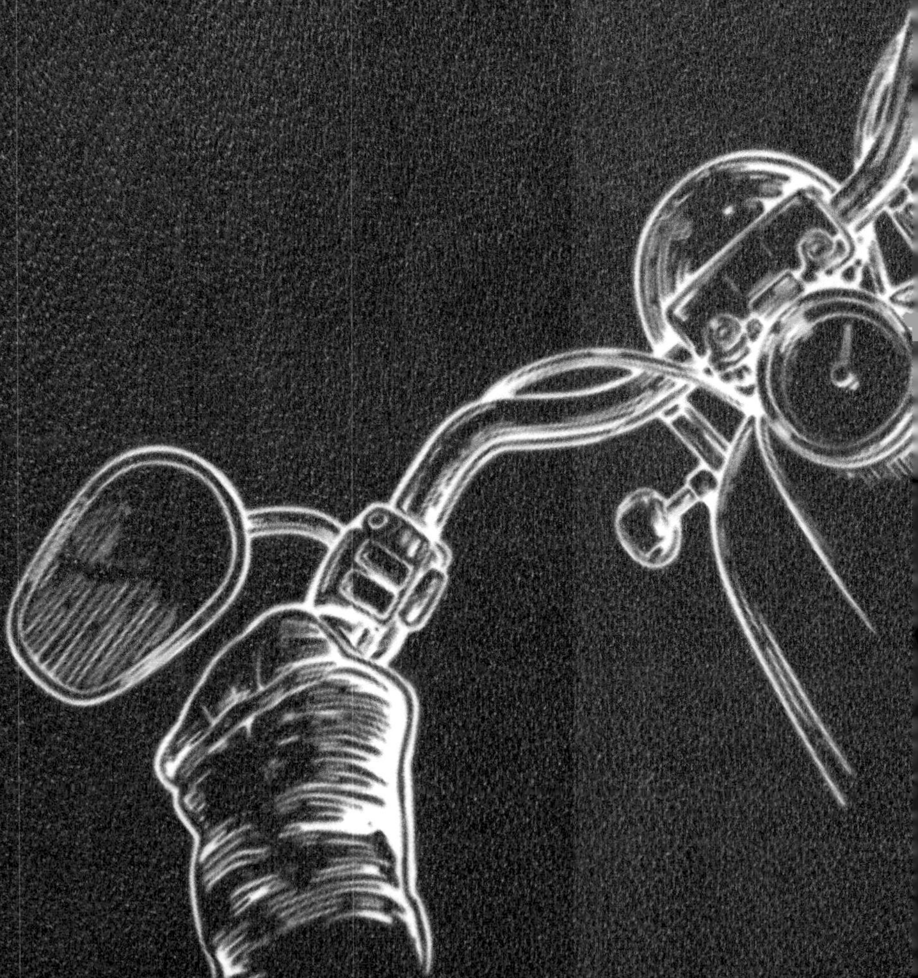

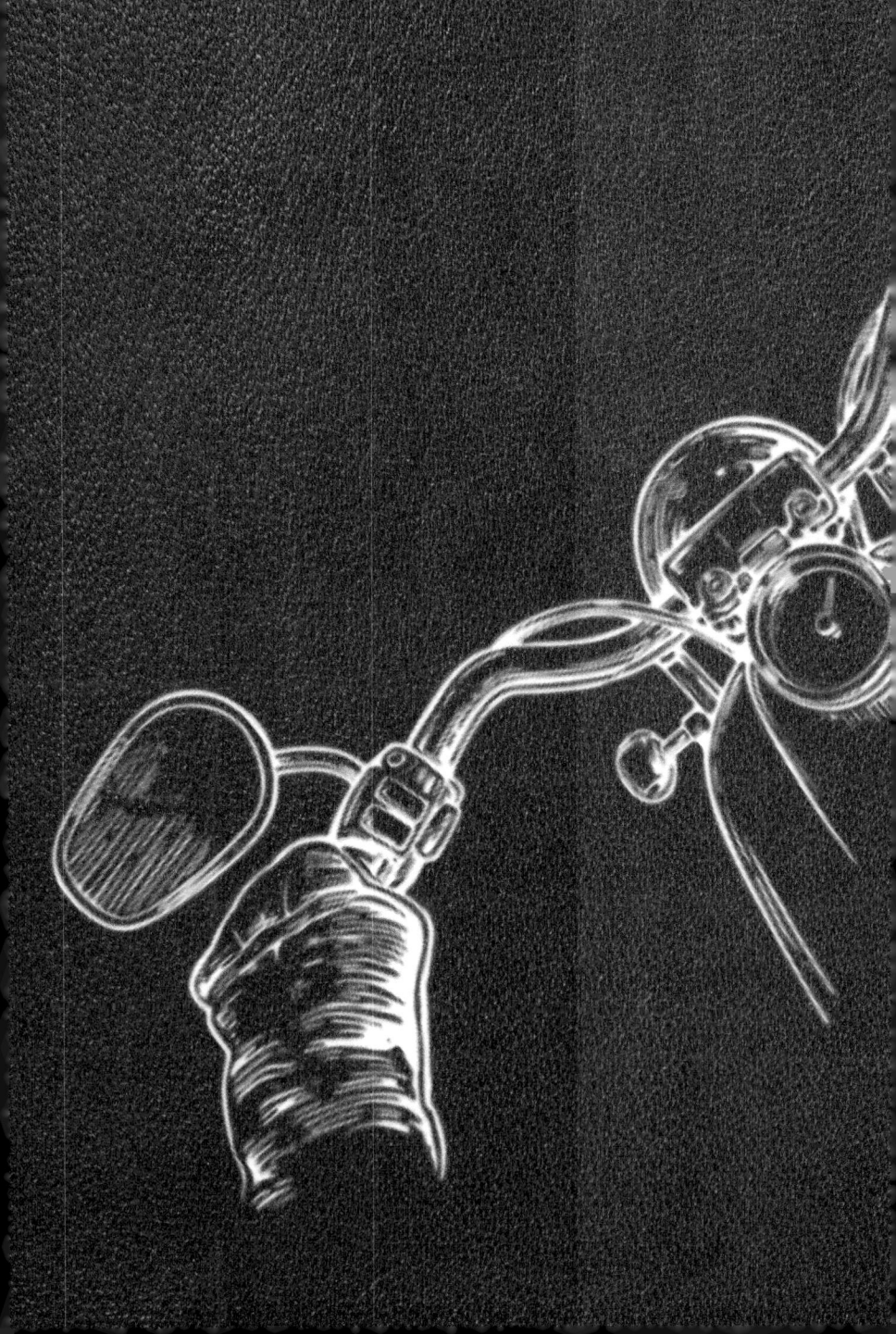

CHAPTER 8

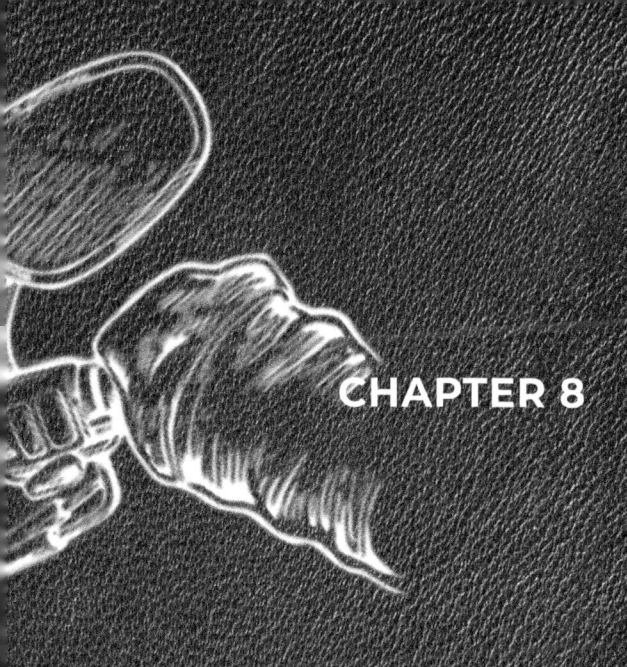

Waking up snuggled next to radiating warmth, Winnie blinked into the darkness. She turned to see Scythe's handsome face lit dimly by the nightlight she kept by her bed. He'd stayed. She'd actually found a man whose word meant something. And he was interested in her. As she smiled into the darkness, a thought leapt into her mind. Was she brave enough?

Moving cautiously, Winnie stretched to press her lips to his neck. She held her breath when he moved, but Scythe simply tilted his head slightly to give her greater access. Emboldened, Winnie trailed more kisses down to the neck of his T-shirt. If only he'd taken this off before stretching out with her.

"Mmm, Winnie," he murmured and rubbed his hand up and down her spine.

"Off, Daddy," she whispered, pulling at the soft cotton.

Without asking a question, Scythe curled up slightly from the bed and reached over his head to grab the material and remove his shirt. Winnie immediately took advantage of access to the expanse of chiseled flesh. Her hand stroked over his skin as she pressed kisses to his chest.

"That feels good, Chipmunk," he complimented her as he

slid his hand under the back of her nightshirt to caress her bare skin as well.

She loved the rasp of his rough fingertips gliding over her. When his hand moved lower to cup her naked bottom, she froze.

"Relax, Little girl. You can tell me to stop anytime. Do you not like my touch?"

The darkness made her brave enough to confess, "I love how you make me feel. I don't want you to be disappointed."

"You could never disappoint me, Winnie."

Scythe tightened his grip on her bottom, squeezing the soft padding. "You're absolutely perfect just as you are."

When she relaxed against him, Scythe rolled toward her, urging Winnie onto her back. He kissed her deeply, dispelling her apprehension. Their kisses escalated the desire already brewing inside her.

She wrapped her arms around his neck, trying to get as close as possible. When he lifted his head, she protested, "More!"

"Daddy wants to unwrap his present."

After turning to press her into the mattress, he ran one palm up her thigh, sweeping her nightshirt up her curves. He caressed the hollow of her waist and swell of her breast as his hand passed along her side. Her shiver of excitement pleased him as she leaned into his touch. She lifted her arms without him asking, allowing Scythe to pull the oversized garment off.

"Good girl," he praised her as he tossed the garment to the floor. In the faint light, her skin glowed like a pearl. "You are so beautiful."

He brushed her tousled hair away from her face and leaned in to kiss her. To his delight, she responded eagerly and rubbed her nipples against the scattering of hair on his chest. Scythe grazed his fingertips down over her sensitive inner arm and cupped her breast. It fit perfectly in his hand.

Winnie moaned softly into his mouth. The sweet sound went straight to his cock. His shaft lengthened, tenting the heavy denim of his jeans. Scythe shifted to ease the pressure. He was sure his Little girl was a virgin. He refused to rush her, even if his body had different ideas.

Lifting his lips from hers, Scythe then kissed a trail down her throat and the other breast he hadn't paid attention to yet. He rubbed his whiskery stubble over the sensitive underside. Her fingers tightened on his shoulders as her body froze.

"Breathe, Chipmunk," he reminded her before turning his attention to her taut peak. Scythe drew it into his mouth, increasing the suction until she wiggled underneath him.

"Daddy, please," Winnie begged.

"We're in no hurry, Little girl. Your Daddy is enjoying your beautiful curves."

He leaned slightly to the side and rolled her nipple between his lips. Scythe trailed his hand over her stomach to ruffle her silky adult hair before squeezing her mound slightly. Her pussy was slick with arousal under his fingertips.

With a pop, he released her nipple before tracing her cleft. He lifted his drenched index finger to his lips and licked the sweet nectar from his skin. "Mmm. You are delicious, Winnie. Have you ever tasted yourself?"

She shook her head.

"Use your words, Little girl."

"No, Daddy."

"No, Daddy what?" he prompted.

Even in the dim light, he could see the blush spread over her cheeks as she completed her answer. "No, Daddy. I've never tasted myself."

"Good girl. I think it's time you did, don't you?"

Winnie nodded eagerly. Her gaze remained glued on his face until he moved. Then she followed the path of his hand as he glided his knuckles down the centerline of her torso. Her eyes closed to half-mast as he stroked over her mound. Scythe dipped into her pink folds, tracing them as he wet his fingers.

Her hips lifted to deepen his caress. Scythe traced her wet opening and flicked over the bud at the top. Her gasp made his cock jump in his pants. Scythe didn't know if he'd ever been so hard in his life. He lifted his fingers to her lips and smoothed the slick juice over them.

The tip of her pink tongue darted from her mouth to slide over her skin. She moaned at the flavor and licked her lips fully as her gaze lifted to his face in amazement.

"Delicious, huh?" he suggested.

"Yes, Daddy."

"I can't wait to fill you with my cock. Perhaps I'll allow you to lick me clean after you've orgasmed a few times."

"Tonight?" she asked eagerly.

"Do you want me to make love to you, Chipmunk? Once I do, I'll never let you go."

"Please, Daddy. Make me yours."

He wouldn't refuse that offer. Scythe kissed her hard. To his delight, she caressed his chest and moved daringly lower to flip the button of his jeans open. When her fingers brushed the soft head of his penis, they froze. Then, as if she couldn't believe his cock would extend to his waistband, Winnie stroked over the tip again.

Scythe couldn't contain the moan at her second tentative caress. Winnie snatched her hand away.

"Did I hurt you?"

"Only in the best way." He cupped himself to slide his zipper down carefully, and his shaft burst through the opening. "I'll be right back."

Scythe rolled out of bed and thrust his jeans and boxers over his hips. He tried to ignore her gasp as she caught sight of his cock. *Damn. Don't think about her staring at you,* Scythe warned his hard-on when it jerked, demanding attention. *We're going slow, remember?* He grabbed a condom from his wallet and tossed it on the bed. Scythe would protect her at all costs.

He stretched out beside her. Immediately, Winnie reached for his shaft, trying to circle it with her fingers.

"Is it supposed to be that big?" she whispered, squeezing him.

"Mine is exactly the right size."

"Maybe you're too thick for me, Daddy."

He could hear the sadness in her voice and knew she didn't think it was possible for the two of them to continue. "We'll match together perfectly, Chipmunk."

"You're sure? I've never had sex. I could be terrible at it."

"I'm positive our parts will align incredibly and that we'll both enjoy ourselves. A lot."

Before she could ask any other questions, he leaned down to claim her mouth. His lips teased hers until she focused completely on his kisses. She relaxed enough to dare to stroke his body with her hands. Scythe encouraged her with growls and "That's so good," comments. He loved that her touch became more confident as he urged her on.

Sliding a leg between her thighs, Scythe wrapped his hands around her sweet bottom and pulled her tight to him. Immediately, she squirmed to get away and then repeated that action deliberately as she bit her lip.

"Do you like that? Never be afraid to experiment. You're safe with me."

"Daddy, I ache," she whispered.

He closed his eyes, controlling his need to move. He forced himself to go slowly, wanting her to discover how magical making love could be. "Let Daddy see if he can help you, Chipmunk. Spread your thighs for me."

Winnie hesitated for a couple of long seconds before she followed his instructions. Scythe cupped her pussy and squeezed firmly. "You're so wet, Little girl. So ready."

Easing the pressure, Scythe explored her pink folds. He

listened to her sharp inhales, noting those spots that pleased her the most and returning to them frequently. When she writhed in front of him, Scythe circled her entrance before gliding his finger deep inside. She clamped down on his digit immediately and bounced, trying to coax as much sensation from it. He slid it from her tight channel and replaced it with two fingers.

"Daddy!"

"Do you feel a burn, Chipmunk?"

"I like it," she whispered before hiding her face against his chest.

"I'm glad, Little girl. I can't wait to fill your tight pussy."

He scissored his fingers inside her. When her hands tightened on his shoulders, he knew she was on edge. Leaning forward, Scythe softly bit the sensitive curve of her neck to distract her as he prepared her. When she relaxed around his fingers, he smiled. His Little girl enjoyed a taste of pain. She was perfect.

He slid his fingers from her and urged her over onto her back. Tearing the condom open, he rolled it onto his cock as she watched him so closely, he could almost feel it. "Daddy's going to make you mine now," he told her.

"Will it hurt?"

"Maybe for a split second. Then I'll make it so much better." Scythe wouldn't lie to her.

"O—Okay," she whispered.

"Wrap your legs around my waist, Winnie."

When she followed his instructions, he placed his cock to her entrance. Slowly, he pressed inside, pausing when her muscles tightened around him as he did farm crop calculations in his mind to distract himself. "Damn, I love being inside you, Chipmunk."

"Daddy, I don't...."

He pushed the last couple of inches inside her, interrupting her statement. "Are you okay, Winnie?"

"If you don't move, I may scream," she hissed into his ear.

Relieved, Scythe captured her lips in a sizzling kiss as he

glided out and thrust back inside her heat. Winnie tilted her head and closed her eyes as if she needed to concentrate on the sensations filling her. Scythe nibbled along the cord of her exposed throat as he experimented to discover what she liked best. He guessed she was struggling to stay quiet as the muscles of her neck contracted under his lips. He couldn't wait to have her at his place, where she could make as much noise as she wanted.

When she trembled under him, he suspected she was close. He reached between their bodies and brushed his fingertip across her clit. She lifted her hand from his shoulders and covered her mouth as she orgasmed, capturing most of the sound.

Her shocked eyes met his a few seconds later. She asked through her fingers, "Is it supposed to feel that good?"

"Oh, yeah, Little girl. And it will get better."

"I may have to rethink that A+ thing," she whispered, completely serious.

Scythe's heart skipped a beat. She was so damned cute. "Let's see if I can convince you."

By the time she burrowed into the crook of his shoulder to fall back asleep, Scythe knew he'd scored the ultimate grade. His Little girl was naturally sensual and responsive. She would be sore tomorrow, but he suspected she'd welcome the reminder. Closing his eyes, Scythe allowed himself to sleep.

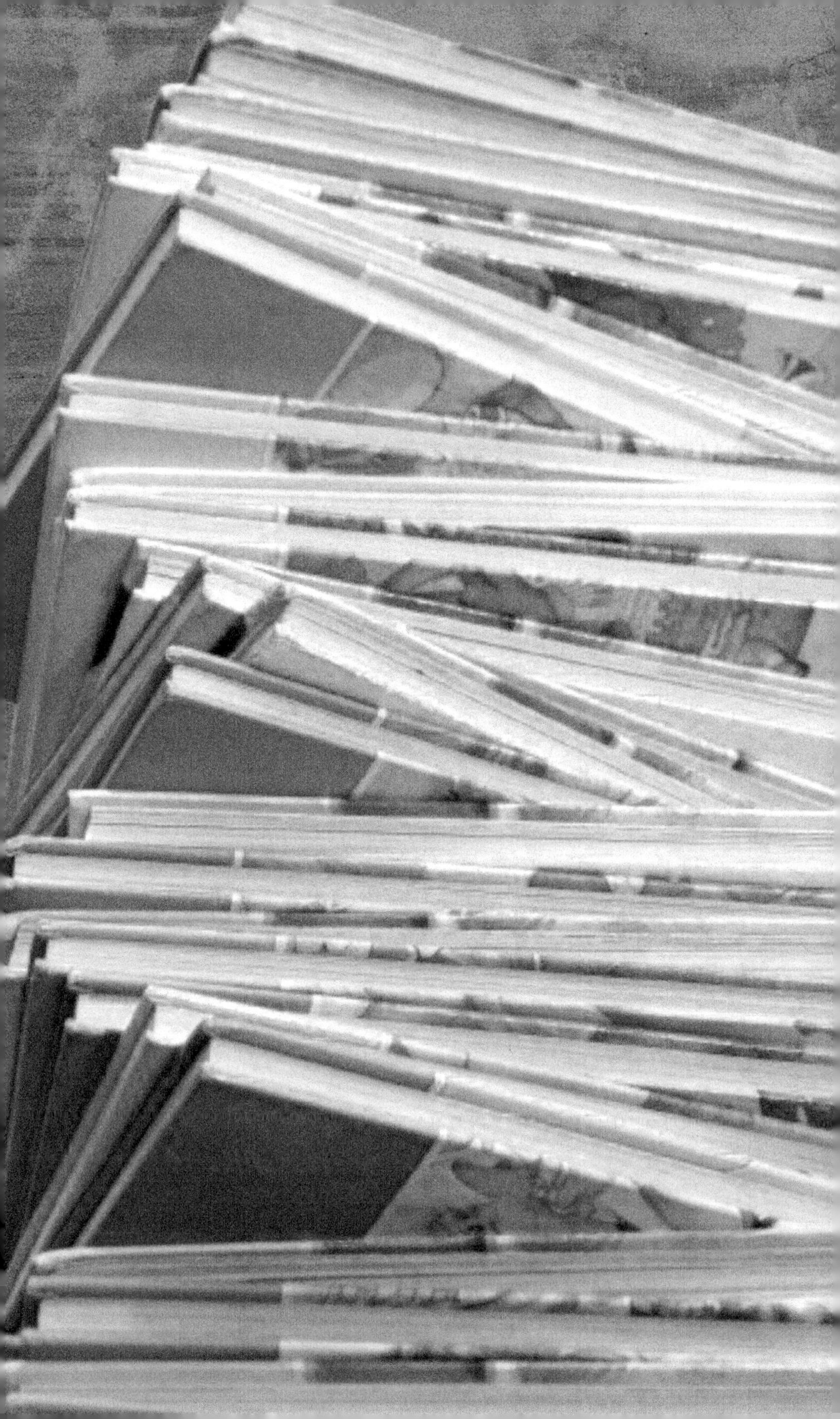

CHAPTER 9

Winnie hoped no one could tell how different she was as she walked into her building fifteen minutes before the requirement. Seeing her principal again standing inside the door distracted her slightly from her life-changing experience. Lorraine placed a mark on the clipboard as Winnie entered. How many mornings was she going to patrol the entrance, hoping to catch Winnie arriving late?

"Good morning, Miss Oberson," Winnie greeted her pleasantly.

"Good morning, Winnie. I'm glad you're on time this morning."

"Of course. Monday was a complete fluke. I figured out that a hundred and ninety contract days for six years meant I was punctual 1139 days out of 1140. That's ninety-nine-point-nine percent on-time arrivals."

"Are you arguing with me, Winnie?"

"No, ma'am. I just thought it was an interesting fact," Winnie assured her. "I'll get ready for the kids."

Walking into her classroom, she listened for the telltale clatter of Lorraine's heels on the linoleum in the hallway. As she suspected, a few seconds after she turned on her computer, her principal left her position at the door to the faculty parking lot. The bitch had waited to try to punish *her* for being tardy for a second time. She didn't care about the others who were delayed on a consistent basis.

Winnie sat down and typed out a message to the faculty union rep. She'd been too embarrassed on Monday to admit she'd gotten in trouble for arriving late because of her car problems. Now that she was sure Lorraine was out to get her, Winnie knew she needed help.

Elizabeth McGower, the building faculty representative, appeared in her doorway two minutes later with her notebook. She listened carefully and took notes. "I would normally suggest a meeting with Ms. Oberson, but she's already told me you are on her list not to rehire or to transfer to a different building. I was on my way down to talk to you when your message popped up on my computer."

"Why? I'm never in trouble." Winnie looked at her in complete disbelief.

"I'm not sure. If I had to guess, she has a friend who wants your position," Elizabeth said.

"Can she do that?"

"She can transfer you to another building without stating a reason. That would allow you to keep your job. If she can fire you, then no one will be around to ask any tricky questions. Make sure you are following each rule she establishes. Be aware her secretary is posting new ones on the office bulletin board almost every day. Go down there before and after school to check."

Winnie shook her head, unable to believe this was happening. She had promised to tell Scythe if she had any problems today. He was going to flip when he heard this.

"Hi, Miss Bradley!" Her first student arrived and rushed forward to hug her.

"Hi, Dakota! I'm glad to see you!"

The faculty rep waved and headed out the door, saying, "Keep me updated."

"Thank you, Elizabeth."

Winnie followed her out the door to supervise the halls around her room as the kids streamed inside. She wanted to send Scythe a message, but Ms. Oberson stood at the hallway intersection blatantly watching. Winnie already had that rule memorized. Teachers were forbidden to use their phones during the school day.

What else could the principal throw at her?

She twisted the doorknob to make sure she'd locked the door when she'd come inside. If a shelter-in-place drill occurred, she would be in trouble if her door was unlocked. Winnie breathed a sigh of relief when she found it secured.

When the bell rang, she quickly took attendance and submitted it on her computer while the kids attacked their bell work. One sweet student who had some health problems requiring frequent bathroom breaks signaled her, and Winnie handed over the bathroom pass from her desk drawer. When Winnie walked into the hallway to supervise her on her way, she discovered her principal leaning against the wall, typing furiously on her phone.

"Good morning," Winnie greeted her before addressing the student. "Go ahead, Taylor. Hurry back."

"Thank you, Ms. Bradley," the student said and raced through the hallway.

Ms. Oberson roared, "Stop running!" Taylor jumped before cupping her hand frantically over her crotch. That shout had scared her student, and as a result, Taylor had an accident.

Winnie scurried to the girl's side and told her quickly. "I'll get someone to clean this up. You go on to the nurse's office. I'll alert her you'll need some help."

"She shouted at me," the child said, with tears coursing down her cheeks.

"Ms. Oberson didn't understand, Taylor. She wouldn't have yelled if she did. I'll explain."

"Do you not train your children to follow the school rules?" Lorraine Oberson demanded as she joined Winnie at the puddle on the floor.

"There's a medical issue involved here with a special requirement. Taylor must hurry sometimes to get to the bathroom. Would you mind standing here so no one slips while I notify the office to call a custodian?"

"I'll take care of that, Ms. Bradley. You've left your class unsupervised for too long. Come in tomorrow morning at eight for a meeting with me."

"Of course. I'll bring Taylor's health plan and ask the nurse to attend as well," Winnie said quickly.

"We will not address the accident, Ms. Bradley. I wish to discuss your extended absence from your classroom."

"You mean now as we're talking in the hall?"

"Obviously." Lorraine turned and stalked off, leaving the mess.

Winnie stared at her stiff spine in disbelief. If the administrator had simply left everything alone, Taylor wouldn't be mortified in the nurse's office. Not trusting that she would take care of the hallway puddle, Winnie returned to her room and grabbed the trash can. With it stationed close to the fall hazard, she returned to her room and called the office. The secretary was extremely surprised. Lorraine had not reported it.

Two hours later, Lorraine waltzed in to sit in a chair at the rear of the room. She scribbled notes as Winnie taught. This was obviously an unscheduled teacher evaluation—which was fine, of course, with Winnie. She'd never had a principal spend ninety minutes in her room. Usually, they appeared for at most a half hour. Combining these events together made it obvious that Lorraine was out to fire her.

At lunch, the other teachers who had the same lunch schedule gathered in her room. The treatment she had gotten appalled everyone. Winnie tried to play it cool, but inside she was a total mess. She fled to the teacher rep's room immediately after school to share what had happened.

Elizabeth promised to be at school with her the next morning for the meeting. She would take notes, and with luck having an observer would curtail Lorraine's targeting. Winnie didn't have much hope.

Returning to her room, she phoned Taylor's mother to inform her about her daughter's accident. Lorraine had already contacted her and placed the blame on Winnie.

"Ms. Bradley, I thought we had a system in place."

"We do, and I followed that. Taylor was startled and had an accident," Winnie explained.

"Because you yelled at her."

Winnie opened her mouth to explain but heard Taylor's voice in the background. They must be in the car on the way home. "No, Mommy. Miss Bradley sent me immediately when I asked. It was that mean lady who yelled at me to stop running."

"Miss Bradley didn't yell at you?"

"Oh, no. Miss Bradley wouldn't ever do that. It was the principal. She's mean."

"It appears I received some incorrect information. My apologies for speaking harshly. I have appreciated all you've done for my daughter this year."

"It's not a problem. I'm glad we got everything straightened out and Taylor is in good spirits. She had a wonderful rest of her day. I'm amazed at how good she is at math," Winnie complimented.

"She does love math. Who do I report the principal to?"

"I have no idea. The superintendent, perhaps, or the assistant superintendent in charge of elementary education," Winnie suggested, crossing her fingers.

"Thank you. I'll investigate," Taylor's mother said before disconnecting.

Winnie typed up the information and sent it to the faculty

rep. She wasted more time making notes for herself and starting a file off the computer. After tucking the printouts of everything into her bookbag, Winnie double-checked her lesson plans for the following day. Lorraine would be back to evaluate her tomorrow. Her administrator wouldn't give up until she found something to use against Winnie.

When Winnie reached her car in the parking lot, she checked her phone and saw a bunch of messages from Scythe. She didn't have a few minutes to linger and read them. She barely had enough time to get home before Belinda would need to leave. Crossing her fingers, she hoped Scythe would understand.

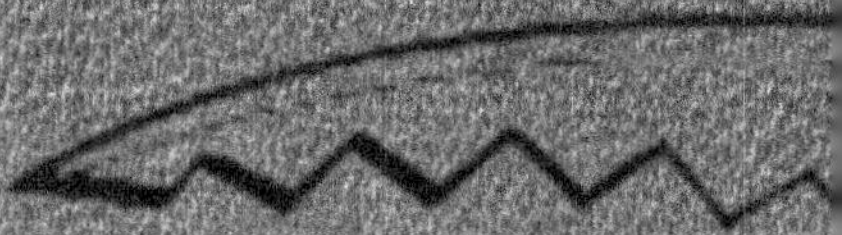

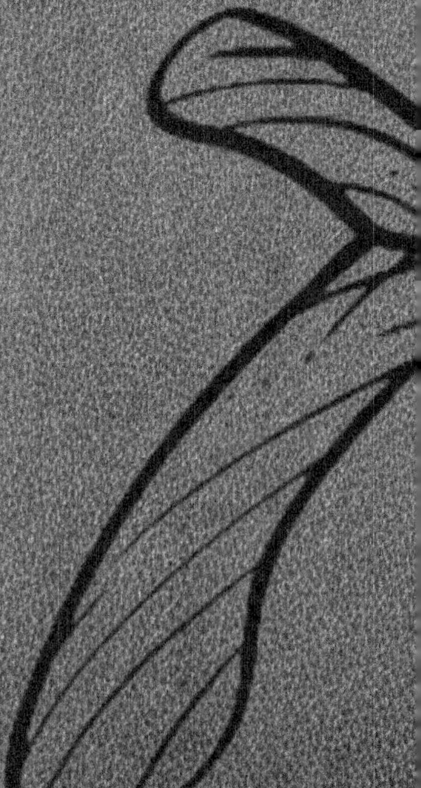

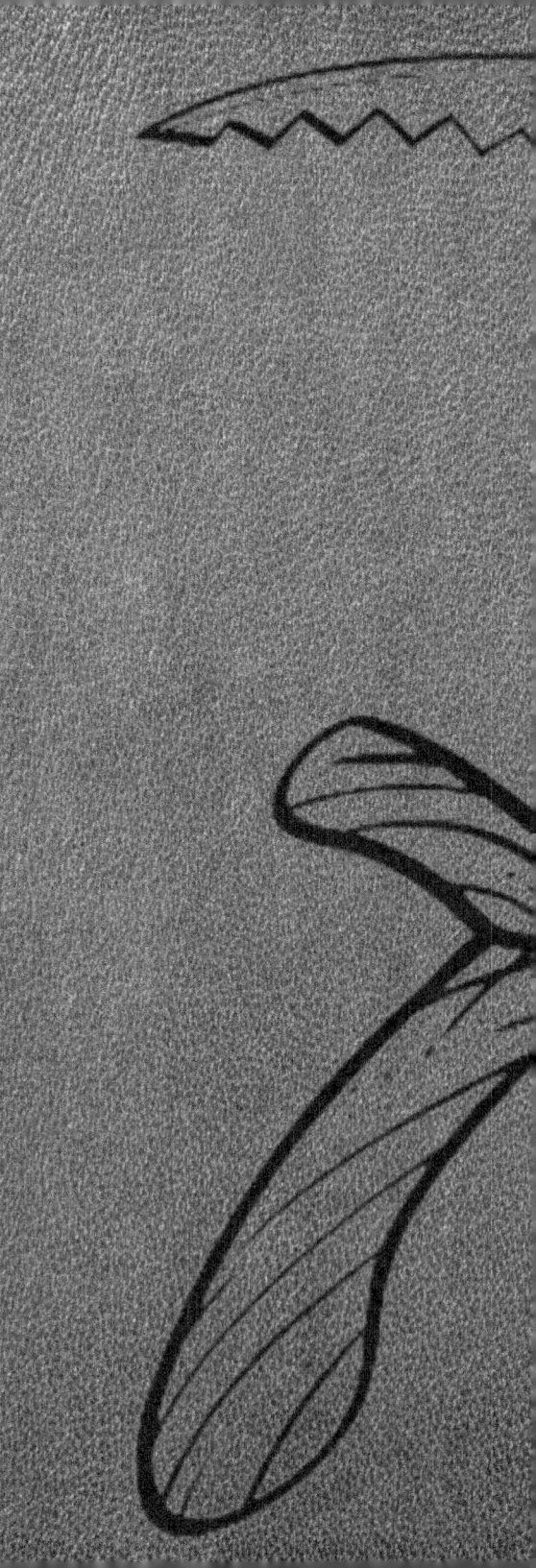

CHAPTER 10

Things at home were not good. All the hassles from her day disappeared as Winnie sat by her mother's bed, listening to her breathe erratically. She'd call the doctor tomorrow with her mother's request to bring in hospice care. Winnie could understand her decision. Her mother was tired of fighting and didn't have any more strength.

A tear ran down Winnie's cheek. She would miss her mother so much. Evelyn Bradley had a heart of gold. Laughter and happiness had filled their home from Winnie's earliest memories until her father had died suddenly of a massive heart attack. Evelyn had focused on comforting memories and the tasks she had to handle.

When her mother met Belinda's dad, Winnie had celebrated. So different from her father, Niles Spencer had helped her mother laugh again. He was jovial and fun-loving at all times. As a child, Winnie thought his laid-back attitude was due to his blue-collar job. He hadn't worn a strangling tie every day to work like her father had.

When Evelyn had fallen ill, Niles had gone to each appointment, treatment, and test. He'd been her rock. In fact, his fatal accident had occurred on his way to pick up a new dose of a trial medication.

With him gone, Winnie had tried hard to bolster her mother's spirits, but the cancer defeated every treatment. She'd need to request a leave of absence soon from work. Winnie knew that would be a huge struggle to get approval from her principal. Hopefully, her request wouldn't be one more reason for her to lose her teaching position. Surely Lorraine wouldn't be that unkind.

Winnie jumped when her phone buzzed in her pocket. She pulled out the device and checked the screen. Scythe. Seeing his name bolstered her spirits.

I've missed you today, Chipmunk. Is everything okay?

I'm sorry. I really wanted to see you, but Mom's not doing well. I'm at her bedside now.

I'm sorry, Chipmunk. Do you want me to come sit with you?

She hesitated. Having someone with her would support her, but her mother would try to rally and interact with their guest. That would drain more of her energy.

I'd love that, but I need to concentrate on Mom. Can I have a raincheck for another day?

Of course, Little girl. You can have anything you want. Promise me you'll call if you need me or change your mind. Time doesn't matter.

I promise. Thanks, Scythe.

Daddy.

Thanks, Daddy.

I'll text in the morning. Try to get some sleep.

Yes, sir.

Yes, Daddy, he corrected her again.

She smiled at the screen and messaged, *Yes, Daddy.*

A million kiss emojis floated across her screen.

How had she gotten so lucky to meet him? Winnie laid her cheek on the bed in front of her and closed her eyes. She'd stay here with her mother tonight.

A few hours later, she felt her mother's hand brush over her hair. Sitting up, Winnie asked, "Are you okay, Mom?"

"Go to bed, Winnie. You need your rest too." Her mother's voice was feathery soft.

Winnie stood and grabbed the ice water off the bedside table. "I will, Mom, if you take a drink."

"Okay, sweetheart." She sucked the smallest sip from the bendy straw and shook her head that she didn't want any more. "Go to bed."

"I'll see you in the morning, Mom."

"I love you, Winnie. Thank you for being such an incredible daughter. You know I'm proud of you, right?"

"I know, Mom. I love you. You could write a book on how to be a phenomenal mother."

"Thank you, sweetheart. Go lie down. You need your rest."

She couldn't argue with her mother, but she didn't want to leave her alone, either. Winnie stood and walked out into the hallway. She listened to her mother's light breathing and decided to go take a shower.

Later, dressed in her worn nightshirt with a faded chipmunk on the front, Winnie peeked into the living room. Did her mother's breathing sound quieter? Winnie crept into the room and stood by the side of the bed.

Her mother's chest rose sporadically. The inhales and exhales were so shallow they were hard to distinguish. Winnie's first thought was to call an ambulance, but that wasn't what her mother wanted.

Winnie took her mother's hand and sat by the bed. She swallowed hard before starting to reminisce aloud about all the fun memories they'd had together over the years. Making snow ice cream and chocolate chip cookies. Family vacations and staycations with a plastic pool in the backyard. Her mother seemed to relax as Winnie talked about how much she treasured having this time with her mother and how much she loved her. Silently this time, she asked her father and stepfather to come to get her mom to end her suffering.

Dashing away the quiet tears that poured down her cheeks, Winnie ignored her breaking heart to reassure her mother. "Mom, it's okay. You can stop struggling to stay here. You've done so much. It's okay to rest."

A peaceful silence settled over the room. Winnie kept thinking about all the happiness they'd had together. When she focused on her mother's face around three in the morning, Winnie knew she was gone. Fresh tears cascaded down her face. She was comforted that her mother wasn't battling cancer. But Winnie struggled to imagine a world without her in it.

Without second-guessing herself, she called Scythe. He answered on the first ring.

"Chipmunk? What's wrong?"

"She's gone."

"I'm on my way. I'll be there in five minutes."

"I'm supposed to do something, but I can't remember what that is," she confessed.

"I'm coming, Little girl. We'll handle this together. Five minutes."

"Thank you."

The emergency techs treated her mother with incredible care as the police asked her questions. Wrapped in her mother's robe that Scythe had found somewhere, Winnie provided them with copies of her mother's "do not resuscitate" order, her list of medications and doctors, as well as the signed consent for hospice they hadn't had time to begin. Winnie held it together with support from the rough-looking man at her side.

When Belinda got home, the house was quiet.

"What are all the lights on for?" Belinda demanded as she came through the front door.

"Mom's gone, Belinda." Winnie broke the news, moving forward to hug her stepsister.

"Why did you send her to the hospital? She didn't want to go back," Belinda demanded, waving her hands to fend Winnie off.

"I didn't, Belinda. I was at her side when she passed."

"She's dead? Why didn't you call?"

"I didn't know this would happen, Belinda. She's been bad before but rallied," Winnie pointed out. Inwardly, she rebuked herself. She should have phoned Belinda. It hadn't even crossed her mind. She'd focused on her mother and filling the space with good thoughts and energy.

"I didn't get to say goodbye," Belinda wailed. "She told me she loved me yesterday afternoon before I got ready for work. Do you think she knew?"

Winnie nodded. "Yes."

Belinda walked blindly forward to hug Winnie. The two hadn't always gotten along well, but this wasn't the time for petty squabbles.

"What do we do now?" Belinda asked.

"She organized all her arrangements in a folder. We just have to do what she wanted."

"O—Okay," Belinda said, stepping away to wipe her tears. "I'm so tired. This is overwhelming."

"Go to sleep, Belinda. I'll take care of this," Winnie assured her.

"Thanks."

As soon as Belinda's door closed, Scythe wrapped his arms around Winnie and pulled her close. He held her quietly for a few minutes before directing her. "Go find the folder. Let's get things in order."

He made everything easier for her. Scythe even reminded Winnie to call in for a substitute. She texted her bestie, Abby, with the location of her emergency sub plans.

Winnie had just sent the message to Abby when her phone

rang. "It's my principal." She met Scythe's gaze, hoping she didn't look as scared as she felt.

"Hello?"

"I have deleted your request for a substitute and will place another reprimand in your file for using paid time off as a weapon to delay a disciplinary meeting. One more letter in your file will result in you losing your job and receiving a negative recommendation," Lorraine Oberson announced.

"My mother passed away this morning," Winnie said dully. Her emotional well was completely empty.

"Right. Bring the death certificate to school, and I'll get you a sub tomorrow."

Winnie stared at the phone in disbelief. The woman didn't believe her? Who would make something like this up?

"What's going on?" Scythe asked.

"She canceled my sub and won't arrange for one until I bring a death certificate in to prove I'm telling the truth," Winnie said to him. She pressed the speaker button on the phone and set it down on the table. Her hand trembled too much to hold it without dropping the device.

"You have an hour to get here," the principal announced coldly.

Scythe growled. His voice was rough with anger. "Reconsider your decision about the substitute or all your secrets will unravel."

Winnie panicked. What was he doing? Scythe didn't understand how vindictive her principal was. She shook her head frantically, mouthing, "Stop!"

"Who is this? Is that supposed to be a threat, Winnie? I'll start writing that third letter."

"You will not, Lori," Scythe told her.

"My name is Lorraine Oberson. Who are you?"

"The man who's stopping this now. Arrange for a sub, Lori."

Winnie's finger hovered over the disconnect button. What on earth was Scythe doing? This was her career. Something in his expression made her trust him. She held her voice, hoping for a miracle.

Silence followed. When she spoke next, Winnie's principal's voice came in a stutter. "I—I don't know what game you're playing, b—but you can't th—threaten me."

"My word is my vow, Lori. If you come after Winnie or harass her in any way, I will turn your life upside down. Call the sub, Lori."

What did Scythe have on her? She was caving to his pressure.

"I'm reinstituting a substitute for you, Winnie," the principal said after another pause.

"Make it a good one," Scythe said firmly and disconnected the call.

"What have you done?" Winnie asked, so anxious she caught herself tugging the side of her hair.

Scythe gently pulled her hands free and held them in his. "Your principal has several secrets she doesn't want to have publicized. She's going to leave you alone."

Winnie stared at him in disbelief. Her mind whirled inside her skull as she tried to understand his words. "What kind of secrets?"

"I will tell you everything later. I don't think this is the time to deal with this. Do you?"

Winnie's phone dinged, and she checked the screen. Opening the device, she pulled up her email and skimmed it before meeting Scythe's gaze again. "My sub confirmation came through. She approved it."

"You're going to contact your district's human resources department later today and set up a leave of absence for the death of a parent," Scythe told her, "but first, you're going to go back to bed and rest for a few hours. There's nothing you can do until the funeral home opens."

"I'll never be able to sleep."

"You will. Come on, Chipmunk."

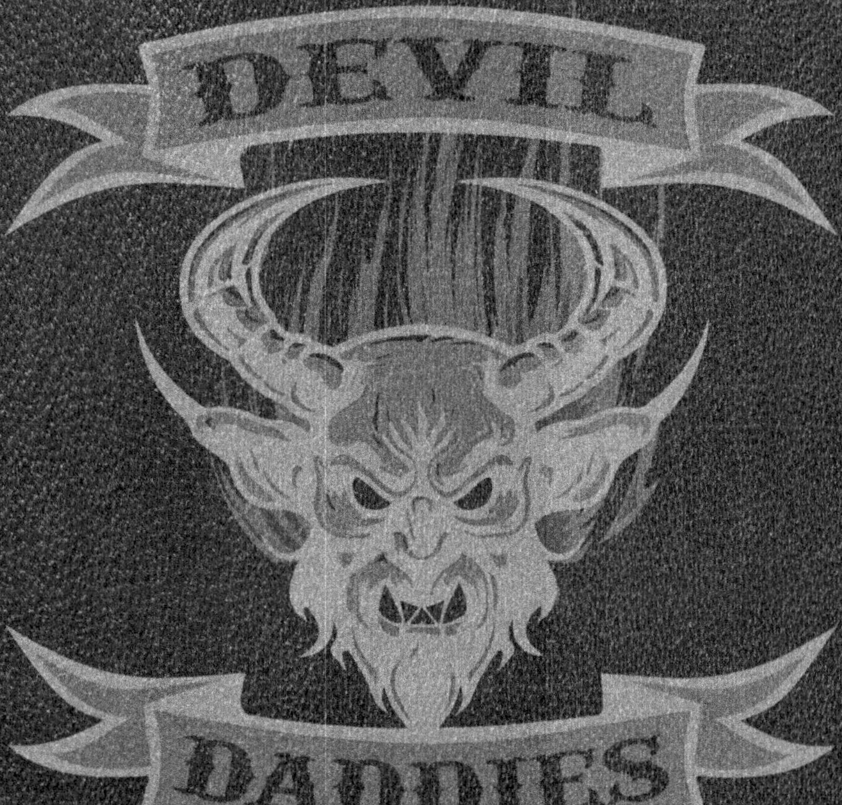
DEVIL
DADDIES

CHAPTER 11

Winnie woke up wrapped in Scythe's arms. The muscular man dominated the double bed in the guest room. She yawned in disbelief, noting the clock. She had slept and so had he.

Taking advantage of the opportunity to study him while he slept, Winnie was amazed he was interested in her. Scythe's powerful frame was trim, seemingly without an ounce of extra padding anywhere. He must work out a lot or his job involved physical activity. What did Scythe do? Just help out at Inferno?

His arm tightened around her, squeezing Winnie tight against him, dragging her from her thoughts. He opened his gorgeous blue-green eyes to meet her gaze. "You're supposed to be sleeping."

"I did sleep. It's almost ten now. I need to get up and attack everything that needs to be done."

"In a minute. First, I need a kiss." He towed her easily on top of his body with one arm.

"Scythe! Let me down. I'm too heavy. I'll squish you."

"Right. Look how hard I'm breathing. Maybe you should give me mouth-to-mouth resuscitation."

Winnie shook her head at his request and dropped a quick

kiss on his lips. Scythe looked up at her with still puckered lips. Sighing like it was a huge imposition, Winnie pressed her mouth to his. Scythe drew his tongue along the seam of her lips, and Winnie allowed him in.

His flavor seduced her. He didn't taste like toothpaste or a snack he'd had late last night but his own unique essence. She squirmed on top of him as he explored her mouth. Enjoying herself, Winnie only lifted her lips from his when she had to breathe.

"You're good at that," she admitted. "I don't know how I ever gave you a C+."

"I'm A+ material with the right woman," he teased before grinning at her.

"I hope you believe I'm the right woman."

"You're absolutely the woman I've searched to find. And the Little girl I need to make my world complete. How about coming home with me after we go meet with your school district?"

"Can I decide later? I don't know how I'll get through all these tasks on the list. I may work until I have to fall into bed." Winnie slid off Scythe to rest on the mattress with her torso propped up on his so they could discuss everything.

"That's not healthy. Assign a few things to me that don't require your personal touch, and I'm sure Belinda will help when she wakes up," Scythe said.

Winnie mentally reviewed the things she needed to do. The funeral home would release her mother at some point when the investigators were satisfied that her death was natural. No one thought the decision would require more than a day when they reviewed her mom's medical files.

"My first priority is the school stuff, I guess."

"Do you want me to go with you?" Scythe asked.

"No. I really need to take care of my request for leave as a professional. Then my sub will need lesson plans. Surely, they'll let me off for a few days," she thought aloud.

"Do you like the staff in human relations at your central office?" Scythe asked.

"I do. She's very sweet."

"We go to the funeral home first to get everything set up. Then we split up. I'll come back here and use the file to notify the medical supply place and the lawyer while you deal with the district."

"You're comfortable doing that?"

"Sure. I can be nice on the phone. Then I'll head to work. You reach out when you're ready to call it a night. I'll come get you and make sure you eat."

"And tuck me into bed with a bedtime story?" she asked with a smile. She'd look forward to that all day.

"Exactly."

"Thanks, Scythe, for being here with me."

"You don't have to thank me for spending time with you. If I had my choice, we'd always be together from now on."

"You don't think you'd get sick of me?" Winnie asked, holding her breath in hopes he wouldn't say yes.

"Not going to happen, Little girl. All right. Go potty, and we'll get that folder."

Winnie patted her blotchy face in an attempt to mask the results from their visit to the funeral home. She sat in her car, pulling together her thoughts for a few minutes before going into her district's HR office.

"Hi, Mandy. I'm Winnifred Bradley. I don't know if Miss Oberson informed you...."

"I got an extensive report about you today," Mandy said with a stern glance.

"I'm here to talk about bereavement leave. My mother passed away in the early morning hours," Winnie told her and watched the woman's expression soften.

"This morning?" When Winnie nodded, Mandy said, "I am so sorry. I didn't have any notice of that. Did you tell your principal?"

"I did. She wanted my mother's death certificate as proof. I don't have that yet."

"Of course you don't. Let me update the reason for your absence. Good. That puts you back in the green zone." She turned from her computer and waved Winnie into a seat in front of her desk. "How long do you need off, Winnie? Your contract allows you to miss up to five days."

"It's Thursday. The memorial service will be on Monday. How about through Tuesday next week?" Winnie suggested.

"Notify me if you want Wednesday as well, but I'll arrange a good sub for you. You'll need to leave plans for her," Mandy warned.

"That's next on my list. I'll send them to you as well, so you'll be aware that I followed through," Winnie told her.

"That's not usually what people do. Is there a reason you want HR to have proof you've created plans and left them organized for the substitute?"

"Yes."

"Gotcha. I can read between the lines of the mistake in your rationale for missing today and the concern that the sub's information will mysteriously evaporate."

"Thank you, Mandy."

"Of course. I'm going to run off some paperwork for you to sign before you get to return to the hundreds of tasks you need to do," Mandy told her before turning back to her computer.

In minutes, Winnie walked out the door with the approval papers in her hands. She drove next to her building and let herself in the entrance closest to her classroom. Apologizing to the substitute for interrupting, she talked to her second graders to explain her absence. Enlisting their help in cooperating with the substitute, Winnie stressed how proud she was of how much they'd learned this year and that she'd look forward to them dazzling her with the information they mastered while she was gone.

With their promises to do their best each day, she sat at a small desk in the back of the room and made her lesson plans, using the teacher textbooks while the sub coached the kids through their afternoon subjects. Taylor walked to the tissue box to blow her nose and stopped next to Winnie.

"Thanks for telling Mrs. Kelley about our signal," Taylor whispered.

"Of course. That's at the top of my list of important things for the substitute to know," Winnie assured her and returned the child's hug.

"I'm sorry about your mom."

Tears gathered in her eyes as Winnie smiled at the young child. "Thank you, Taylor. Now, go back and learn all you can."

The sweet student slid back into her chair and immediately focused on the substitute. Winnie quickly finished her lesson plans and sent them to the printer as well as to the other second-grade teacher, and Mandy at the district office, and her bestie, Abby, in case something happened to the printed copies she left for the substitute. Scythe might think Lorraine would stop causing problems, but Winnie didn't trust her at all. After straightening her area and returning the teacher's editions for the sub, she slipped out of the classroom and headed for home.

Pulling into her mom's driveway, Winnie burst into tears for what felt like the tenth time that day. She didn't want to walk in there. The house wasn't the same without her mother.

A soft knock on her driver's side window made her look up in surprise. Scythe leaned close, studying her with a concerned expression. "Unlock the door, Chipmunk. I need to hold you."

Winnie hit the unlock button fast, allowing Scythe to pull it open. As she tumbled out of the car, he wrapped her in his arms and hugged her tight to his hard chest. Stroking over her hair, he whispered soft words that she couldn't focus on. They reassured her, nevertheless.

"She's not here," Winnie whispered.

"She's not. Your mom is with your dad and stepdad in heaven, wondering why you're so sad," Scythe told her.

She bit back a rueful laugh. "You're so right. She wouldn't be happy with me."

"She'll love you forever, Little girl."

"I know. It's just hard." Winnie tried to pull herself together. She pushed on Scythe's hard chest, and he relaxed his grip on her.

"Okay. Let's go check that file and see what we need to do next," she suggested.

"We've checked off every item that can be finished now, Winnie. The medical equipment people were in the area, so they already stopped by to retrieve their stuff. We have an appointment in a half hour with the minister."

"Wow! Thank you." Her eyes landed on a duffle bag sitting on the driveway. "What's that?"

"I packed some of your things. You're coming to stay with me, Little girl."

"I am?"

"Yes. Do you trust me, or would you like to see if I missed anything?"

"As long as I have underwear, I'm happy. How did you sense I didn't want to go in there?" she asked, looking back at the house.

"I know you, Winnie. Follow me over to the church and we'll get everything started. Then, I'll take you home."

Home. That word echoed in her head. Her mom had made this place a home. "I came back to live here when she needed my help."

"You were a very sweet daughter, Winnifred Abigail Bradley."

Her gaze rebounded to meet his. "How did you find out my middle name?"

"Your sister and I picked out photos for the funeral service.

She was good at finding fun pictures to show how much your mother enjoyed her life. I spotted a birth announcement in your baby book. Ten pounds, five ounces. You were healthy when you were born." He stroked a hand over her spine to cup one of her butt cheeks. "You still have the same cute badonkadonk."

"Oh, my, God! You saw the naked picture of me as a baby."

"I did." Scythe waggled his eyebrows up and down suggestively.

"You!" Winnie slapped his chest, laughing. Only Scythe could change her mood in a flash.

CHAPTER 12

Winnie followed Scythe along the winding road behind Inferno, enjoying the scenery of his broad shoulders and tight butt. A few fantasies roamed through her mind as he led the way. Thank goodness for his brake lights warning her he was stopping. Winnie stepped on the pedal sharply to halt behind him.

A gate? Scythe lived in a gated community? That seemed odd. He talked to someone inside the booth, gesturing back at her car. When he pulled forward, she trailed behind. When Vex appeared in front of her car, Winnie slammed the car to a stop.

"Hi, Winnifred," he greeted her warmly.

"Winnie," she corrected automatically. "Didn't your parents teach you to look both ways before crossing the street?"

"They tried to *teach* me a lot of things. Some stuck in my brain, others not so much," Vex answered, completely unfazed by the close call.

"Vex won't always be at the gate, Winnie," Scythe explained as he walked back to join them. "He'll need your license to put on record, and everyone will let you in when you arrive without a question."

"My driver's license?" she asked, grabbing her purse and

searching through it for her wallet. Of course, it was lost somewhere inside. Winnie grabbed a handful of things and dropped them on the passenger seat as the men watched. Finally, she found it.

"Got it!" Winnie flipped it open and yanked out a card for Vex. "Ta-da!"

"This is your library card, Winnie," Vex told her.

"Crap!" She snatched it out of his hand and muttered something about how much the two looked alike.

"Okay, this is it!" Winnie waved her license around before pulling it back to double-check. "Yep! I found it."

The guys didn't point out her library card was pure white while the license was tan. Vex carried it inside to scan and returned with his phone to hand her license before capturing pictures of her car and the plates.

"Why the high security?" she asked.

"Very precious people live inside," Scythe answered.

"Bikers?" Winnie asked.

"They're not the special individuals we want to protect," Vex explained. "The Devil Daddies can take care of themselves."

When she glanced at Scythe, hoping to get a clearer answer, he said, "Vex is referring to you, Chipmunk. You are one of the precious people living in our community."

"Oh."

"All done," Vex announced. "If you arrive by yourself, tell whoever's at the gate that you're Scythe's. They'll review this information and let you in." Returning to the booth, he raised the gate and waved her in as Scythe jumped on his bike.

Scythe led her to the last cottage on the right. He drove into the far side of the garage and waved her in next to him. He turned to rummage in the workbench near his bike. When she hesitated, he walked down the driveway to her side. "Go ahead and pull in, Chipmunk."

"I don't want to hit your motorcycle. Bad things happen to me at the worst time."

"You're not going to hit my bike."

"I might."

"If I drive your car in, can you back it out safely?" he asked.

"Definitely." She unlocked her door and scrambled out. When she lost her balance in her rush, Scythe's powerful hands wrapped around her waist to steady her. "Thanks."

"I got you." Scythe kissed her gently before smacking her bottom. "Go stand by the door."

Seeing him try to squeeze into her car without adjusting the seat made her giggle. Finally, shaking his head, he found the lever and eased it back. Scythe clipped something to her visor, and Winnie realized it had to be a garage door opener. He was moving her in as if she were going to stay for a while.

When he rejoined her, she asked, "How long are you planning for me to be here?"

"Forever, Chipmunk."

Stunned by his response, she stared at him. *Could he really mean that?*

"Come in. Let me show you around."

He opened the door and ushered her inside. The garage entrance led into the sunny, yellow kitchen with an attached screened-in porch. A feathered creature walked past outside. "Is that a chicken?"

"I brought the last few from my parents' farm with me. Only two are left now. That's Fluff. You'll see Patches soon. They roam around together."

"You grew up on a farm?" She eyed his muscles. That made sense. Hard labor had honed his physique from a young age.

"I did. Unfortunately, life interfered with my plans to be a farmer. Come, let me show you around."

Winnie ran her hand over the old-fashioned, red-gingham oilcloth that protected the table as they walked into a large family room. A large leather couch and a huge double-sized recliner dominated the space. A picture popped into her mind of sharing that chair with him as they watched Saturday cartoons.

She could see the influence of his former country lifestyle on his decorations. "Your place is lovely, Scythe."

"It works for me. We'll change anything you don't like. And add more to make it your home as much as mine."

"Is that a scythe on the wall?" she asked, pointing to a weathered wooden handle with a long, rust-dotted blade. She could tell it wasn't a simple decoration. It was an actual farm implement.

"A memento from my parent's farm. It was in the family for a long time."

"I bet that's where your name came from. Silly me. I keep picturing Death with his lethal scythe."

She jumped as her phone rang, preventing him from responding to her guess. Winnie dug into her bag and retrieved the device. Checking the screen, she said, "It's the funeral home."

"Hello?"

"Miss Bradley? It's Russell at Key's Funeral Home."

"Yes, this is Winnie."

"I wanted to inform you that we received notice that the doctor has signed your mother's death certificate. They've released her body."

Relief flooded through her. Her mother had grown to hate the hospital in the last few months. "That's wonderful. You'll go get her now?"

"Our driver is already on the way. She'll be here in less than an hour."

"That's wonderful. Thank you." Winnie disconnected the call.

"The investigation concluded, and the hospital is releasing your mom's body?" Scythe guessed.

"Yes. They're headed there now." Winnie couldn't stop the tears from rolling down her cheeks. Winnie was so glad she wouldn't be there for much longer.

Scythe picked Winnie up in his arms and carried her into a

small bedroom. He sat in a rocker and set it into motion to soothe her. She melted against his chest, loving how his strength supported her. He kissed the top of her head as they glided.

"Close your eyes for a few minutes, Chipmunk. Everything is going well. You can relax."

"I already took a nap," she protested.

"You don't have to sleep again," he promised.

The slow movement of the rocker soothed her emotions. With her ear pressed to Scythe's hard chest, she could hear his steady heartbeat, reassuring her he was healthy. Absorbing his warmth, Winnie relaxed.

"Thank you," she whispered to Scythe.

"Thank you, Daddy," he corrected and kissed the top of her head.

"Do you want me to call you Daddy all the time?"

"I would love that. When we are with other people, judge what is safe for you. Teachers are often held to a different standard than others in the workplace."

"I can't imagine what Lorraine would say if she heard me call you Daddy," Winnie said with a shudder.

"I don't like how this woman treats you, Chipmunk."

"Wait until you hear what happened today." Winnie quickly ran through her encounter at the school district's head office and how Lorraine must have coded her absence in to make her look bad. The human relations director had corrected it for her and helped with the paperwork to fill out to protect her job during her bereavement leave.

Scythe's jaw tensed, and Winnie knew he was pissed at her principal. "Don't do anything to Lorraine, Scythe. I can't lose my job. I'll never get hired by another district if I'm fired for some fabricated reason."

"I'm listening, Chipmunk."

Winnie noted that wasn't a promise, but she figured it was the best she'd get right now. She noticed a familiar figure on the wall and pointed to it. "Is that a chipmunk?"

Scythe's gaze focused on the creature now attached to the wall. "Yes. That's a Siberian chipmunk. He has stripes on his face."

"You recognize the different species of chipmunks?" she asked, squirming to the side so she could see his face clearly.

"Maybe not *all* the different types. I'm not sure if that is a baby long-haired chipmunk or an eastern chipmunk," he confessed, pointing to one in the far corner.

She peered over his shoulder and shook her head. "Babies are hard."

Now that she was checking out their surroundings, Winnie finally noticed how unique this area was. Not only was it decorated with cute fuzzy characters, but she'd never seen furnishings like these. It was as if she'd walked into one of her favorite age-play novels.

"Is that a crib?" she asked, pointing to the beautiful oak crib with carved spindles creating a railing around it.

"Yes. You can nap there on the weekends. I'd rather you sleep with Daddy at night if you're comfortable with that," he answered smoothly without any indication that this wasn't a normal bed to have in a room.

"But it's adult-sized!" Winnie stared at it, secretly enthralled by the thought of curling up on the fluffy covers and truly being Little.

"Of course. You need to be comfortable to sleep, Little girl."

She forced herself to look around. "Is that a toy chest?"

"It is."

"Is anything inside?"

"Yes, Chipmunk. I gathered playthings as I created this nursery that I hoped my Little girl would enjoy."

"It is a nursery!" she exclaimed.

"Not just a nursery, Winnie. It's *your* nursery." He stressed that one word, driving it home for Winnie.

Scythe had put this room together with the conviction that he would find his Little girl. It was adorable and so perfect for her.

How had he guessed what she would like? Struggling to process how incredibly well he'd envisioned this room. Winnie craned her head to see the wall behind her. And froze.

"There's a changing table against the wall. Are those diapers? I'm a big girl. I don't use diapers," she protested, hearing her voice slide into Little space as she thought about the padded garments.

"Sometimes even big girls need to be super Little. Can you try new things for Daddy?"

Winnie froze as her mind whirled inside. Could she be that brave? "At home with Daddy?" she asked finally.

"If that's how you're most comfortable, I think that's a smart idea."

"You won't laugh at me or tell other people?"

"I wouldn't do that to you, Chipmunk. I'd lose my right to be a Daddy for life if I betrayed your trust."

"That would be bad."

"The worst punishment for a Daddy ever," he agreed.

"Worse than a spanking?"

"Far more severe. Your bottom will recover after a couple of stingy days. My heart would never rebound if I'd screwed up my chance to be a Daddy."

Winnie nodded. He made perfect sense. "What do we do now?" she asked.

"Would you like to explore your nursery before dinner? Then we can watch some TV or a movie and relax."

"Don't you have to go to Inferno?"

"No, Chipmunk. I took the next few days off to be with you. They'll do fine without me."

"Lucien looks mean, but I think he's a softie," Winnie said with confidence.

"To Littles, definitely. Someone who wrongs him gets an entirely different Lucien," Scythe warned.

"I'll be good."

"Of course you will. Do you want to get Chippy before you check out everything in here?"

"Did you bring him?"

"Of course. He wouldn't let me pack without jumping into the top of your duffle bag. Let's go find him."

In a few minutes, Winnie sat on the floor in front of the toy chest with her stuffie. She loved everything he'd collected. A few games made for several players filled one side and some activities that she could do alone.

"Will you play with me, Daddy?"

"Of course. What would you like to do first?"

"How about dress-up? I found all this play jewelry and makeup," she said, opening the case to show him.

"Little girl." Scythe shook his head wryly. "You want to put makeup on Daddy, don't you?"

"I bet I could make you pretty," she cajoled, trying to hide her smile.

"Where should I sit?" he asked and winked at her.

"How about in that chair at the table? I can lay out my supplies. You know, if you grew your hair out a bit longer, I could braid it."

"Not happening, Little girl," he growled, moving over to the seat she indicated.

"Okay, Daddy. I'll brush it until it shines. Did you bring my hairspray?"

"No hairspray," he declared.

Winnie smiled. He had brought it. This was going to be so much fun. "Here, you hold Chippy."

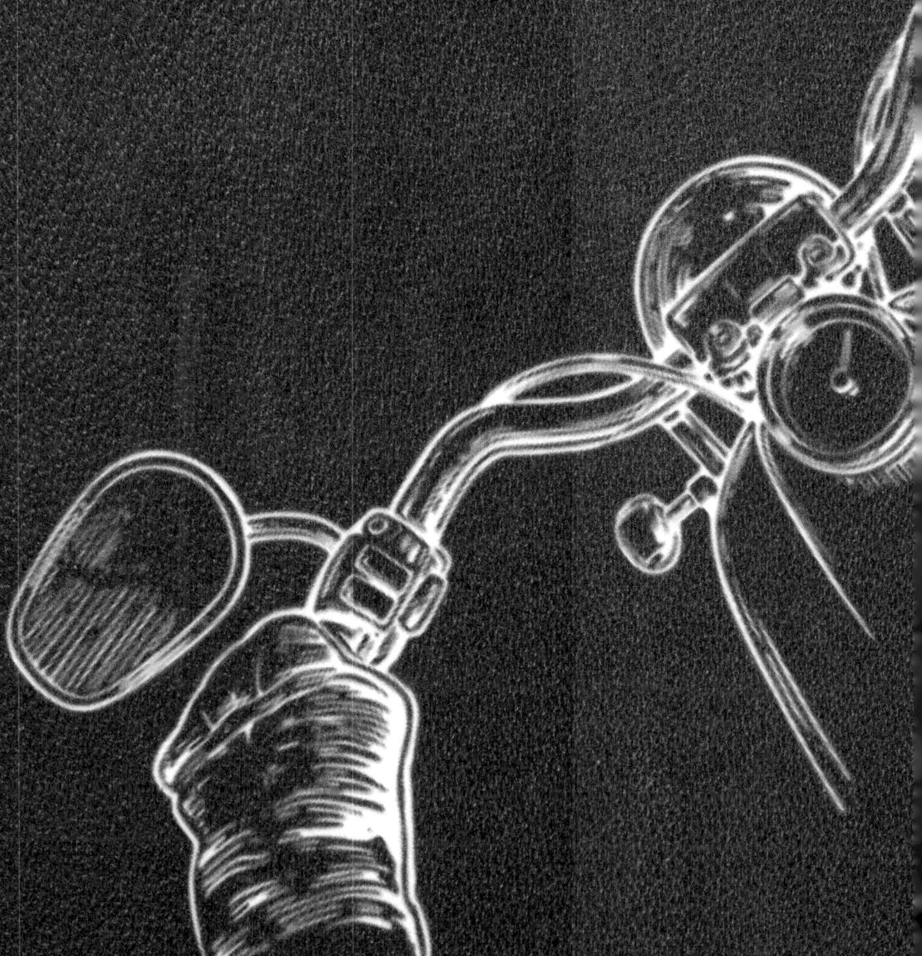

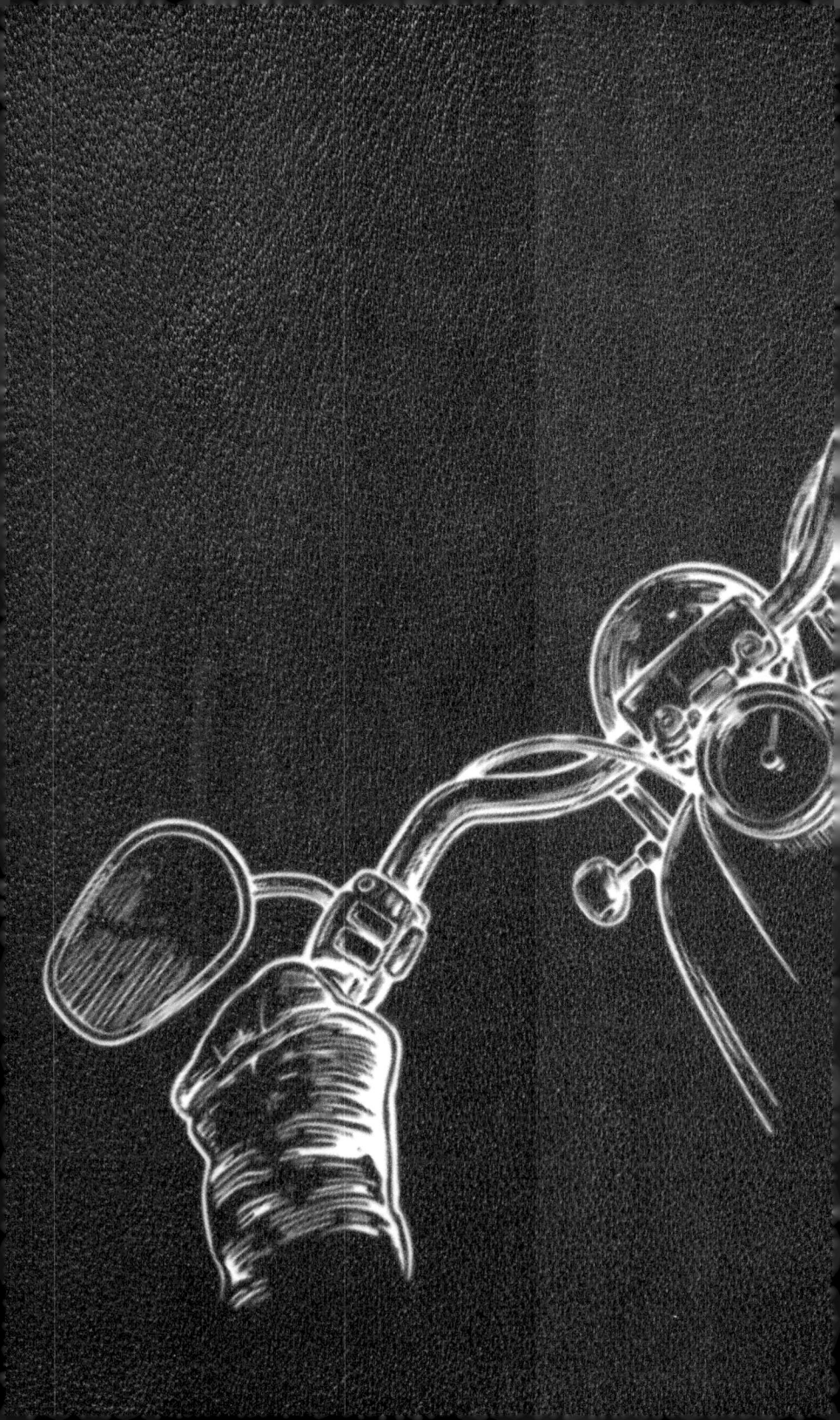

CHAPTER 13

Scythe had fun despite the extent of the beautification process his Little girl undertook. It was the first time since he'd met her that her face wasn't drawn with grief and worry. He was confident she wasn't thinking about her mother's illness and death or work. Letting her have a blast was well worth the makeup she layered on him.

When a booming knock came at the door, Winnie looked at him with an "uh-oh" expression. "I can go answer it, Daddy."

"Not happening, Chipmunk." Scythe stood and walked toward the entrance with Winnie trailing him.

"I might have overdone it on the blush, Daddy. Let me wipe a bit off."

"You did a wonderful job, Winnie. I'm prettier than ever."

"Daddy, wait!"

Scythe turned the doorknob and threw open the door.

Wraith's face contorted as he tried to control his expression. "Looking good," he finally got out. The curvy woman next to him giggled.

"Who is it?" Winnie asked, sliding into the opening with Scythe. "Oh, hi!"

Winnie considered the other visitor. "Wait! Do I remember

you from Inferno?" Winnie asked. "Wraith is always at the door, but you were there the last time I visited. I'm Winnie."

"Hi! I'm Caroline. We did meet at the door. You wore a strappy dress and sky-high shoes."

"My stepsister's," Winnie confessed. "Those shoes were toe-killers. I might have gotten a bit too enthusiastic with the makeup."

"Your Daddy is gorgeous," Caroline told her. "Maybe he needs more lipstick."

"Does he? I thought that might be over-the-top," Winnie said.

"There's no way more lipstick is over-the-top."

Winnie turned to consider Scythe's appearance. "Maybe you're right. I'll go brighter next time."

The two men exchanged a glance.

They make brighter? Scythe wondered before focusing on the women.

"Are you...."

"Am I Little? I would tell you if you wanted to be my friend," Caroline answered.

"I'd love to be your friend. I'm new to this," Winnie confessed.

"Then, we'll be friends. I'm pretty new as well. I just found my Daddy," Caroline confided.

Winnie rushed forward and hugged Caroline. When she stepped back, the duo held hands and bounced with excitement. Scythe met Wraith's gaze, and they nodded at each other. Wraith's idea to put the two together was brilliant.

"I'm so glad you're here. Daddy said there could be other Littles living in the cottages. Do you have a nursery?" Caroline asked.

"I do. Want to see it?" Winnie said, welcoming Caroline inside.

"A half hour, Precious," Wraith called as the two skipped down the hall.

"How'd you know she was here?" Scythe asked, waving

Wraith inside. He walked to the kitchen and grabbed two beers from the fridge. After handing one to Wraith, he opened the top of his.

"This is definitely a new style for you," Wraith commented.

"Think I can wash it off without Winnie being upset?"

"Definitely. Those two will be thick as thieves in there."

"Thank God." Scythe set down his beer and flipped on the water in the sink. Five minutes and almost a roll of paper towels later, his skin felt clean. "Did I get it all?"

"You're good. That lipstick will take a while to fade," Wraith told him.

"That sounds like you're speaking from experience."

"Vex suggested that kit for your toy box, didn't he?" Wraith asked with a smirk.

"He did. Sounds like he needs a special project at Inferno when I'm back," Scythe suggested.

"Grab me another beer and I'll help you think one up," Wraith offered.

"Help yourself. I'm going to check on the girls."

Scythe didn't wait for Wraith's response. He headed through the house. As he entered the hall, Scythe could hear female voices. He peeked inside and found the women had emptied everything out of the toy box. They lay on their tummies, playing a board game as they chatted.

"Are you both okay?" he asked.

"We're good, Daddy," Winnie assured him.

"Perfect! Winnie's letting me win," Caroline shared.

"What an excellent hostess," he praised. To his delight, Winnie's shoulders moved back as if more confident. "Come get a snack and juice when you're ready."

"Yes, Daddy!"

"Okay, Scythe! Could you tell my Daddy I might need some extra time?" Caroline asked.

"I'll tell him," Scythe assured her. He paused outside the door, out of the way to listen.

"My Daddy is the best," Winnie shared with Caroline.

"I would argue that mine is better, but I think we both ended up with great Daddies. You haven't known Scythe for long. How do you feel about him?"

"He's my Daddy," Winnie said.

"I'm so happy for you. It's your turn. See if you can land on the bonus space."

Scythe nodded as he walked away. Finding his Little girl was the best feeling ever. As he entered the kitchen, he discovered Wraith sitting on the screened-in porch. He grabbed his beer and went to join the large man.

"Settle in. You'll be here for a while. I have wings to throw on the grill. Want to stay for dinner?" Scythe suggested.

"Can you make them hot?"

"Hotter than your mouth can handle," Scythe promised.

"Not possible. You'll have to make some mild ones for the girls."

"Definitely. I have broccoli and apple slices to go with them."

"Crap. I've been eating healthy so Caroline eats her veggies. I avoid broccoli like the plague. Any chance you'd make something different?" Wraith asked.

"Now that I know you don't like broccoli, I'm serving it every time you eat over here."

"Of course you are." Wraith held out his beer bottle, and Scythe clinked his against it. "Congratulations, brother. I'm glad you found her."

"Thank you, Wraith. I guess we should thank Caroline. She's the one who convinced you to let her enter Inferno."

"Oh, I'll put an extra sticker on her chart tonight."

"You have a sticker chart? Tell me about it. I think Winnie would like that as well."

The two Daddies settled in for a long chat. Scythe was glad to have someone to bounce ideas off. He and Wraith had been friendly since he joined the Devil Daddies. Now, they had a common bond—a very special one.

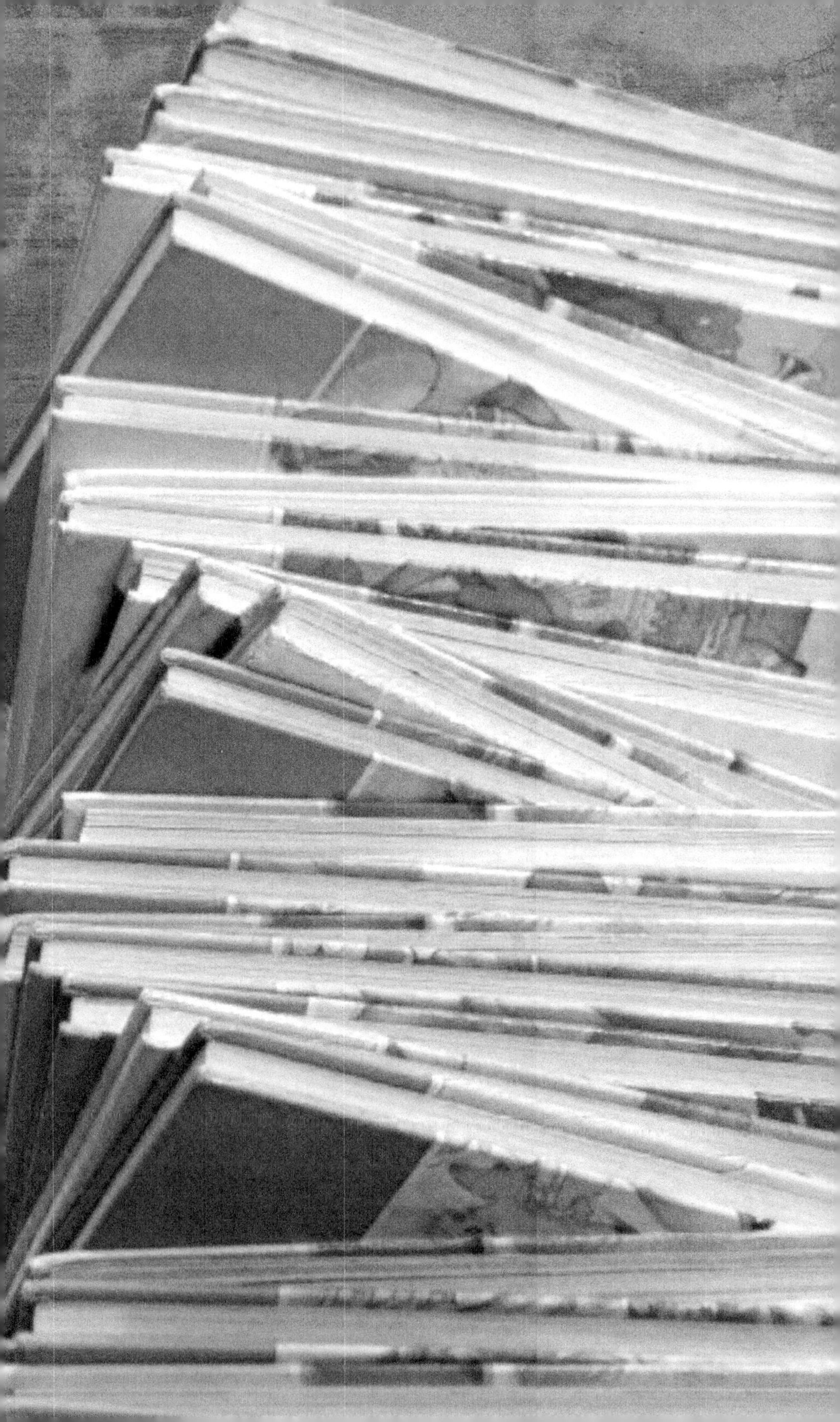

CHAPTER 14

"Daddy, I had so much fun with Caroline. She was really nice when I remembered about my mom and started crying."

"You should have come to see me or let me know you were upset," Scythe said, wrinkles of concern forming on his forehead.

"It didn't last long, Daddy. I was sad for a few minutes. Caroline patted my back to comfort me."

"She is very nice," Scythe agreed. "Do you think she'd make a good Little friend?"

Winnie bounced with excitement as she nodded. "We're going to get together in her nursery next time. I can't wait to see it."

"That will be fun. Come with me, Chipmunk. I think you got wing sauce on every inch of your skin," Scythe said, taking her hand and leading her down the hallway.

"They were yummy. Will you make them again? Wraith's face was almost scary when he put extra hot sauce on the habanero wings. He doesn't really have a mouth lined with asbestos."

Scythe chuckled. "He definitely drank a lot of milk, trying to cool everything down."

"You like hot wings too. I can't handle them. I always end up getting sauce in my eye or smeared on my skin. That hurts, Daddy."

"It does. Let's get you cleaned up before bedtime." He stopped by the big tub in the enormous bathroom connected to the main bedroom. As she watched, he turned on the water.

"I won't be able to sleep for hours, Daddy. I'm too wound up."

"I know. I bet a hot bath and a bottle will help."

"A bottle?" Winnie had never tried using one.

"A bath first. Come here, Chipmunk. Let's get these sticky clothes off you. Maybe I need to buy some bibs like Wraith described." He sat on the edge of the tub and drew her between his thighs.

"Those that are made like a towel with a hole you put your head through?" Winnie asked as he tugged her T-shirt over her shoulders.

"Those are the ones we should try. What do you think?" Winnie crossed her arms over her chest, trying to seem cool about him undressing her but inside freaking out a bit.

"No hiding from Daddy," Scythe said sternly as he pulled her arms away and guided them down to her sides.

"Sorry. I'm not used to anyone seeing me." Winnie forced herself to stay in place as he reached around her to unfasten her bra.

"I'm not just anyone, Chipmunk. I'm your Daddy. Maybe tomorrow needs to be naked as a blue jay day for you." Scythe eased the cups of the lacy garment from her breasts and slid the straps down her arms.

"What's that?" she asked.

"While you're inside the house, you don't wear clothes. Or only a diaper."

"I can't do that, Daddy."

"Why is that, Chipmunk?" he asked as he pulled her leggings down.

"I have things to do for my mother's service, and I need to meet with the lawyer. You know… I have important, clothing-required tasks," Winnie stressed.

"And you will definitely get dressed for those," he agreed before tapping on the toes of her left foot. "Lift this, please."

She followed his directions before asking, "But not at other times?"

"Not tomorrow." He tapped on her other foot, and she shifted her weight so he could remove her leggings completely. "Good girl."

"Can I have bubbles?" she whispered.

"Of course. Let me check the water's temperature." Scythe caressed the length of her arm she had rigidly next to her side to keep from covering her nakedness.

"You are lovely, Winnifred Abigail Bradley. I am a very lucky Daddy." Scythe reached down to adjust himself in his jeans, drawing Winnie's attention to how her shape affected him.

Suddenly, her nakedness registered more as a temptation for her Daddy than exposure for her. Winnie straightened and drew her shoulders back. Scythe groaned. Maybe naked as a blue jay day would be fun.

"Temptress," Scythe growled. "Let's get you in the water before I bend you over the tub and fuck you."

"Sorry, Daddy," she said, giggling, and realized she wasn't apologetic in the least.

"Bubbles. Let's get those started," Scythe said, visibly forcing himself to turn and check the temperature before pouring bubble-gum-scented bubble bath into the cascading water.

She allowed him to help her into the tub as white foaminess spread. Immediately, she sculpted a series of peaks across the surface in front of her. Winnie darted a glance at Scythe to judge the distance between them before smacking her palm down on top of one foam mountain. A plume of water arced through the air, drenching the front of his T-shirt. The surprised look on his face made her laugh and do it again before he could react.

He caught her hand before she could do it for a third time. "Chipmunk. The water needs to stay inside the tub."

"It was a total accident," she swore, trying to appear innocent.

"Right. That might have worked for the first splash but definitely not for the second and third. I'm going to have to wear a raincoat to bathe you," he muttered, reaching over his shoulders with one hand to grab a handful of his T-shirt and yank it over his head. He threw it into the sink, where it landed with a wet-sounding splat.

She struggled to control her giggles, and a snort escaped from her nostrils. That made her laugh harder. When Scythe shook a warning finger at her, she pressed her lips together, struggling to stop, and snorted another time.

"Do I have a chipmunk in the bathtub or a hedgehog?"

"Hedgehogs snort?" she asked, instantly intrigued. They were so cute.

"I believe so. We'll do some research when we finish your bath," he promised.

"That's a good idea. I need to check my phone to see if I have any messages."

"We'll worry about those in a few minutes. First, bath. Close your eyes, Chipmunk, and I'll wash the wing sauce off your face," he instructed, picking up a fluffy blue washcloth. He finished without getting soap in her eyes or mouth.

"You're good at that, Daddy," she complimented.

"Thank you, Winnie. I have some toys for you to play with if you promise not to be a splash monster."

"I promise!"

"That's my good girl." He leaned to the side to open a cabinet and pulled out a package. Zipping open the sealed top, he emptied the plastic toys into the tub. Some floated, and others sank from view.

Exploring all the fun shapes, Winnie was too busy to notice as Scythe cleaned her back and shoulders. He coaxed one arm away and washed it before repeating the process on the other side. Winnie's attention ricocheted to him when Scythe swept the washcloth across her collarbones.

"I could help you, Daddy," she suggested, grabbing the wet material.

"Daddy's job, Little girl. Your job is to play."

Focusing on the toys was so challenging as he carefully smoothed the washcloth over her chest. Did she imagine that he gave special attention to the sensitive under slope of each breast? When he moved on to her stomach, she tightened her muscles as much as possible to make her tummy flatter.

"Relax, Chipmunk. You're supposed to have curves. Daddy has them too."

"But yours are grooves chiseled between massive muscles," she pointed out.

"You flatter me, Little girl. I'm glad you like my body. Yours is special as well. Spread your legs, Winnie."

She followed his directions without thinking and froze when he whisked the wet cloth over the tops of her thighs and each side. Her breath caught in her mouth as he attended to her inner thigh area and stroked the cloth through her pink folds. Could he tell how turned on she was by him?

Don't squirm. Don't squirm.

"It's okay, Chipmunk, to enjoy your Daddy's touch."

She nodded, unable to talk, and then exhaled a shaky breath when he shifted to wash her legs. The brief massage of her feet and toes made her long for more. After standing for so many hours on a tile-covered, concrete floor as she moved around the room to work with children, Winnie's arches usually ached by the end of the day. She dared to tell him.

"I liked that, Daddy."

"Thank you for sharing, Winnie. I'll try to remember to rub your feet from time to time. Remind me if I forget," he said.

"Yes, Daddy." She beamed at him, so excited to have someone who cared and wanted to help.

"Up on your knees, Winnie. Daddy has one more place to pay attention to."

Not quite following what he needed to do, Winnie followed his directions. When he whisked the washcloth between her buttocks, she almost slipped on the bathtub surface. He stabilized her easily and continued to wash her bottom thoroughly.

"Daddy!" she protested. Her face flamed with embarrassment.

"I will take care of every part of you. You'll grow accustomed to my touch on your bottom," he said easily.

"My—My bottom?" she stuttered.

"Oh, yes. Daddies care for their Littles in all ways. I think you're free of sticky sauce now. Would you like to stay in your bath and play, or would you like to get out?"

"Out, Daddy. My fingers are pruney." She held up her fingers to show him the wrinkles.

"Oh, no! It is time to escape." Scythe scooped her out of the water and set her feet on the soft rug that squished with the liquid she'd splashed on him earlier.

"Oops!" she said, trying to prevent a smile.

"You aren't sorry at all, Little girl!" Scythe kissed the top of her head, letting Winnie know he wasn't upset with her as he dried her skin with gentle strokes of the thirsty towel.

"Okay, story time before bed."

"I can't go to sleep now!" she protested.

"Daddy's rule. Early bedtime for Little girls."

"Daddy!"

"Little girls who argue with their Daddies earn spankings. Is that what you need, Chipmunk?"

"No. I think I'm tired."

"Telling lies is not good either, Winnie. Let's see how you really feel when you're tucked into bed with Chippy."

She nodded eagerly without saying anything else that could get her in trouble.

Scythe picked her up and balanced her on his hip. He rubbed

his whiskers against her neck as he carried her out of the bathroom. After pulling down the covers, he set her on the crisp sheets and tucked the covers around her. "Stay right there. I'll get Chippy from your nursery."

He returned with a thick book and her stuffie. Scythe also carried something wrapped in a plastic protective bag. She pointed to it and asked, "What's that?"

"It's a present for you. A special blankie." Scythe ripped it open and pulled out the gray fleece material. After shaking it out, he laid it over her.

"Look, Daddy. That embroidered image is the same as the one on your vest."

"It is exactly like the one on my cut," he assured her.

"I love it." She rubbed her face on the soft fabric. "Does this mean I'm a biker in the Devil Daddies MC?"

"No, Chipmunk. You're protected by the MC. Lucien purchased them for each of the members. I only have one blanket to give to my Little, so they know you're important."

"Oh," she said, brushing her finger over the stitches. "I love it. Thank you, Daddy."

The importance of receiving this resonated inside Winnie. No one had ever thought she was unique and special except for her mother. She burst into tears as grief overwhelmed her again. Winnie scrubbed at her cheeks. She had to stop crying

"I'm sorry. I'm being silly," Winnie said as Scythe sat down on the bed next to her and gathered her in his arms.

"You are not. It's better to let grief out, Winnie. If you bottle it up inside, grief either explodes at the worst time, or it eats at you. I was young and stupid when my dad died, and the farm was repossessed. Both were drastic blows to my life. I only dealt with the death of my father. Tell me how you and your mom were alike?"

"She taught first grade for thirty years."

"And you teach second. I bet some of her lessons she taught

you as a young child show up in your activities with your students," Scythe guessed.

Incredulous, she stared at him. "They do! I always have my students write three things they want to learn on a card for me at the beginning of the year. Mom always had me do that on my birthday. What did I want to be able to do when I was nine or ten or eleven?"

"And the kids love checking to see if they can do those things at the end of the year like you did the night before your special day?"

"They do. I hadn't thought about how much she'll always be entwined in who I am. Thank you, Scythe. That helps a lot." Winnie relaxed against him. Her heart felt better.

"You're welcome. Stretch out, Little girl. Let's tuck your blankie under your chin so you're toasty warm." Scythe set Chippy in her arms before moving to sit on the other side of the bed. "How about if we start with the first story and see if you enjoy this book," he suggested.

His voice was low and rumbly. She closed her eyes to concentrate on the tale and wiggled a bit to get comfortable. A few minutes later, her Daddy seemed to talk softer, and she lost track of the story.

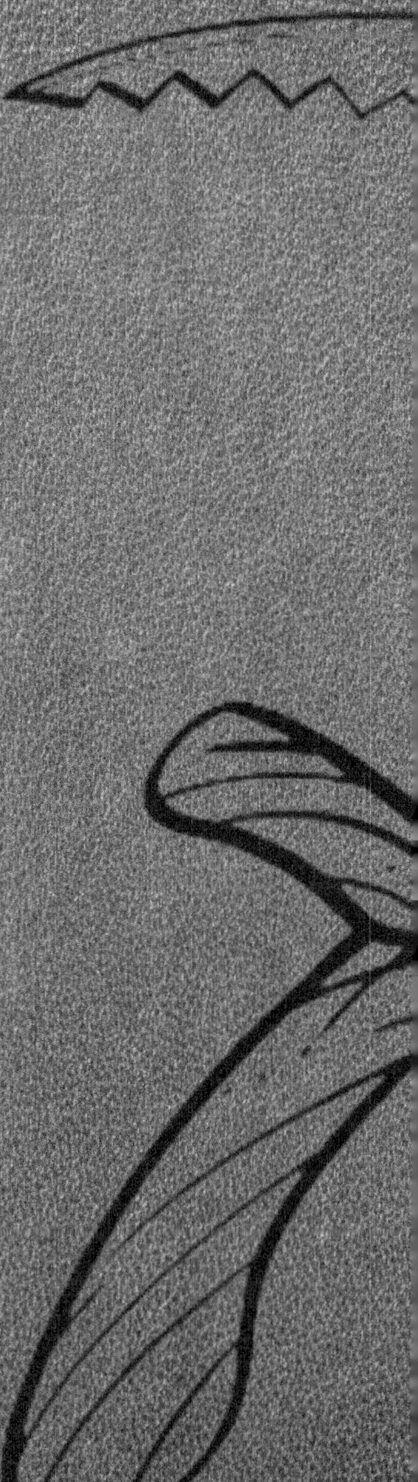

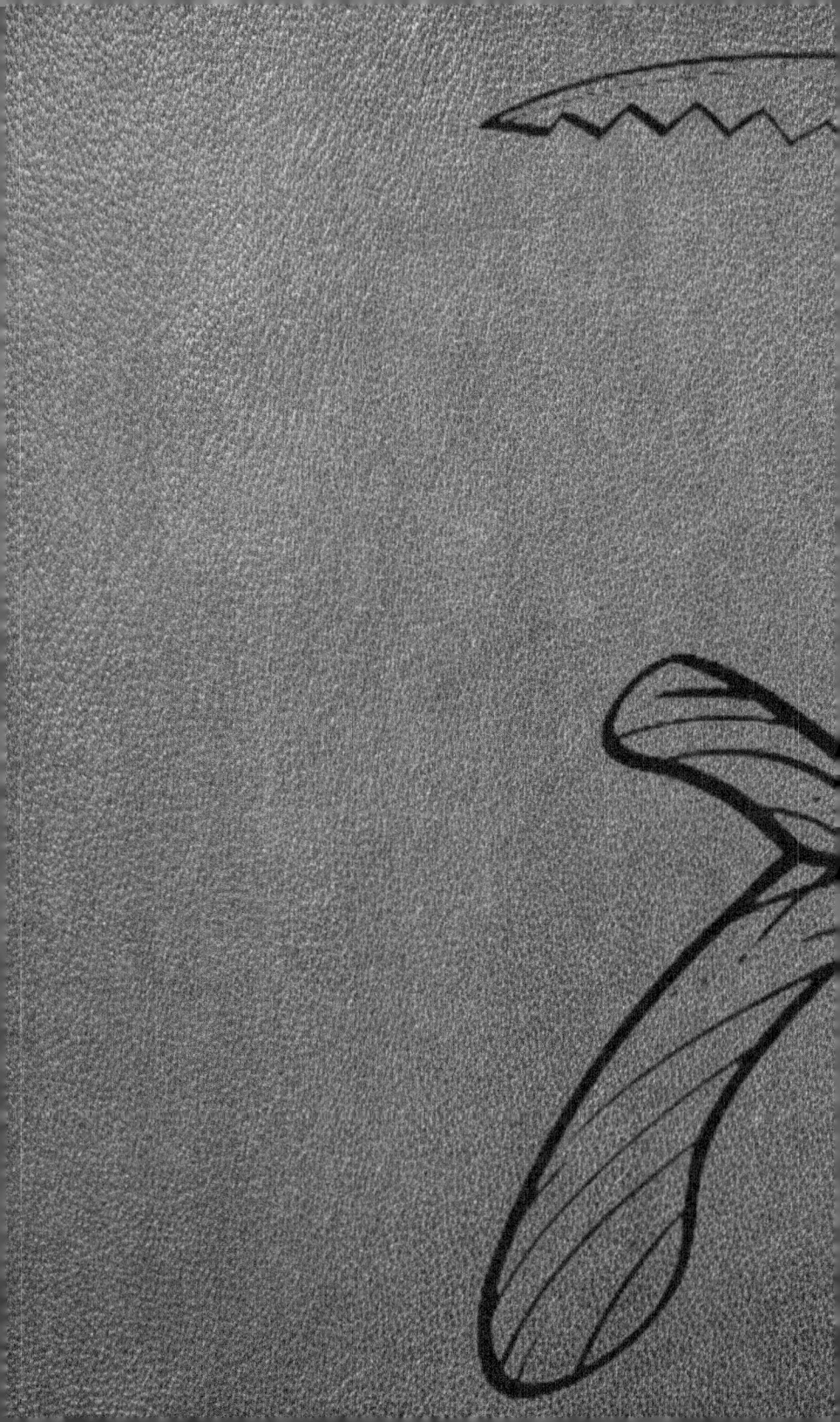

CHAPTER 15

"Stop throwing books! No, sit down! Don't pull her hair!"

Scythe sat up, instantly on guard as he scanned the dark bedroom. An elbow whacked his ribs, sending a jolt of discomfort through him. "Winnie! It's okay. You're having a bad dream," he said, instantly focused on her.

He turned and dropped to his forearm to comfort her. Scythe rubbed her shoulder and got a double jab of that dangerous elbow to his midsection. An "oof" gusted from his mouth.

"Chipmunk, you're okay. Stop beating up on Daddy."

"Daddy isn't in my classroom." Her whispered response told him she was waking up.

"If your students are as dangerous as you are, no way am I visiting."

"Daddy?" She turned in bed to face him. "Oh!"

"Just me, Winnie. You were having a bad nightmare. Want to tell me about it?"

She shuddered. "That was awful! Kids all over the room doing dangerous things!"

"I'm so sorry, Winnie. That was a scary dream."

"I wish it was only a dream. Sorry I woke you up. Want me to go sleep on the couch?"

"Your class is that awful?" he asked, appalled.

"The worst I've ever had. Lorraine selected the lowest-achieving kids and the ones with behavior problems from each of the first-grade classrooms and put them in my second-grade room. Their previous teachers shuddered when they scanned my roster at the beginning of the year. I must have been dreaming about how terrible their behavior was on that first day."

He shook his head. That bitch had done that on purpose. How long had she been after Winnie, trying to get her to leave her position? "What happens if a teacher quits in the middle of the year?"

She yawned and rubbed her eyes. "The district can keep their teaching certificate. They could never teach again in that state."

Winnie ran her hand over his jaw. "Go back to sleep. I'm totally awake now. I'll go out to the family room so I won't disturb you."

"Not happening, Little girl."

Scythe leaned over to kiss her lips hard. He wanted to grab her attention and wipe the terrible memory of that dream from her mind. After a split-second hesitation, Winnie responded eagerly. She reached up to weave her fingers through his hair and pull him closer.

Scythe loved how Winnie responded to him. She wasn't a practiced femme fatale, thank goodness. He didn't doubt her motivation or interest. Winnie was completely into him, just as he was to her. She could arouse him with an innocent look.

He stroked over her bare skin, loving her shiver of excitement. When she moved closer, he whisked the covers from her. Scythe lifted his mouth from hers to peruse her. He took his time enjoying her beauty.

"Damn, Little girl. You take my breath away."

"Make love to me, Daddy. Please."

Her request corresponded well with his intentions. Scythe

kissed her lips passionately before trailing kisses down her throat. Inspired by the cute sounds she squeaked as he lavished attention on her breasts, Scythe lingered a few minutes before continuing his path over her body.

Sliding between her legs, Scythe spread Winnie's thighs. Her heat radiated toward him. He knew she wanted him as much as he desired her. Winnie lifted her hips to urge him on as he kissed her mound before inhaling her sweet aroma. *Fuck!* He needed more of that.

Scythe pressed against her inner thigh to display her thoroughly to his view. Thank goodness for the dim glow of the night-light that allowed him to see her. He glided the tip of his tongue through her slick juices, savoring Winnie's flavor. Lifting his head, Scythe deliberately licked his lips to reassure her he enjoyed her flavor.

"Little girl, you are officially my favorite treat," he growled before lowering his mouth to her once again.

Taking his time, Scythe flicked his tongue over her pink folds to tease her. He pinned her down to the mattress with a firm hand to her thigh when she lifted her hips to guide his attention. "Daddy's in charge, Chipmunk."

She met his gaze and nodded eagerly. Her muscles contracted under his touch. His Little girl was so new to intimate play he knew her thoughts battled between titillation and worry.

"Mmm!" Eager to reassure her, Scythe hummed his enjoyment as he explored her.

"Oh!"

He suspected the vibration pushed her desire even higher. Scythe praised her, "You taste so good."

Winnie propped her head up on a bent arm so she could see better. When Scythe met her glance directly as he circled her clit with his tongue, Winnie bit her lip as if struggling to control her sounds. He'd take care of that.

Circling her clit with his lips, Scythe sucked gently on the small bud. He teased her opening with a fingertip before sliding it inside. She attempted to arch her back, but he held her firmly in place. When he replaced one finger with two, she cried out with pleasure. Scythe's cock jerked, eager to fill her.

When he pulled his mouth away from her, a wordless protest tumbled from her lips. As he shifted to grab a condom from the nightstand near her, he said, "Don't worry, Little girl. I'm going to make you come again and again."

She nodded, completely focused on Scythe and lifted her arms to beckon him toward her. Scythe lingered for a few long seconds to kiss her, allowing Winnie to taste herself on his lips. Then, he quickly tore open the condom and rolled it onto his shaft.

Scythe pressed his tip into her tight channel and pushed forward slowly to press into her. Gritting his teeth, he controlled his urge to thrust forward, filling her completely. After several pauses, he slid fully into her and groaned as she clenched around his cock.

"Damn, I love being buried inside you."

She tugged him down for a kiss before whispering, "I don't know where I end and you begin. I feel so close to you."

He understood what she meant. Making love to Winnie was different than ever before. The bond between them blew his mind. Scythe wrapped his arms around her torso and rolled to his back. Her shocked expression made his heart skip a beat. He loved introducing her to new sensations.

"Daddy, what do I do?" she asked.

"Sit up, Winnie." His hands helped her change positions. As her weight settled on his pelvis, driving him deeper, her eyes widened even more.

Scythe gripped her hips and bounced her slightly. A gasp tumbled from her lips. He shifted her forward to rub her clit on his pelvis, and she quickly repeated the action, grinding herself against him.

"Play, Little girl. Make yourself come."

He captured her hands and pressed them to his abdomen.

Immediately, her fingers explored his body. Each time she moved, his cock glided inside her. He held himself still, only shifting when she bounced or stirred on top of him. Quickly, she realized she had the power and could help herself feel good. He guided her at times to show her how different angles could make this position become completely new.

Soon, her breathing increased, and her fingers gripped his torso tightly. She was almost there but struggled to push herself over the brink. "Help me, Daddy."

Scythe seized control and made love to Winnie. Drawing on her experimentation with what brought her pleasure, he pushed her arousal to the edge. More turned on by this shy woman than ever before, he tried to memorize how good she felt wrapped around him.

Her cute squeal of pleasure signaled her climax. Winnie's pussy tightened around his cock like a velvet fist. He couldn't resist. Thrusting quickly into her tightness, Scythe triggered his own orgasm. His shout echoed throughout the room, ricocheting off the walls.

As their movements slowed, he drew her back to stretch out on his chest. Her heart rate slowed against him as her breathing settled. Scythe kissed her temple as he eased her down to his side to rest, cuddled close to him. Her soft protest as his cock slid from her warmth went straight to his heart. He quickly took care of the condom and relaxed.

Damn, I love this woman.

Sex was definitely his favorite bedtime story to help lure her to rest. Scythe closed his eyes. He waited until Winnie drifted to sleep before joining her.

DEVIL
DADDIES

CHAPTER 16

Winnie stared at the door into the garage. The motorcycle had roared away fifteen minutes ago, but she kept hoping that the door would reopen, and Scythe would come back in. He hadn't wanted to leave her, but Lucien had called. She'd assured him repeatedly that she would be fine without him.

I miss him already.

As much as she loved teaching, hanging out with Scythe was a much bigger thrill. Winnie forced herself to go grab one of her outfits from Scythe's closet. He had insisted on unpacking her clothes and putting them in drawers and on hangers before he left.

She liked that he wanted her to be with him. He'd talked over breakfast like the decision had already been made for her to move in permanently with him. Crossing her fingers, she continued to get dressed. Staying here with Scythe would be a Little girl's dream.

Remembering work, she sighed and grabbed her laptop. Sure enough, an email from Lorraine had arrived stating Winnie hadn't left lesson plans for the sub. Before she could panic,

Winnie found a message from Abby, who'd checked with the substitute before school and had given her a copy of Winnie's detailed notes for the day.

Winnie messaged her thanks to her bestie on her phone before replying to her principal's nasty email and copying the human resources department director. She attached her previous email to Lorraine in the office and Mandy in HR, along with the timestamp of when each had opened the documents. She also responded with the message, "I'm sorry, the district email system isn't working. Thank goodness I left several copies with teachers around the building, just in case. Let me know if the sub runs into any other problems."

She rolled her eyes as she closed her laptop and stowed it away. Hopefully, Mandy would have something to say to Lorraine. She'd have to deal with her when she got back. Lorraine was going to be pissed when her deception and attempts to prove Winnie had not fulfilled her professional responsibilities flopped. Pushing that out of her mind, she focused on the tasks at hand.

Not bothering with makeup, she headed out in the garage for her car and discovered the remote control attached to her rearview mirror and a house key. She smiled at Scythe's efforts to care for her. A couple of minutes later, she realized she was daydreaming about how swoon-worthy her boyfriend was.

Daddy. She corrected herself. Scythe would be proud of her.

Her first stop that morning was at the small chapel her mother had chosen for a cozy service. She'd already talked to the minister but wanted to take over a printed sheet with a few facts about her mother so he could personalize her memorial service on Friday.

With that finished, she drove to her mother's house. All the lights were on at ten o'clock in the morning. Wondering what was going on, Winnie let herself into the house, finding chaos. Cabinets stood open with items falling out of them. Someone had tossed everything from clothing to potholders across the carpet. The contents of boxes spilled over on the sofa cushions and coffee table. Had someone broken in?

"Belinda? Are you here?" she frantically called from the doorway.

Her stepsister appeared in the living room. Her hair was frazzled and dark circles were under her eyes. Winnie knew immediately she hadn't slept well.

"Are you okay?" Winnie asked, walking close. "Did someone rob us?"

"Are you kidding? There's nothing here to steal. Just a lot of pictures, mementos, and crap," Belinda spat.

"You did this?"

"Parents are supposed to leave you a ton of money, right? I can't find where my dad or your mom stashed anything! All that's here is the money from the guns."

"I have the will here. We've gone over it before," Winnie told her, waving the folder her mother had put together before she got too ill to move around.

"They had to have some investments or a nest egg to fall back on. Are you hiding something from me?" Belinda accused.

A shiver of fear ran down her spine. Belinda was out of control. "No, Belinda. We can sit down and go over their assets. Your dad's life insurance went to fix the car of the person they hit in the accident. Mom only had this house left. We'll have to sell it to pay off the loan."

"What happens to the money leftover from the sale of the house?" Belinda demanded.

"We'll have to use any extra to pay for the funeral and mom's last expenses. Whatever is left, we're supposed to split," Winnie told her.

"What do we do with this junk?" Belinda asked, pointing to the many boxes she'd dumped.

"Keep what's important to each of us and get rid of the rest.

We could have an estate sale. Someone might like the furniture," Winnie said.

"I want all of that. What are you going to do, throw me out in the street with nothing?"

"Of course not. Belinda, have you had any sleep? Everything will seem better after you rest. These are decisions we'll have to make after the will is settled and we have time to figure out what we want to do. None of this goes quickly. I promise we'll talk every step of the way."

Belinda stopped frantically looking around. Her shoulders dropped into a less tense position. "You promise?"

"Of course. We're sisters," Winnie stressed. "Mom loved you. We won't get much after all the medical bills and her final arrangements are paid, but whatever happens, we'll do this together."

"Okay," Belinda said and exhaled heavily. "I came home, and you were gone. The house was dark and abandoned."

"I'm sorry. I'm going to stay with Scythe…. Hopefully forever."

"The motorcycle guy? He's handsome, but really? A biker and a second-grade teacher? How's that going to look?"

Winnie hesitated for a minute, searching her heart. "I don't care what anyone thinks of our relationship. I care about how it feels."

Belinda seemed to consider her answer before commenting, "Maybe I need to spend some time at Inferno. That dress seemed to work magic for you."

"I got lucky, Belinda. But it's a fun place." Winnie smiled at her and added, "It's going to be a big change for both of us, Belinda."

Her stepsister sighed dramatically, cluing Winnie in that she'd solved the conflict for now. More sparks would fly in the future, but hopefully, they could resolve those as well.

"I know," Belinda said sadly. "We're the only ones left now."

"But that's the good part. We still have each other," Winnie said with a smile and walked forward to hug Belinda.

"Yeah." Belinda scanned the house, taking in the mess she had made. "Want to help me put this stuff away?"

"Let's do this," Winnie agreed.

In an hour, they'd restored most things to their rightful places. Belinda headed to her bedroom to sleep as Winnie went through the folder for what felt like the thirtieth time. She made some phone calls to relatives and canceled some credit cards. Finally, she packed a few more clothes and keepsakes from her room.

If Belinda was ransacking different areas, Winnie wanted to grab those items precious to her. Winnie could store them in her trunk if her stuff took up too much room in Scythe's tidy house. Slamming the trunk lid down with all her force, she managed to secure everything she wanted to keep.

Heading back in the house, Winnie checked off the tasks she'd needed to complete from her list. She left a note on the table telling Belinda to call if she needed to talk and asked her sister to order food for the house in case the relatives visited. Hopefully, with something special to do, Belinda wouldn't freak out again. Crossing her fingers, Winnie headed to the lawyer's office.

Why didn't I go to the bathroom at the lawyer's office? She squeezed her legs together and kept driving. Giving herself a pep talk, Winnie reminded herself she was almost to Scythe's. Just a few more minutes. Winnie pressed down on the gas, hoping she wouldn't attract the attention of a cop.

She came in hot to the gate to the Devil Daddies complex. Lurching to a stop at the entrance, Winnie swallowed hard as a heavily tattooed biker emerged from the gatehouse to check her out. When he stopped at the side of her car, she squeaked, "I'm Winnie." And then she remembered to say, "Scythe."

The stony-faced man's face transformed as he smiled. "Winnie. I'm glad to meet you. I'm Pirate."

"Hi, Pirate. It's nice to meet you too. Am I okay to go inside?"

"Definitely. Let me raise the gate. Enjoy your evening."

Winnie drove through with a carefree wave while inside her heart was beating a thousand times a minute. *Pirate.* All he needed was an eye patch. Or a parrot.

An image popped into her mind of the dangerous-looking man with a parrot on his shoulder, and giggles erupted. She was laughing so hard as she pulled into the driveway. She was afraid to get out in case she wet her pants. When the garage door went up, Scythe stood in the middle of the open space. Just seeing him, blew her wavering control to pieces.

Winnie shifted into park and threw open the door. Rolling out of her car, she laughed harder at the surprised expression on his face. That was it. She lost control. Standing by the side of her car, a torrent of pee raced from her to stream down the driveway.

She was almost hysterical now, as her amusement blended with mortifying embarrassment. Winnie covered her face with her hands and hoped to disappear. Scythe was at her side immediately. He wrapped his arms around her, shielding her.

"Scythe," she whispered frantically. "Let me go. I'm wet."

"I don't care."

His tone was final. He really didn't give a fuck. When she finished peeing, Scythe kissed her head and asked, "You okay?"

"Yes... I wish the ground would swallow me up."

"Not happening," he told her firmly. He scooped her up into his arms and carried her into the house.

"Scythe! My car's still running."

"It's fine. One of the Devils will turn it off," he told her as he headed for the bedroom.

"Someone saw?" She hid her face against his chest.

"A Devil Daddy will drive by in a bit and take care of it. The MC watches out for each other."

After breathing a sigh of relief that no one had watched, Winnie pressed a kiss to his jaw as he carried her into the bathroom.

"Let me throw a towel on the ground, and you can set me down. That will wash easily."

"Daddy's got you. That's what I'm here for."

Scythe carried her into the large walk-in shower. Before standing her up, he balanced her with one arm so he could slip off her shoes. He dropped them in the corner.

"Those are goners," Winnie said sadly as he set her on her feet.

She turned to him to apologize again and noticed the front of his T-shirt and jeans were wet. Winnie pulled the material away from his skin. Mortified, she whispered, "I'm so sorry. Take this off."

"You, first. Then I'll get myself sorted."

"Okay. Sorry!"

"Look at me, Little girl. Do I seem upset?"

"Not as much as you did when I tried to bribe my way upstairs to talk to Lucien."

"Exactly. I'm not concerned about this at all." He unbuttoned her first button and glanced up at her as he continued, "Tell me what made you laugh."

"I should have used the restroom at the lawyer's office. My brain was tired, and I only wanted to come home."

"Understandable. I'm not concerned about you peeing, Little girl. Everyone pees. Well, I'm not worried about it unless you have a medical problem we need to investigate." He looked at her meaningfully.

"No problem here unless Pirate starts walking around with a green parrot on his shoulder." Giggles welled up from inside her, and although she tried to control her mirth, that mental image got her. "P—Polly w—ants a cra—cracker!" she choked out as she struggled to laugh and talk simultaneously.

"Oh, Pirate was at the gate," Scythe commented with a knowing nod.

That made everything funnier. Her Daddy followed her weird sense of humor with no explanations. She loved that he got her. Winnie dropped her head on his shoulder as she wrapped her arms around his neck to support her. Scythe never paused in his efforts to remove her wet clothing. By the time her second round of amusement petered out, he had her naked.

Scythe turned on the water, keeping her safely out of the cold spray until it warmed up. "Okay, Little girl. Let's get you under the showerhead to stay cozy while Daddy gets undressed."

She nodded and plodded forward. She stumbled slightly, and her Daddy caught Winnie with powerful hands around her waist to stabilize her. Exhaustion clung to her like a heavy blanket. "I'm so tired, Daddy."

Scythe yanked his T-shirt off over his head as he said, "I know, Chipmunk. You've had a very involved day. Those giggles were fun, but they totally wiped you out."

A shower and a nap are exactly what you need," he said as he bent down to untie his work boots.

A couple of minutes later, he stepped in behind her and tugged her gently against his powerful frame. Winnie leaned against him heavily. "Let's get cleaned up, precious Little girl."

Gently and efficiently, Scythe soaped and rinsed her full body. His reaction to her nudity thrust against her, but Scythe didn't stray from his purpose. When he turned her around to rinse her backside, Winnie checked out his thick cock that had pressed against her.

"I could...," she offered, reaching a hand toward his erection.

"Definitely not."

Her face fell, and she dropped her hand to her sides. He didn't want her bumbling caresses. "I'm ready to get out."

"You will give me a blow job in the future, Chipmunk. I can't wait to be buried deep inside your sweet mouth. Today, when you're exhausted, is not the day." Scythe guided her out of the water and wrapped a fluffy towel around her.

"Oh. That's better. I thought you weren't interested." Winnie threw herself into his arms to hug him tight.

"When I see you, think about you, or touch you, I'm interested. You're mine. I have intimate, smutty plans for you." Scythe held her gaze for a short time before setting her away from him and walking forward into the water. When he dunked his head under the spray for a couple of seconds, she knew he was struggling for control.

When he emerged, Scythe continued, "But not when you're completely worn out."

"Smutty plans?" she asked.

"The very smuttiest," he said, turning off the water. He dried himself roughly before patting the moisture from her skin.

"I feel so much better," she told him as he wrapped a fresh towel around her.

"I'm glad."

Scythe carried her to the nursery. He threw back the covers and stretched her out on the soft bedding. Enchanted by the way he showed how much he cared with every action, Winnie blew him a tired kiss.

He left her side for a moment to grab something from a drawer in the dresser nearby. When he returned, Scythe threaded the thick panties over her feet and up to her calves. Instantly, Winnie stiffened as she struggled with how to react. This level of care challenged her to face how much she craved being Little.

"Shh! You're okay, Chipmunk. Daddy loves you so much. Now, you don't have to worry about having an accident. These are padded to absorb anything." He pulled them over her thighs and lifted her pelvis with one powerful hand under her bottom to slide them into place. Setting her down, he straightened the elastic before blowing a raspberry on her belly. That bit of silliness reassured her that she was safe with him.

"Daddy!" she said.

"Giggle all you want, Little girl. This will keep you dry." He pulled the covers up around her neck. "Let me get Chippy."

A short time later, Winnie turned onto her tummy with her stuffie cuddled against her. The new panties were bulky between her legs. She wiggled to find a comfortable position. Then she closed her eyes and let her brain relax for a while as he rubbed her back. She remembered nothing after his kiss to her temple.

CHAPTER 17

The afternoon sun shone weakly through the windows, leaving shadows here and there as she sleepily glanced around the nursery. She'd tossed off the covers at some point because the room was warm. Scythe must have turned up the heat.

She turned to roll out of her crib, but the railing was up. Winnie rattled it. It didn't budge. Rising to her knees, she examined the railing and tried to figure out how it lowered. There must be a latch somewhere she couldn't reach.

"Daddy?" she called, looking toward the door. "Oh! You're here."

Scythe lounged against one side of the door frame. "I heard you wake up. You slept well."

She rubbed her eyes. "I guess so. This is stuck."

"Nope. It's doing its job to prevent a Little girl from falling out of bed." He did something to unlock the railing and slid it down out of the way.

"But…. You don't have to put that up. I won't tumble out…." Winnie leaned too far over as she dramatized her point and saw the ground coming up toward her.

"Gotcha." Scythe caught her with an arm around her waist

and set Winnie safely on her feet. "The railing will go up when you're in your crib."

Winnie shrugged. She couldn't argue with him now. When his gaze strayed to her face as she moved, Winnie remembered she was only wearing the special panties. "I need some clothes, Daddy."

"It's plenty warm in here, Little girl. You need to get used to being just in your skin. I'll let you wear these for the rest of the day," he said, patting her padded bottom.

Before she could think of something to counter that declaration with, he took her hand and led her to the bathroom across the hall. Once inside, he left the door open and pulled her underwear down. She collapsed to the toilet and, to her embarrassment, immediately tinkled.

"You don't have to stay with me," Winnie assured him.

"Chipmunk, I've already seen you pee. There are no secrets between a Little girl and her Daddy." He grabbed a few squares of toilet paper and tugged Winnie to her feet. Bending her over, he efficiently wiped her while she tried to figure out if she was turned on or horrified.

His hand lingered on her bottom. "You're warm. Do you feel okay?"

"I'm fine, Daddy." She reached down to tug up her underwear, but Scythe brushed her hands away and scooped her up in his arms.

When he returned to the nursery and stretched her out on her side on the changing table facing the wall, she suspected she was in trouble. Winnie tried to turn over, but Scythe held her firmly in place as he drew a wide strap over her ribcage and attached it snuggly. He hooked another restraint around her calves and tethered them bent against the back edge of the padding.

When she tried to unfasten the closest strap, he swatted her butt hard. "You are fine, Little girl. I won't hurt you. I am going to check to see if you're sick. Do you need me to tie your hands to keep you from getting into trouble?"

She nodded without thinking.

"Good girl." Scythe didn't ask any more questions.

"I'm kidding, Scythe. You don't need to do that."

"Daddy," he said, wrapping an inch-wide strap around her hands and securing them above her head.

"Really, Daddy."

"Pick a safe word, Chipmunk."

"A safe word?" she asked as he opened the drawer below her and pulled out a large tube.

"Yes. Something that you'll remember but wouldn't normally say. Red always works."

"Red." She seized on that idea.

"Good girl. I'm going to take your temperature. Little girls have their temperatures checked rectally. That's the most accurate way." He unscrewed the lid and set it behind her.

"In my bottom?" she repeated, staring at the thick ointment he squeezed onto his fingertip.

"This may be a bit cool. It will warm up quickly."

She squealed as he lifted her top buttock and dabbed the mixture on the tight ring of muscles he'd revealed. He held her firmly in place as he pressed his finger inside.

"Relax your muscles, Chipmunk. You are very narrow, but I won't hurt you. Daddy needs to start plugging this cute bottom, so you'll be ready to enjoy my cock here."

"No, Daddy." She shook her head rapidly to dissuade him of that idea. What would lovemaking there would feel like? She clenched her thighs together as her body responded to his electrifying caresses. He didn't seem convinced as he concentrated on her bottom, moving his finger in and out to spread the lubricant everywhere.

The sensations overwhelmed her. Her juices welled from inside her, responding to his treatment. Could he tell she was aroused? She hovered between completely embarrassed and so turned on as he touched her in this forbidden spot.

Scythe's finger pressed deep inside her and paused. Winnie

glanced back at him. Hunger etched his face. It released something inside her. She didn't need to pretend with this man. He got her.

"I'll pay attention to every inch of your precious body, Winnie. We're both going to enjoy it."

She nodded before she realized what she was doing and then rushed to say, "Daddy, I've never...."

"You will now. Daddy won't let you hide from all the things you desire. Do you know why?"

"Why?" she whispered.

"Because you are the bravest Little girl I've ever met." His finger stroked in and out of her. "Can you tell Daddy you'd like him to explore your bottom?"

His gaze wouldn't allow her to look away or hide. Winnie swallowed hard and whispered, "Yes."

"Use your words, Chipmunk. What do you want to say?"

"I—I like." Her voice broke, and she cleared her throat. "I like you touching me there."

"You like me touching your bottom?" he asked, sliding his finger out of her bottom and squeezing more lubricant onto the tip.

She understood he was going to make her say the whole thing. Her cheeks flamed as she gathered her courage to bare everything to him. "I like you touching my bottom, Daddy."

That thick finger glided back into her as a reward on a flood of slickness. She could hear it crackle as he moved his digit in and out. "That's my good girl. I think that deserves a reward."

He reached for something else in the drawer and pulled out a thin wand vibrator. Raising it to his mouth, he gripped the flat end with his teeth and twisted the wand to turn on. She shivered at the sound of the vibration as his finger continued to tantalize her.

"I'm going to press this to your pretty clit, and you're going to come hard for Daddy, aren't you?"

She nodded eagerly, and then when he tilted his head,

signaling to her that wasn't quite enough, she blurted, "I'm going to come hard for you, Daddy." Winnie's cheeks didn't heat this time. She was too turned on to be embarrassed.

"I can't wait to watch you fall apart."

With her thighs bound together, he slid the wand through her pink folds. He observed her closely to judge when he had it in the correct place. When the vibration brushed over her clit, she gasped and immediately orgasmed. She shook from the intensity of her pleasure.

"You're so beautiful when you come, Winnie."

Scythe slid the wand away just before it became too much, and Winnie melted onto the padded surface as she tried to regain her breath. His finger slid from her bottom as well, brushing across the nerve-sensitive opening. She shuddered as the pleasure rebounded.

"You're fine, Chipmunk. Daddy's preparing you."

She nodded and closed her eyes. Winnie zoned out for a few seconds before she heard him rustling around behind her. Then the cold tip of something pressing into her warm bottom jolted her. It was thick and filled her tight passage. Winnie tried to clench her muscles to keep it out, but he'd prepared her with so much lubricant she couldn't stop it.

"Daddy, no!" she pleaded, peeking over her shoulder.

"This thermometer will go in your bottom frequently, Little girl."

"It's cold," she whined.

"It will warm up," he promised.

She didn't want to admit he was right, but Winnie was reassured that he wouldn't lie. He always told her the truth. She liked relying on him.

"How's your tummy, Winnie?"

"It feels funny now."

"Daddy will give you some medicine to see if that helps."

"I don't need anything," she promised.

"Daddy is in charge. When do you start your period, Chipmunk?"

Winnie would have struggled to share such intimate information with him but having him take care of her like this made it seem normal. "Next week."

"We'll put that on our calendar so Daddy can help you keep track. Are you interested in being on birth control? I'll always protect you, Winnie, but if you are concerned, Razor can prescribe some medicine for you."

"Maybe that's a good idea. Can that come out yet?" she pleaded. Winnie wasn't falling for his distractions.

"Two more minutes."

She snorted softly.

"Be good, Chipmunk."

Winnie wrinkled her nose and didn't look at him. When the thick tube finally slid from her bottom, she immediately struggled to get up. He couldn't keep her there now. The sting from a firm smack to her butt convinced her he could. She froze in place as he cleaned up the thermometer and put it away.

More rustling happened from the drawer below her. Winnie peeked over her shoulder to see him open a jar and pull out two, thick, bullet-shaped items. "What's that?"

"Medicine," he told her. "This will help your tummy."

"I can't swallow those," she protested.

"That's not a problem. These go into you where they'll work immediately to soothe you."

"Daddy, no," Winnie wailed as she clenched her thighs together. Her skin felt coated with her slick juices. She tried to hide her reaction to his words. Having someone care for her so completely was scary but totally arousing.

"Try to relax, Chipmunk."

He rubbed her buttocks until she forced herself to stop squeezing so hard. The anticipation of his treatment became more daunting than just allowing him to finish. "That's my girl."

Scythe separated her buttocks and inserted the first one

against her tight opening. He pushed it as deep as his finger would go. Again, the thick lubricant nullified any of her efforts to stop him. He slid the second into place, nudging the first even deeper.

The intruders filled her tight passage, reminding her constantly of their presence. The thought popped into her mind to push them out, but she had the feeling that would be a very bad idea. Especially while he was watching.

"Can I get up, Daddy?"

"Yes, Little girl, as soon as I get a diaper on you to make sure you don't have an accident."

He released the restraints and quickly wrapped her in the padded garment. "Let's get you down to play."

"Can I have a top, Daddy? I'm cold."

"No clothes for the rest of the day, remember? Let's get some warm socks on you, and you can cuddle with your blankie. Those will help keep you warm."

In a few minutes, Winnie settled at the small table to work on a colorful puzzle. She smiled as her Daddy sat with her. "Help me with the pink pieces, Daddy?"

"Let me find all I can, Chipmunk, before I need to go work on dinner."

"I like mac and cheese," she shared.

"I do too. Thank you, Little girl, for telling me what sounds good."

He plucked a pale pink piece from the jumble in front of them. "Is that the color you're looking for?"

"That's perfect, Daddy." She shifted on her padded bottom. The thick lubricant still coating her intimate area made her buttocks slide against each other. The intruders inside didn't seem so distracting. She didn't have any trouble ignoring them as she concentrated on fitting the puzzle together.

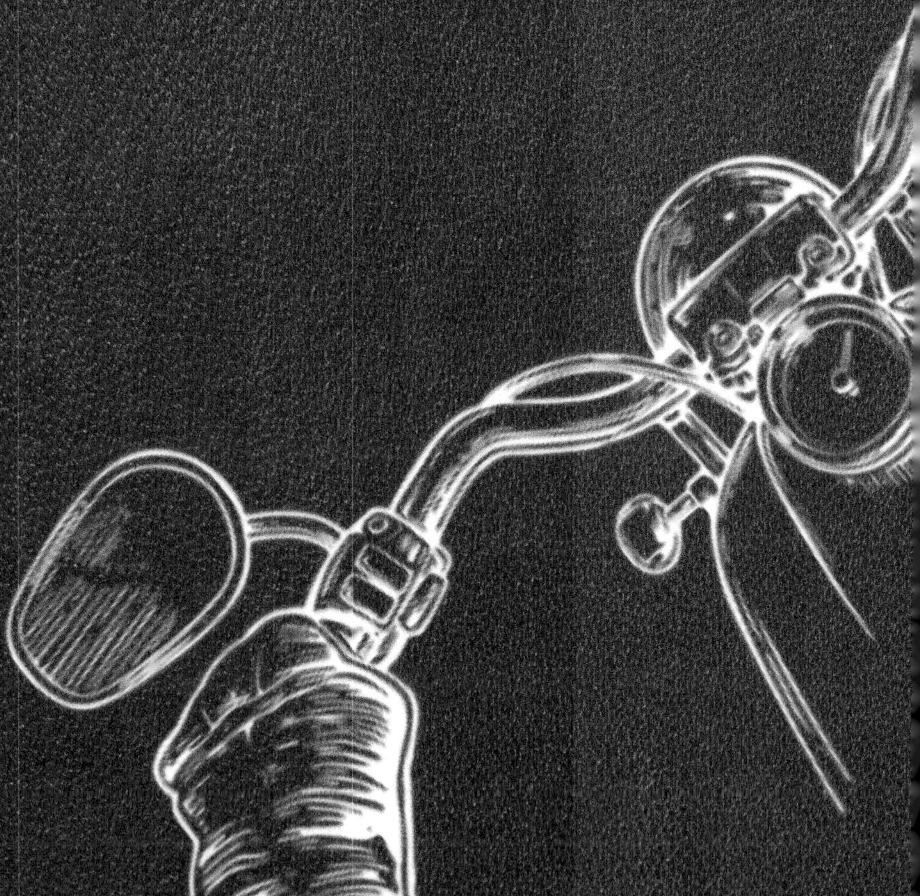

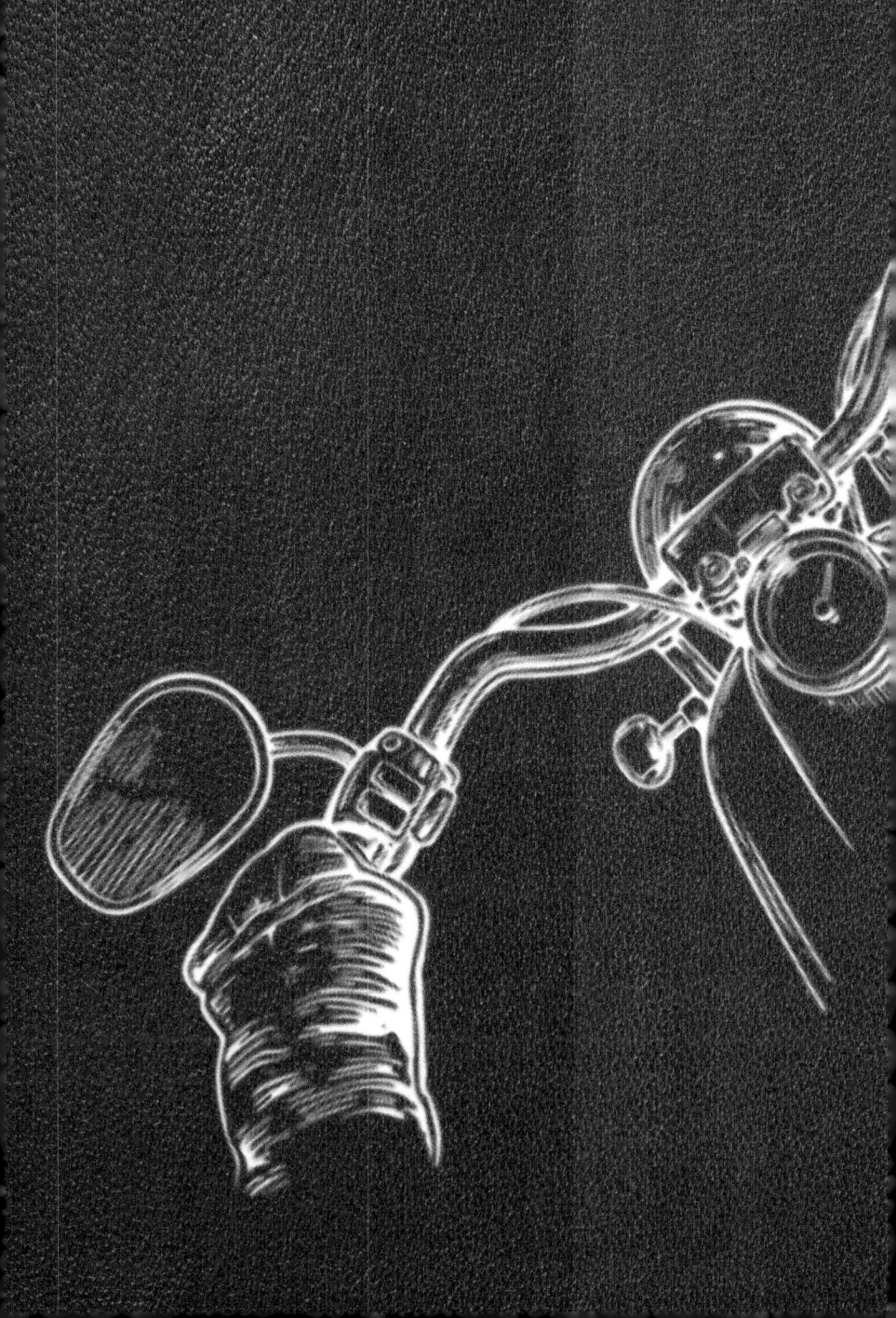

CHAPTER 18

"Five more minutes, Chipmunk." He smiled at his Little girl as she squirmed on the wooden chair.

"Daddy. I need to go now." Her sweet features beseeched him to relent.

"The medicine has to work thoroughly, Winnie, or I'll have to repeat the treatment."

"Nooo," she wailed. "Please!"

"Come here, Chipmunk." He walked to Winnie and plucked her from the seat. Carrying her to the rocker, he sat down with her cradled on his lap. He rubbed her tummy in a counterclockwise circle as he held her. She relaxed against him as the cramps eased.

"Better, Daddy." She sighed in relief.

"I'm glad, Winnie. You're going to feel so much better."

He checked the clock. The longer the medicine stayed in her bottom, the more effective it would be. Scythe told her funny stories about people at Inferno as they rocked. To his delight, she made it fifteen minutes before she begged to use the restroom.

"I think the medicine has done its job. Let's go." He helped her to the hall bathroom and freed her from the diaper. She raced to the toilet and waved him away.

"I'll give you some privacy, but the door stays open," he stated firmly as he walked out.

"Daddy, no!"

"Daddy's in charge, Chipmunk. Call me when you're finished." He returned to the bedroom and collected another pair of the padded training pants and grabbed a diaper from the nursery. He slipped them onto the bathroom vanity.

"Choose whichever one works best for you when your tummy is finished. Call Daddy for help with the diaper."

"Daddy! Go away."

"What?" he asked, stepping fully into the bathroom.

She took one look at him and stammered, "Sorry, Daddy. I'll yell if I need you."

"Better, Chipmunk."

Going to the kitchen, he listened for her as he started boiling water. If his Little girl wanted macaroni and cheese, he'd be glad to give her a treat. Winnie came to lean against his side after fifteen minutes in the bathroom. She rubbed her tummy as she stood quietly plastered to Scythe.

He wrapped an arm around her and kissed her forehead. "You okay, Chipmunk."

"My tummy exploded," she whispered.

"You needed that medicine, hmmm?"

Silence answered his question, but she hugged his torso to get a bit closer. He let her think as long as she needed. He handed her a cooled noodle from the batch boiling on the stove. "Want to taste test for me? Is it done?"

"Perfect, Daddy. I'm really hungry."

"I'm so glad. Stand here for Daddy, so you're safe." He moved her to a safe spot so he could carry the boiling pasta to the colander in the sink. I hope you like Daddy's macaroni and cheese."

"Yum," she hummed and rubbed her tummy again.

"Does your stomach hurt, Chipmunk?"

"No. It's better now."

"That medicine helps Little girls' tummies work their best. We'll remember that. You let Daddy know if you need its help, and Daddy will keep a close eye on your bottom. And your other cute bits," he teased. She was absolutely adorable in her pink polka-dot padded panties. Her blush was icing on the cake.

Winnie reported the shenanigans over her lesson plans, testing Scythe's ability to keep his cool. That principal had to go. For some reason, she thought she was invincible.

Winnie ate two servings of macaroni and cheese, along with a baked chicken leg and some apple slices. She didn't seem to notice Scythe was steaming inside. He chatted easily with his Little girl as he debated how to best deal with the problem. A meeting in the school or district office? A visit with the school board members? Scythe needed to keep Winnie safe from any type of backlash.

"Is everything okay, Daddy?" she asked.

"Perfect, Chipmunk. I was waiting to see if you noticed the chart on the refrigerator."

"Really?" She twisted in her seat. The appliance was a few feet from her. "That has my name on it."

"It does. You'll get to put a sticker next to the things you do. If you get seven stickers in one day, you get a treat."

"What kind of a treat?" she asked, reading all the entries on the chart.

"It could be something sweet, a fun excursion with Daddy, or a Winnie's choice, and only you can choose what you want," he explained. "Shall we go check the chart and see how many stickers we need?"

She nodded eagerly and ran to the chart. Her breasts bobbled deliciously, affecting the tightness of his jeans. He followed her and patted her outstretched bottom as she leaned over to read the lower choices.

"Look, Daddy! I see a naked as a blue jay day spot. Do I get to put a sticker there?"

"I think you'll earn a half sticker tonight since you wore clothes this morning."

"But if I skip my clothes tomorrow, I'll get one?" she asked eagerly.

"Yes, Chipmunk. Here's a box you can fill with a sticker today." Scythe pointed to a section.

"Temperature or anal plug time! You checked my temperature. I definitely get a sticker there!"

As he suspected, earning a sticker would encourage her to submit to his care. "Do you see another one in that medical section?"

"Accepted bottom medicine or enema? Yes!" She celebrated and then sobered. "I don't want an enema."

"Who's in charge, Little girl?"

"Daddy," she said, plucking at the thigh-high socks she wore.

"Daddy will always take good care of you," he promised. "Now, let's get the stickers, and you can decorate the chart."

She nodded eagerly. Scythe reached up into the top cabinet over the refrigerator and removed a plastic container. Opening it, he pulled out two sheets. "Frogs or rainbows?"

"Rainbows!"

He carefully peeled off one. "Tell Daddy which one you're going to celebrate. Announce proudly what you did to earn this sticker."

"You took my temperature."

"No, that's what I did. What did you do to earn this sticker?"

"I was a good girl and let Daddy take my temperature when you were worried I had a fever."

"Excellent. Add this sticker on the chart," he said as he handed over a rainbow.

The tip of her tongue poked out of her mouth as she carefully placed the sticker. Winnie scanned the chart and chose her next target. "I let you put medicine in my bottom, and I didn't try to push it out."

"You didn't. You were a very good girl. Best of all, the medicine made your tummy better, didn't it?"

"The best, Daddy!" Winnie agreed, dancing in front of him with eagerness.

"I think that space needs a rainbow with a pot of gold," he suggested and handed it over.

In the end, Winnie received five stars. She was upset. Adorably so.

"Daddy, I don't get a reward." Tears shone in her eyes as she looked up at him.

"But the best thing is you see what you need to do to get seven stars tomorrow. If you'd eaten a few green beans or if you'd drunk all your milk at dinner, you would have seven stars. Your chart is always up on the refrigerator. You can check to see your progress whenever you wish."

"But I want a treat."

"It's tough when you want something so bad, isn't it? Let's celebrate with a fun activity before bed. Would you rather watch cartoons or play in your nursery?"

"Cartoons, Daddy," she selected, bouncing on her toes in anticipation.

"Let's go see what's on, Chipmunk. If you're lucky, one featuring Chippy's relatives might be playing."

"I love them. Come on, Daddy." She rushed forward to grab his hand and pull Scythe toward the couch.

A few minutes later, she curled up next to him, cuddled under her new blankie. She seemed entranced by the cheerful characters dancing around the screen. Scythe kissed the top of her head and relaxed on the sofa. His MC brothers understood he needed to bond with his Little girl, especially after the death of her mother.

He hoped Winnie would enjoy spending time at Inferno in the future. If she didn't, he'd have to step out of his role as the road captain for the Devil Daddies. They needed someone heavily involved with the MC to have the pulse of the members. He pushed that concern from his mind. For now, he'd concentrate on protecting Winnie.

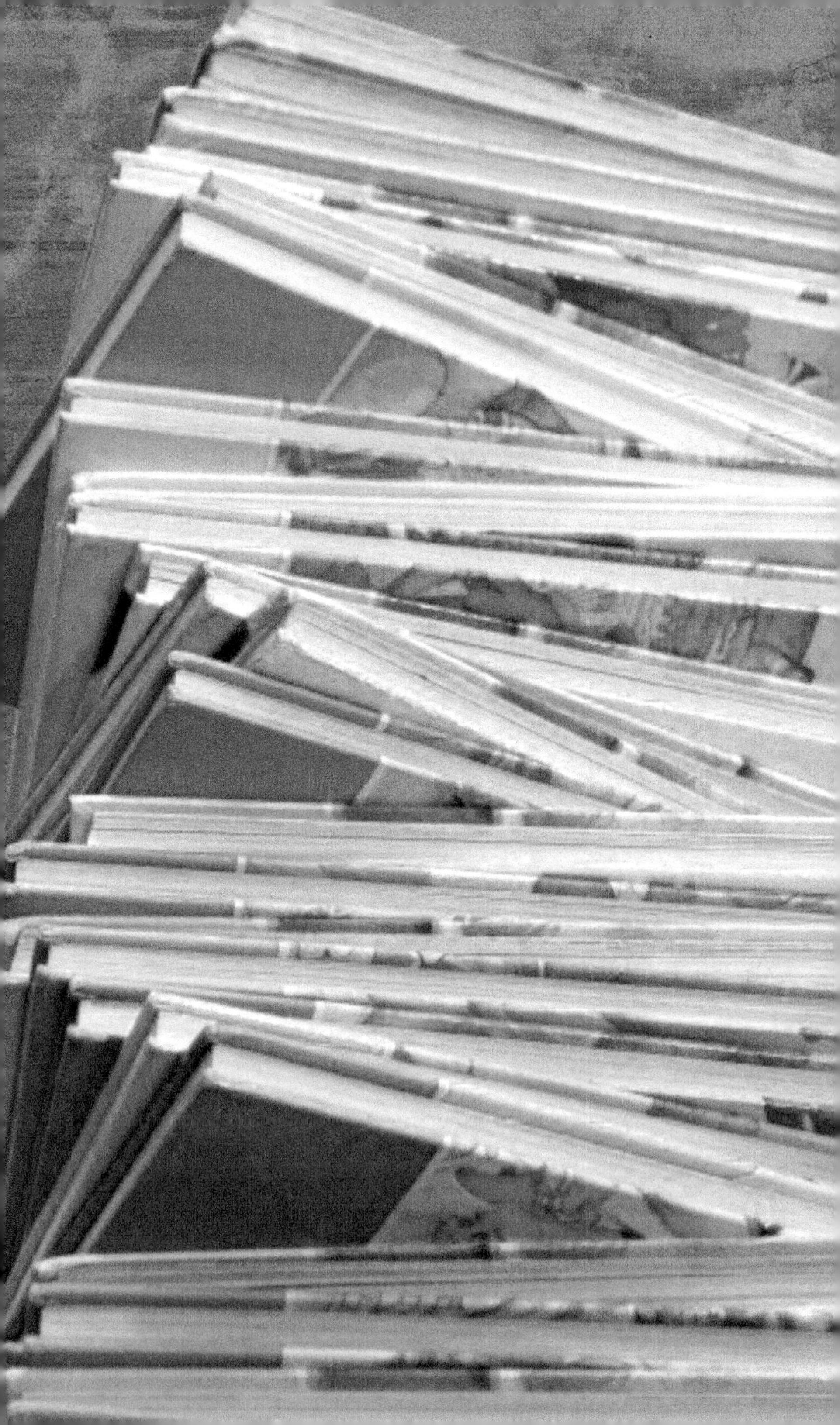

CHAPTER 19

After spending the morning in naked as a blue jay time, Winnie had earned her first sticker on the chart today. Scythe hadn't allowed her to wear the training panties today, since she hadn't had an accident. Winnie hadn't even thought about being nude until he announced he needed to dress her to go out to lunch. She'd had her blankie, Chippy, and her Daddy. What else could a Little girl need?

It turned out she needed a lot if she was riding on a motorcycle. Protected by the layers, Winnie had climbed onto her Daddy's bike, and off they'd gone on an adventure. He'd stopped to introduce her to Hellcat, who manned the front gate today. Everyone looked fierce until they met her, then their faces softened.

She guessed all Daddies loved Little girls. To her surprise, she liked being claimed by Scythe. It wasn't like the bikers would report her to the superintendent.

After a delicious hamburger and onion rings from the lunch menu at Inferno, Scythe had taken her on a tour. He'd even shown her where he worked in the warehouse. It was buzzing with activity on a Saturday afternoon.

"What do you do here?" she asked.

"Whatever Lucien decrees."

"That's cryptic. Are you good or bad guys?"

"We helped you out. What does that make us?" Scythe asked.

"Good guys."

Scythe nodded but didn't add anything else. Had he really answered her question? Winnie knew that she was naïve about a lot of real-life stuff. Lucien had helped her with the guns and had provided additional money to pay for them—more than Winnie had anticipated. Maybe in reality, lines weren't simply drawn between good and bad.

Scythe interrupted her thoughts by stroking a powerful hand gently over her hair. "Do you have any more questions?"

Winnie studied his face for a minute. She trusted Scythe. Slowly, she shook her head. "No, Daddy."

"Come on, Chipmunk. You have a visit with Razor this afternoon."

"With Razor? Why?"

"He's going to help us with birth control. He's got an office set up in that building over there." Scythe pointed to a building across the paved lanes to a window with a large red cross on a white background with the words 'Medical Office'."

"He works on Saturdays?"

"For us. Yes."

"Okay. I'll answer his questions fast so he can enjoy his weekend," Winnie promised.

"There's no rush, Winnie. How long has it been since you were at the doctor's office?"

"Several months ago. I did a telehealth visit during the winter when I had a sinus infection."

"When did you have a physical last?" Scythe asked, studying her closely as they walked.

"Sixish years ago? It was when I got hired to teach. I had to get a TB test and some immunizations to be in the classroom."

"I don't think Razor will find that acceptable. But no worries. He'll take care of you from now on."

"For birth control, right?"

"Yes. And anything else you need," Scythe assured her as he opened the door.

Inside, she discovered a traditional waiting room at a doctor's office, with chairs and tables with magazines. There was a small fridge with bottles of water and snacks on an island in the middle. Scythe escorted her over to the tablet set up on a stand.

"Go ahead and enter your name. Check that you have an appointment and the box by the L. When the space shows up, type in Scythe." He spelled it for her.

She grinned at him. "I know how to spell, silly. I give lots of spelling tests."

He winked at her. *Damn, he's handsome.* How had she gotten so lucky to catch his eye? "Did you only notice me because I wore that fancy, almost-not-there dress?" she asked when the concerning thought popped into her mind.

"No. That stringy garment was hideous. I really paid attention to you when Caroline signaled to Wraith to let you in. I realized she'd picked up on something I had been too busy to notice. When I watched you that evening, I knew I'd been a fool to not have snatched you up immediately."

"Oh!" The raw honesty in his voice convinced her he was telling the truth. "Hideous, huh?"

"Definitely. I brought something for you," Scythe told her.

"You did? What?" Curiosity pushed away her nervousness.

Scythe opened the bag he'd pulled out of his saddlebags when he'd parked the bike. He held it open for her to look in.

"You packed my blanket?" Winnie reached in to grab the soft fabric and drew it out of his bag. She rubbed it on her cheek and held it to her chest. "Thanks. I'm kind of scared."

"I know. Everything will be fine, Little girl."

She nodded, holding the blanket tightly.

"Come on, Chipmunk Let's sit down."

"No need. I'm ready for Winnie. Come on back," a deep voice instructed from a now open door.

"Hi, Razor. I'd like to introduce you to my Little girl, Winnie. Winnie, this is Razor. He's got more degrees than anyone I've met, including an MD and PhD."

"Hi," Winnie said, nervously. Her fingers tightened on the blanket.

"Hi, Winnie. I'm glad to meet you. I see you have Scythe's blanket. I mean your blanket, of course. My congratulations to both of you. I'm envious. I've been searching for my Little for many years."

"I'm sorry," Winnie rushed to say.

"That's sweet of you, but I'm sure she's out there. I just need to keep my eyes open. Step into the exam room, and we'll talk about what brought you in today," Razor said. He waved them through the doorway.

They entered a hallway with several closed doors and an open area with file cabinets and a counter with storage.

"Go into room one," Razor said.

Scythe opened the door into a regulation exam room. It was equipped with everything Winnie expected to see: an exam table, instruments, supplies, a scale. Scythe guided her to the chair near the desk. Razor sat on a rolling stool and opened his laptop.

"Do I call you Dr. Razor?" Winnie blurted and felt even more awkward.

"You can call me Razor or Doctor, Winnie. I'll answer to both."

She nodded and hesitated. Was she supposed to say something now? Scythe saved her.

"Razor, Winnie hasn't seen a doctor in quite a while. She's never been on birth control. We were hoping you could help us with that," Scythe told him without a hint of embarrassment.

"Of course. We'll do a screening for any communicable diseases as well to make sure you're both safe," Razor stated.

"I don't need that." Winnie rushed to reassure him. That sounded like a blood draw. She hated needles.

"It's smart to have the testing done, whether you have symptoms or not, to protect yourself and your new partner," Razor explained gently.

"What if there's never been an old partner?" she asked and then blushed as Razor lifted a questioning eyebrow and turned to check with Scythe. Winnie seriously considered hiding under her blankie.

"I'm Winnie's first and only lover," Scythe stated, looking sternly at Winnie. She nodded to reassure him that was her plan as well.

"I screen the Devil Daddies regularly, so that means you're both safe. Have you had a physical in the last year, Winnie?" Razor asked.

"Oh, no. I'm never sick. I'm a teacher. We're exposed to so many germs every year. I think I've got super immunity." Winnie rushed to reassure both men.

"No matter how healthy you are, Winnie, you need to have a doctor monitor your health. Do you have a primary care physician?" Razor asked, and Winnie understood he wouldn't let her shy away from his questions.

"No. I never chose one."

"If you would like, I'll be glad to step into that role for you," Razor told her.

"Are you any good? Can you take my insurance?" Winnie blurted. She'd never selected a doctor for fear of getting the wrong one. Her mom's first physician had ignored her symptoms until it was too late.

"He's excellent, Chipmunk. He's patched everyone up in the Devil Daddies and watches us like a hawk. Heaven forbid you have a cheeseburger when he knows your cholesterol is borderline," Scythe said.

"Borderline is still too high," Razor corrected him.

"You need to work on that, Daddy," Winnie told him and

clapped her hand over her mouth when she realized what she'd called him.

"He does need to lower it. You can help him by hiding the cheese," Razor suggested, not bothered by her use of Daddy.

Scythe rubbed her knee. "I've got a good reason to stay in tip-top shape now. I'll pass on the cheeseburgers."

Winnie beamed at him and linked her fingers with his, holding his hand.

"To give you birth control, I'll need to examine you. Several brands are available and effective, but each has a risk. It's important to match your health history and plans with the right medicine. The alternative is condoms and spermicide," Razor told her.

Studying his face, Winnie reflected on the things she'd noticed about Razor. By the size of the waiting room out there, the Devil Daddies visited him often. She liked how he talked to her. Not in stuffy doctor verbiage but like he was a real person.

"Can you take my insurance?" she repeated that question. Teachers didn't earn a lot of money. Covering an expensive exam could be pricey.

"Visiting my office won't cost you anything," Razor told her.

"Oh. That's great. Let's make an appointment," Winnie suggested.

"We can do that now. I'll step out and get the supplies we'll need. Scythe, help your Little change into a gown. She'll need to remove everything," Razor said.

"Everything?" Winnie squeaked and tightened her fingers around Scythe's hand.

"Yes. Would you like your Daddy to stay with you during the exam or wait in the lobby?" Razor asked.

"With me."

"I think I would have had a tough time getting him out of here," Razor said with a chuckle before meeting Winnie's gaze. "But I would have kicked him out if you preferred that."

"Thank you." She didn't doubt that he would have followed her wishes exactly.

Before Razor walked out of the room, he pulled a patient gown from a drawer under the exam table. "I'll give you a few minutes to undress. Everything, Winnie."

"Yes, sir."

The minute he closed the door, Winnie turned to Scythe. "He's pretty intense."

"He's extremely good at what he does. I trust him or I wouldn't have brought you here. A poor doctor would have simply written a generic prescription for birth control. Razor will make sure he chooses the one you need," Scythe shared as he stood and tugged Winnie to her feet. "Let's put your blanket there for a few minutes."

When she set it down on the chair, he immediately lifted her shirt over her head and turned her around to unfasten her bra. Winnie felt very conspicuous, standing half nude in the doctor's office. What if Razor walked in?

"Razor will knock before he enters." Maybe Scythe could read her mind. Maybe she was staring at the door too much.

"Let's put on your gown, Chipmunk," he suggested.

When covered, she relaxed immediately. Gathering up the bottom of the enveloping garment to get it out of the way, Winnie allowed Scythe to finish undressing her. She wrapped the fabric around her as best as possible, thankful Razor didn't use those awful paper gowns. Grabbing her Devil Daddies' blanket, Winnie felt less exposed. Scythe helped her sit up on the exam table and drape it over her lap.

"You're fine, Chipmunk."

"He's going to look at me there, isn't he? I've never had one of those exams," she whispered.

"I'll be right by your side. You can squeeze my fingers as hard as you'd...."

A knock at the door interrupted him. Winnie hoped she didn't hurt his fingers as she clamped her hand around his.

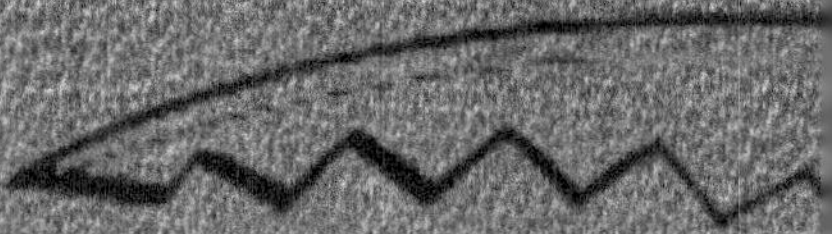

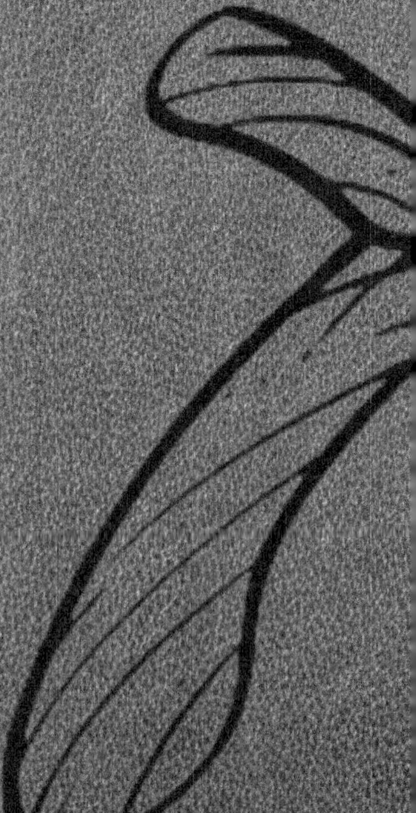

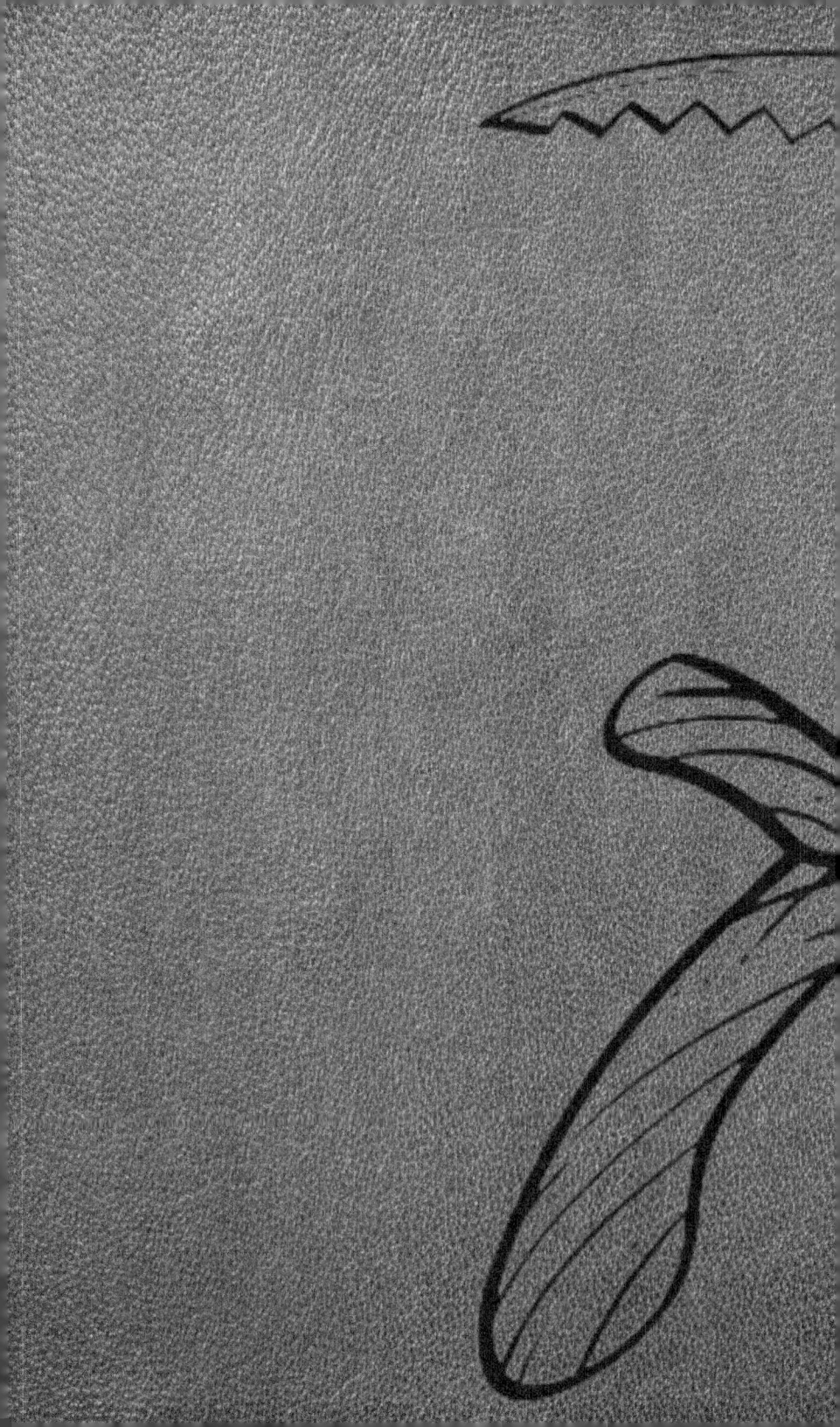

CHAPTER 20

"Okay, Winnie. Let's get the easy stuff out of the way. Step on the scale for me and we'll get your height and weight."

Winnie avoided meeting Scythe's gaze. She hadn't thought through all the things he'd learn about her. She needed to stop having an afternoon snack while she graded after school. "Ummm, maybe you should wait for me in the other room?"

"Chipmunk, I know how much you weigh. I've carried you a dozen times already."

When she didn't answer, Scythe added, "I'll close my eyes, and Razor will never tell me."

"Deal!" Winnie scrambled off the exam table like it had become electrified. The gown billowed around her, but she didn't pay any attention. To her delight, no one asked her to put down the lightweight material. "Close your eyes."

Razor followed her over to the scale and wrote down her weight and height. "I've got everything recorded, Winnie. You can go sit down."

She paused for a minute to move the sliding levers to the left on the old-fashioned scale, zeroing out her weight. Then she darted to the exam table and claimed her spot.

"I think I'll wait a few minutes to check your blood pressure, Winnie. How about if I check your ears, eyes, and nose?" Razor asked, grabbing the familiar lighted tool from the wall.

Winnie grabbed Scythe's hand before saying, "Ready."

The exam was similar to ones she'd had since she was a child. She could take deep breaths. This was easy. Her tense muscles relaxed as she did her best to calm down. In a few minutes, he measured her blood pressure.

"That's perfect for a young lady your age. Your pulse is a bit fast. I'm going to blame that on you sitting in the doctor's office," Razor told her.

"You're pretty nice," Winnie complimented.

"Thank you," Razor answered. "Lie back on the table, please. I'm going to check a few last things. You are doing very well. I bet your Daddy already has a reward in mind for you. Can you let him hold your blanket for a bit?"

Winnie met Scythe's gaze, and he winked. That reassured her. Winnie swallowed hard and stretched out on the table as she kept an eye on the blanket thrown over Scythe's powerful shoulder. Razor pulled out the table extension to support her legs horizontally. She closed her eyes and tried to focus on the great rewards her Daddy might get her—ice cream, a vanilla cola, a walk in the park, candy. *Hey, what about a puppy?*

Razor checked the pulse at her ankles before shifting to press in various places in her tummy. "Let me know if anything is tender. Does that hurt?" he asked.

"No," she answered, interrupting her greedy thoughts. When she tried to recapture them, the thoughts dancing in her head floated away. Winnie peeked up at Razor's face. He didn't seem concerned.

He shifted until he was even with her chest. "Do you check your breasts, Winnie?"

She hesitated and then shook her head. She might as well put the truth out there. "I forget. I'm too rushed because of doing things for everyone else—my mom, my students, my friends—I don't have time."

"Scythe shared that your mother just passed. I'm sorry, Winnie. We're going to take this off your plate, Winnie, and assign this to your Daddy. He'll make sure to put you first."

"Definitely," Scythe confirmed.

"Oh, I don't want him to have to…."

Scythe interrupted. "Taking care of you is what I love to do."

"O—Okay," Winnie agreed hesitantly. She was torn between being relieved not to even think about this and anticipation of Scythe doing this for her.

"Scythe, fold her top down on your side, and I'll examine Winnie before I show you what to do."

Winnie felt like she'd been transported into a bad porno. How was she ever going to look at either man in the future? *Bow chicka bow wow* played in her mind as they exposed her. To her surprise, Scythe was focused. He watched Razor and then followed his directions with a serious expression. Making sure she was healthy was important to him. Winnie felt more cherished than ever before.

"Check once a month. After her period is usually best," Razor shared. When Scythe nodded, the doctor re-covered her chest and patted her on the shoulder. "You're being an excellent patient, Winnie. Let me do your pelvic exam, and I'll have almost all the information I need."

"I'm scared," she whispered.

"I'll share what I'm doing as I proceed, Winnie. Your Daddy is right next to you."

She nodded, trying to be brave.

"Good girl. Okay, you're going to scoot to the bottom of the table," Razor instructed as he pressed the table extension back in its storage spot. As Winnie bent her legs to put her feet on the padding to wiggle down, Razor moved the metal stirrups into place.

"A few more inches, Winnie. I know it must seem like you're

going to tumble off, but I won't let that happen. Almost there. Perfect," Razor coached her into position. "Scythe, place her foot in the metal cup and wrap the support around her ankle."

She tried to move her feet and found them bound into place. Winnie squeezed her Daddy's hand hard when he returned to her side. She didn't like being tied.

"You're okay, Winnie. Razor is making sure you don't hurt yourself by falling. Remember, you're right on the edge," Scythe told her as he returned the throw to her. "Hold your blankie."

She opened her mouth to answer, but the snap of gloves captured her attention. Winnie grabbed a handful of the material and held it under her chin. Razor threaded his fingers into the other glove. He pulled a lamp closer and turned it on as he sat on the rolling stool. Winnie freaked out inside. He was sitting at eye level, looking at her pussy.

His hands folded the extra material of the gown, creating a drape that prevented her from seeing what he was doing. She bit her lip to keep herself from begging to get up. Her heart pounded.

"Winnie, you're doing very well. Inhale a couple of deep breaths with your Daddy as I tell you what I'm doing. First, I'm checking to ensure you don't have any lumps or spots that concern me, and you don't. I'm going to touch you now," Razor told her. "Your tissue is pink and healthy. I can see some signs of stretching, which is perfectly normal when someone has sex for the first few times. Your Daddy may need to add a bit of lubricant to assist your natural responses."

He explored her clit, pulling the hood back slightly. Even that professional exploration aroused her. Winnie tried to shut down her reaction. The heat of the lamp focused on her intimate space, her widely spread legs, and the binding around her feet shouldn't have been stimulating, but they were.

Scythe moved closer to Razor so he could see as well, and Winnie closed her eyes. Now, her exposure had doubled. Razor traced along her opening with a fingertip. "Here are the slight abrasions, Scythe. More lube will allow her to take you painlessly. Especially when you stop using lubricated condoms, you'll need to address this."

"Would oral sex help?" Scythe asked, and Winnie squeaked in embarrassment before draping her blanket over her face. "It's okay, Chipmunk. Razor will keep you healthy."

"Definitely, anything that increases her response is great. Perhaps an orgasm or two before intercourse could be all that's needed. Many lubes would work well to prepare Winnie for intercourse. I'll send home some samples for you to experiment with, Scythe."

"Thank you, Razor. Don't you want to thank Razor too?" he prompted Winnie.

"Thank you," she whispered, with her face covered. She was glad her Daddy had reminded her to say something. Winnie would have been embarrassed later if she hadn't.

"You're welcome, Winnie. Now, I'm going to check inside. First, I'll insert my finger. No, don't scoot away," he reprimanded her sternly.

Scythe wrapped his free hand around her thigh and pinned her in place. "Gotcha, Little girl. I'll help."

"Sorry," she whispered. Winnie continued to hide as Razor explored her passage thoroughly. Thank goodness Scythe was there to guide her in following directions. Winnie melted onto the table when Razor withdrew his gloved finger.

"You'll feel me insert a speculum. Would you like to see it?" Razor asked.

"No!" Winnie answered urgently. That would make this worse.

"Try to relax," Razor suggested, as he pressed the instrument deep into her vagina. "Good job, Winnie. Now, I'm going to widen this so I can peek inside."

Winnie tried to scoot up the table as the device inside her spread. Scythe said a warning, "Chipmunk," and she halted. With a final click, the medical instrument held her open. The doctor adjusted the light slightly, and the heat warmed a new spot on her inner thighs.

Winnie hoped she wasn't wet. He kept messing with her. It was hard not to think of her handsome Daddy watching and seeing her most intimate spaces in the spotlight. What he was thinking? Winnie peeked out from under her blankie to see.

"Hi, Chipmunk. Is something wrong?"

He wasn't staring at the display. Scythe focused on her. He squeezed her hand, and she remembered to answer his question.

"I'm okay, Daddy. Is it almost over?" she asked.

"Almost, Winnie. Everything is healthy here. I'm going to take a few cells from your cervix to run some tests. A gentle poke, Winnie."

Winnie recoiled automatically as Razor used a long swab to brush against her deep inside. But Scythe restrained her firmly in place. She kept her gaze on him. Her Daddy made everything better.

"Okay. I'm going to step out for a minute to deal with this sample. Scythe, I'm going to let you play doctor for a moment. First, wrap that wide strap across Winnie's ribcage. She's wiggly today and having trouble staying still."

"Sorry!" Winnie whispered.

"It's perfectly understandable, Winnie. Your Daddy was glad to help, but he'll be busy for this next part," Razor explained.

He met Scythe's gaze. "Grab some gloves and insert that suppository in Winnie's vagina. You'll have to hold it in place until it starts to dissolve and then rub the mixture around a bit. Be sure to add some around her inner lips where I showed you the marks. This will heal those stretched areas."

As Scythe moved between her legs, Razor walked to Winnie's side. He held two swabs in one gloved hand. Razor had already removed the other glove.

"Winnie, this medicine warms as it heals. You may find it arousing. It's perfectly normal if you orgasm while your Daddy touches you. That's why I'm turning this treatment over to him.

Stay in this position. I'll return shortly to finish your exam by checking your rectum."

He nodded at Scythe before walking out the door.

Winnie stared at Scythe. He picked up a glove and started fitting his fingers into the right spots. "We could just say you gave me the medicine."

"Razor knows what he's doing, Chipmunk. We will always follow his instructions."

Scythe picked up the suppository and studied it. Winnie could see that it was thicker than his finger and about an inch long. He pressed the rounded tip to her opening and gently pushed it deep. Holding his finger inside, Scythe brushed his thumb over her clit. "This isn't too bad, is it?"

Winnie shook her head. It seemed normal until…. "Daddy, it's getting hot. Take it out."

"It's medicine, Chipmunk. It needs to stay inside you. It's melting now. Let me rub it around. That will help," Scythe told her.

Shaking her head as his fingers spread the warm mixture, Winnie struggled to stomp down the pleasure building from the heat and his treatment. She bit her lip as he carefully applied the medicine along the areas Razor had shown him and plopped a glop on her clit before rubbing his fingers around to coat the walls. Sensations whirled over and inside her.

A moan tumbled from her lips as he brushed over her clit with his thumb. "Daddy! I'm going to explode."

"That's a good thing, Little girl. Come." He pinched her clit, and everything building inside Winnie exploded.

She clapped a hand over her mouth as she shrieked with pleasure. The orgasm seemed to go on and on forever. The heat continued, keeping Winnie on edge.

"Good girl," Scythe praised her. "You are so responsive."

The door opened, and Razor entered. Winnie covered her face, trying to hide. Razor said nothing, but Winnie heard him snap on gloves once again. Scythe patted her inner thigh and moved.

"Last place to check, Winnie. Take a deep breath," he instructed as he placed something at the entrance to her rectum. "Blow that breath out."

Winnie puckered her lips and exhaled. If only the heat would dissipate. She struggled to control her response. Razor's finger slid through her tight ring of muscles and into her bottom in a steady thrust. Still on edge, she climaxed strongly around the inserted digit as he explored her thoroughly. She tried to stifle her excited sounds.

When Razor's finger withdrew, she decided for sure she could never see him again. Her Daddy had to be upset that she'd orgasmed at the hands of another man. One of his MC! Her cheeks flamed hot with embarrassment.

"Winnie, look at me," Razor said firmly.

She shook her head, keeping her face covered. *Could someone die from embarrassment? Maybe spontaneously combust?*

"Chipmunk, let us see that you're okay. Look at Razor." Scythe pulled her hands away easily. She obviously needed to build her muscles up.

She glared at Scythe before reluctantly meeting Razor's gaze.

"You aced your physical exam, Winnie, and you appear perfectly healthy. I'm going to do a few blood tests simply because a doctor hasn't monitored you for several years and I don't want to miss anything. Your Daddy is going to release you and help you sit up."

Scythe quickly followed Razor's instructions. Within a couple of minutes, Winnie sat on her bottom, still feeling the heat of the medicine. She wiggled restlessly. Somehow, Razor's business-like attitude reassured her that everything was fine. That it was normal for her to have come during the exam. Razor certainly didn't treat her differently.

The slight sting of the needle faded quickly as Razor drew

four tubes of blood from her before winding pink bandaging around her arm.

"Good girl." Razor praised her when she didn't cry or protest.

"Winnie, you're done here. I'm going to call in a prescription for three months of birth control. One pill each day, starting when you finish your next period. Scythe, put the packet on the kitchen table and choose the best time to take it—Every day!" he stressed.

"Got it," Scythe agreed.

"The medicine may affect your cycles for the next couple of months. Your body will adjust, and your periods should get lighter and with less pain."

She sat up straighter at that thought. Her cramps were usually awful.

"Are your cramps bad?" Razor guessed.

"The worst. Two days before and two days after," she admitted.

"Heavy flow?" Razor asked.

She nodded. "It's hard to teach and not have accidents because I can't get to the bathroom."

"I can imagine. I'm going to change my prescription based on that information. Anything else I should know?"

Winnie shook her head. "Nothing. Thank you." She'd never had a doctor who actually listened to her like Razor did.

"You're welcome. And congratulations for finding your Daddy."

Razor turned to Scythe. "That medicine will continue to work. No baths or cleanup for three hours. She can have as many orgasms as she can handle. A diaper is a good idea for the discharge." He opened a drawer and retrieved one, setting it on the counter. "I'll give you a prescription for some ointment to use if she's sore after sex. It heats slightly."

"Thank you, Razor. I owe you one," Scythe told him.

"Get me on that ride?" Razor asked.

"I'd love to, but Lucien says no. He always wants you safe," Scythe told him.

"I'll be on call," Razor assured him. "Be good, Winnie. I'll see you around, I'm sure. And no, I don't share what happens in my exam room."

"Thank you," she said. Winnie was a bit embarrassed but reassured by his calm demeanor. Winnie didn't doubt he was a man of his word. She also knew her blankie had to contain magic. It had made this scary experience okay.

When he'd left the room, Scythe asked, "Can I stow your blanket in my bag so we don't forget it?"

"Please, Daddy. Thank you for bringing it."

"I'll always watch out for you, Chipmunk."

DEVIL DADDIES

CHAPTER 21

Waking up with Winnie plastered over his body was the absolute best. His Little girl had crashed so hard by the time he'd let her sleep. The aftereffects of her doctor's appointment had lingered all evening. Scythe had enjoyed alternating pleasure with bottles and snackies. Caring for her soothed his soul as she claimed a spot in his heart.

He needed to do some work on the ride today. He brushed Winnie's hair from her face as he plotted. Before he made any decisions, Scythe wanted to talk to Lucien. The Devil Daddies' leader hadn't shared the purpose of the ride with him. Hopefully, it wouldn't be a long quest. He had one more thing he wanted to take care of that evening.

Something needed to be done about his Little girl's boss. Scythe didn't give a flying fuck if she was gaming the system and had become a principal with no credentials. What he did care about was her constant attempts to target Winnie. Those were going to stop.

"Daddy?"

"Good morning, Chipmunk. Did you sleep well?"

She dropped a kiss on his lips as she propped herself up on his chest to look down at him. "I always do when I'm with you,

Daddy. You keep the bad stuff from me and Chippy. Well, you and my blankie. It's magical too."

"Of course it is. The Devil Daddies MC wouldn't have non-magical blankets!" he said in mock disdain.

"No way!" she agreed before sighing deeply. "I need to spend a few hours with the relatives coming in today for the funeral. Most will gather at the house for a few hours to chat. I'm sorry I don't get to hang out with you all day."

"You let me know what time you need me, and I'll be there," Scythe assured her.

"I'd love that. Maybe you could join us for dinner out somewhere?" Winnie asked hesitantly. "They'll return to their hotels early, so you'd only miss a couple of hours at Inferno."

"That works perfectly. Text me the location, and I'll meet you at the restaurant. Unless you'd rather I pick you up to drive you to dinner?"

Winnie shook her head. "No, I'll drive away from the house. That way I can escape after dinner to come home."

He liked how she differentiated from her mom's house to this place as home. She might not have processed it yet, but he wasn't letting her go. Ever.

"That's an excellent plan, Chipmunk." He wrapped his hand around the back of her head and drew her down for another kiss. This one was hot and passionate. He was totally in control, dominating Winnie completely. He loved how she submitted eagerly to him without reservation.

When he released her, they were both breathing hard. "Did you have a fun doctor day yesterday?" he asked, watching her expression closely. Her brightly flushed cheeks enchanted him.

"Yes. That medicine was…." Her voice trailed off as she searched for a word to describe it.

"Effective. Daddy will check on you today to see if you're healing. I bet you'll need some of the ointment Razor prescribed for you. I'll go pick up your prescriptions today."

"I can go get them. I have a copay."

"Not happening, Little girl. Your Daddy will take care of you."

She hesitated and opened her mouth as if she was going to argue. Scythe popped her on the butt. "Ouch! That hurt!"

"It was supposed to."

"You can't just spank me."

"Are you using your safe word?" he asked.

"No."

Scythe slapped her butt again. "Then I'll swat your cute bottom any time you've earned it or I need you to alter what's going on in your mind."

"You don't know what's going on in my mind."

"You have a very expressive face, Chipmunk. Right now, you're wondering how long I've been able to figure out what you're worrying about."

"I… I am not!" she answered and then added, "Ouch!" when he swatted her.

"No lying, Winnie."

Her mouth gaped open as she stared at him. "You see too much," she finally whispered.

"Daddies do. I can also tell you're hungry."

Her stomach growled loudly in response. "How did you guess that?"

"I've learned I need to feed you when you get sassy. Let's get up before this cute bottom is pink."

She nodded eagerly as he squeezed her butt. "I have to potty, Daddy."

"Go, Chipmunk. I'll meet you in the bathroom to wash your face," he said, raising his hands to release her.

An hour later, Winnie backed her car carefully out of the garage, and she was on her way to visit her family with a full tummy.

Scythe turned from the window, missing her already. He grabbed his keys and headed for his bike. Lucien should be at Inferno.

As he drove in, Scythe noted the parking lot was filling up. He walked inside. No one monitored the door at this time, so he didn't need to relieve anyone. A bartender waved at him, and Scythe headed behind the bar.

"Hey, I'm glad to see you," Sherry greeted him. "Could you help me catch up with orders? I'd expect a lot of folks to be at church at this hour, but it must be empty. Everyone is here drinking mimosas."

"Sinners love the fancy stuff," Scythe said, grabbing the next order. Sure enough, three mimosas and a tequila sunrise. Shaking his head, he picked up the champagne bottle.

An hour later, the crowd had settled down a bit. A few Devil Daddies members had stopped to ask him about the ride tonight. Scythe had assured them he'd speak to Lucien as soon as possible. He signaled to Sherry that he was heading up to talk to the boss.

"Thank you, Scythe. We all decided we're going to make you the Mimosa King," Sherry shouted his way. The other bartenders bowed in his direction as if he were truly royalty.

Shaking his head, Scythe ducked out of the bar and headed for the stairs. "Ride prep," he told Toxin, who was on guard duty.

"About time. Can we do some crunching tonight? I'm ready to rumble," Toxin suggested as Scythe stepped onto the stairs.

"I'll take that request under advisement."

He knocked on the door to Lucien's office a few minutes later. Hearing the biker call for him to enter, Scythe walked inside. "Hey, Lucien. About the ride tonight at midnight—do you have a target?"

"I do. A shipment is arriving at the airport. We need to intercept it."

"That's interesting. What time is it coming in?"

"Scheduled for two a.m.," Lucien said with a smirk.

"You're expecting it will get there a few hours early?" Scythe guessed.

"I also know it will be something other than the parts listed on the manifest," Lucien said.

"Do we need firepower?"

"Yes, but we should surprise them. With luck, we'll be in and out. No need for the flamethrower we currently have stored in the warehouse," Lucien assured him.

"Damn. I really wanted to try that thing out."

The corner of Lucien's mouth turned up slightly. Scythe took advantage of the MC leader's amusement.

"I've got a problem I may need the help of the Devil Daddies with as well. It involves my Little girl." Scythe paused, monitoring Lucien's expression.

"Go on."

"Pirate discovered that the principal of Winnie's school is a fraud."

Lucien nodded. "The superintendent's daughter who changed her name and doesn't have a college degree?"

Scythe should have known that Lucien would be up on any investigation Pirate had undertaken. "Yes. That's the problem. She's targeting Winnie to fire her."

"That can't happen." Lucien's tone was definite. "She's one of ours now. Appearing together at the superintendent's home is a great show of force, but that won't help Winnie."

"That's what I think too. I'm planning to take care of it alone after the ride. I may need some help sharing this information with the press if they don't do the right thing."

"I'll be glad to make a phone call if that's needed," Lucien agreed. "You go organize the storage of *random parts.*"

"On it. And thanks," Scythe said.

"We protect our own. Keep me updated."

Scythe headed immediately for the warehouse. If the heat got turned on for whatever was coming in on that plane, he needed to assess if the Devil Daddies' warehouse was the safest place for it. As he walked through the depth of the supplies, he quickly decided they didn't need anyone with a search warrant entering the property.

By the time he'd decided where to stash the incoming material, it was time to head out to meet Winnie's family for dinner. Scythe paused outside Inferno to send out a cryptic text to those joining the ride.

Midnight departure from the warehouse. Destination mini-wings. Boy scouts only.

The MC would go to the small regional airport prepared for everything. He entered Inferno, noting his MC brothers checking their phones as the message arrived. Nods of understanding came his direction as he headed for the door to leave.

Once on his bike, Scythe sent a message to Winnie that he was on his way.

He pulled into the pizza shop's parking lot and nodded at a group walking in together. They quickly jumped on the sidewalk, obviously suspicious that he would drive over them. A negative view of bikers didn't surprise him. He hoped these weren't….

"Hi, Scythe!" Winnie darted to the rear of her car, waving furiously.

Almost simultaneously, the jaws of the group on the pavement dropped open. She hadn't told them. Scythe grinned behind his tinted face guard on his helmet. This was going to be fun.

He stopped his bike next to Winnie and flipped up the visor on his helmet. Winnie rushed forward to hug him.

"I'm glad to see you," she said. Her words and glassy eyes told him a lot. She'd had a tough afternoon grieving her mother.

He held her close for a few seconds before saying, "I'm here now, Chipmunk. Let me park my bike, and we'll go in together."

"I'd like that."

Winnie stepped back as he positioned the bike in an empty spot close to her sedan. She scurried to his side as he took off his helmet. He wrapped an arm around her as he unbuckled it with one hand.

"You okay, Winnie? Did you have lunch?"

"It's been a whirlwind at the house. Belinda hadn't stocked the fridge for company."

"That's a no then. Come on. You need food," he said, guiding her safely across the parking lot to the entrance where her relatives waited.

Scythe held the door. As her family members walked in, Winnie introduced them to Scythe. When he followed the group in, the hostess hurried to seat them. He could hear the whispers from a few of the relatives who guessed that the staff feared him.

At the table, everyone jockeyed for seats. It appeared no one dared to sit next to him. An older woman charged forward and claimed that seat. Not sure how to react, Scythe held the chair for Winnie and then sat next to her. He pulled her chair close so she could lean against him. Scythe didn't like the trembles coming from her.

"Scythe! Always good to see the Devils here," the owner, Salvador, greeted him.

"Salvador, thank you for having space for us tonight," Scythe said. "I've got someone special here who missed lunch. Could you bring something for her while the pizzas cook?"

"I'll bring some rolls out to you immediately. It's a pleasure to have you dine with us."

He returned with several baskets of rolls as the waitress asked for their drink order. A minute later, Salvador returned to set a cup of pasta fagioli soup in front of Winnie. "Try this for me. I'm perfecting my recipe."

She dipped the spoon into the beef and vegetable soup and devoured a big bite. Winnie wiggled happily in her chair. "This is amazing. I wouldn't change it at all."

"You keep eating. Maybe you'll have some suggestions when you're finished," Salvador instructed. "Scythe, let me know if you need anything else."

"You're the best, Salvador. I owe you one."

The restauranteur nodded solemnly. He understood Scythe didn't promise anything lightly. A commitment from the Devil Daddies could come in handy.

When Scythe felt a tap on his shoulder, he turned. He met the gaze of an older woman he thought he remembered was an aunt.

"You take good care of Winnie," she observed.

"Yes."

"I might decide I like you. I'm Beatrice. Winnie's mother is—was my sister."

"It's nice to meet you, Beatrice. I'm sorry about your sister. I didn't get to know her, but she produced Winnie. That makes her incredible in my book."

Winnie paused in eating her soup to nudge him. Scythe dropped a kiss on that naughty shoulder when she straightened. A second poke made him turn back to Beatrice.

"I like you, biker guy. What's your name?"

"Scythe."

"Where did that come from?" Beatrice asked.

"Aunt Bea! That's really none of our business," Winnie jumped in. Scythe could tell she was concerned what he would say.

"I grew up on a farm. Believe it or not, when it sold, one of the things I saved was an antique scythe my great-grandfather used to cut hay years ago when he started his farm," Scythe explained.

"I like that. You remember your roots and your family," Beatrice stated firmly and glared across the table. "Scythe is good people. Be nice."

Instantly, the tone at the gathering changed. The relatives went from whispering and avoiding eye contact to chattering easily with each other. A cousin asked his opinion about a couple of bikes he was debating about buying. Winnie's hand wrapped around his thigh and squeezed. He dropped his over hers and returned the gesture. It appeared that whoever Beatrice liked, the family would accept.

CHAPTER 22

Spotlighted by the security lighting interrupting the midnight murkiness, Scythe scanned those gathered near the back warehouse. They joked and gave each other hell. The Devil Daddies were close. Working, playing, and living together had forged bonds between the bikers. Scythe didn't know how Lucien had created this group, but he was glad Lucien led the MC.

A hush fell over the crowd when Lucien arrived last. The Devil Daddies clustered around him, eager to find out what tonight's ride entailed.

"We're going to intercept a shipment coming in. Our arrival and acquisition will not be expected. Use whatever force required to achieve our objective."

"Do we need a truck?" Toxin asked.

"No. Our bikes will handle the volume of goods. Make sure you have room in a covered place. We go in cloaked. No visible Devil Daddies' logos," Lucien instructed. "You'll leave in five after you're prepared and your Road Captain shares the details."

Immediately, the bikers returned to their motorcycles. They opened their saddlebags and pulled out the inner liners of each storage area. After setting those safely by the warehouse, they shrugged out of their cuts and grabbed the additional armor shields. Hooking this reinforced leather to the back of their cuts, they covered the Devil Daddies' patches from their shoulders to their waists.

As he shrugged into his refashioned cut, Scythe scanned the group, doing a last-minute check to make sure he had an accurate count on the men joining the ride. He noted each member in his mind. Scythe never left anyone behind.

He sensed a presence behind him and turned to meet Razor's gaze. "How you can move without making a sound even in biker boots baffles me," Scythe said, shaking his head.

"I'm part panther," Razor told him with a straight face.

"Of course you are. I'll keep you updated," Scythe promised, knowing the doctor was there to respond in case of an emergency. "You're sticking around. It may be a while."

"I'm here. I have a cot in the medical bay."

"A good reason to put in all those hours of study," Scythe said with a smile. Sleep was not in his immediate future.

"You could take me with you," Razor pointed out.

"Lucien says no."

Razor thrust his hand through his short hair in exasperation. "That man is as stubborn as an ox."

"That I am," Lucien said quietly.

Razor gave Scythe a killer glance for not telling him that Lucien had approached before turning to the MC boss. Lucien simply held up his hand to stop Razor's argument.

"You're never going. Too valuable," Lucien stated bluntly. He looked at Scythe. "Your task is important, but be careful. I want to see everyone home safe."

"Do you want to tell them what we're doing?" Scythe asked.

"Your job, Road Captain," Lucien said, handing him a manifest before stepping back into the shadows.

Scythe knew each member was aware he was there. Lucien's presence alone would underline the importance of the ride. "Gather round!" Scythe shouted over the casual conversations.

He scanned the paper and shook his head as the Devil Daddies fell silent and moved closer to hear the details from Scythe. Of all the possible weaponry the Ravagers could be importing, this struck too close to home.

"The Ravagers are receiving a shipment tonight. We're intercepting it at the private airstrip off Chipman Road."

"What is it?" Toxin called.

"A new design of armor-piercing bullets," Scythe answered. "We do not wish to face these on the road."

Answering noes of agreement rumbled from the small group.

"Hey! Won't they just bring in more?" Fury asked.

"We'll have company join us after we've stashed half of the load on our bikes. A few local cops will arrest the crew and seize the remaining shipment, including the plane," Scythe told him. "We get in and out before they arrive."

The Devil Daddies nodded. They'd trust him to ensure their safety. Their confidence in him came with responsibility.

"If no one has any other questions, mount up. Vex, Fury, Hellcat, we'll give you a ten-minute head start to take out the guards," Scythe announced.

Immediately, the three men jogged to their bikes and headed out. The three worked well together and would clear the way. The others strapped on their helmets and straddled their bikes. Scythe watched the time as he moved down the drive to allow the other bikers to line up after him. When he accelerated, the Devils followed.

The entrance was quiet as they entered the airport. Scythe kept an eye out and spotted Fury concealed under a tree. When he nodded, the biker faded from view. They were in position and would guard the club's back. Lucien had trained them well.

Scythe checked the time. The neighbors in the area would have contacted the police as soon as they'd heard the large group of bikers converge on the airport. Vex, Fury, and Hellcat would have arrived separately. A single rumble of a cycle wouldn't have concerned anyone.

He drove to a shaded area off the runway and signaled Dead Eye. The quietest member of the club moved up beside him and stepped off his bike. He drew his well-used sniper rifle from its usual location concealed under his cut and headed into position.

Less than a minute later, Scythe noted the rumble of an approaching plane engine. It sounded rough. He hid a grin. Pirate had hacked into the transport company's computer system and arranged for the cargo to arrive three hours before the Ravagers had contracted them.

The bikers strolled out onto the runway, and those inside the plane opened the hatch, lowering the stairs. Scythe walked forward to greet the man who descended. As they shook hands, Dead Eye took out the tires, rendering the plane helpless. Scythe used that distraction to overpower the man and held a knife to his throat, as he used the new arrival as a shield.

"Tell your men to surrender or you're dead," he growled into his captive's ear.

"We'll kill the Ravagers," the man threatened as he thrashed to get away.

Scythe didn't correct the man's mistake in believing they were the rival club. He'd celebrate if the Ravagers were wiped from existence.

A ping of a bullet sounded. Dead Eye had fired again. A man fell from the door of the plane, where he must have attempted to target the Devil Daddies. The bikers scattered as the gun tumbled down the stairs. When it didn't discharge, Scythe shook his head. "Your guys don't know how to take the safety off?" He chuckled into the man's ear.

When his captive thrashed, Scythe whacked him over the head with the hilt of his blade, knocking him out. He dropped him onto the pavement. One of the bikers would restrain him.

He climbed the stairs cautiously. The pilot sat frozen in his seat. A red dot over his heart kept him pinned in place. Scythe scanned the cargo hold, not spotting anyone. The fools had come with only three on board?

"Tie up the pilot," Scythe growled to Street, who appeared behind him. It was foolhardy of the new MC member to follow him before he got the all-clear, but Scythe appreciated the reinforcement. His intuition told him there had to be another man to unload the cargo.

A glint of moonlight off metal warned him, and he threw his knife. The scream that followed confirmed the danger was over. Soon, four men stretched out on the pavement with varying levels of injuries. All still lived to greet the cops when they arrived.

"Take half. Move fast. We leave in three minutes."

After a flurry of activity, the Devil Daddies exited in different directions with laden saddle bags. The wail of sirens reached Scythe's ears as he navigated a farmer's path through a field without his lights. Street and Vex were hot on his trail. Dead Eye had departed as soon as they'd secured the men and he was no longer needed.

When they were several miles away, Scythe stopped in a parking lot. The two others pulled alongside him and flipped open their visors.

"Head back to the warehouse. I'll return soon," Scythe instructed.

"Where are you going?" Street demanded.

"I have a visit to make."

"Want help?" Vex asked.

"No. This is something I need to do myself," Scythe said.

"Got it. See you in a couple hours?" Vex asked.

"Less than that," Scythe assured him as he lowered the stand down on his bike. He had a few things to prepare before his next stop. Scythe unwrapped the items stowed on his rear carrier and got to work.

Sliding the keycard into the scanner at the exclusive gated community, Scythe didn't hold his breath. Pirate's skills were good. The bar rose, allowing him to coast inside easily. The rear camera would get a picture of a different motorcycle brand logo and an altered license plate. He'd arranged that before driving here.

Steering through the empty streets, Scythe noted the houses sat silent and dark in the exclusive neighborhood. The three to five-car garages protected the vehicles while everyone slept. He crept forward slowly, keeping the rumble of his bike motor at a minimum. When he reached his target, Scythe turned off the engine and parked underneath a gigantic oak tree.

He blended into the shadows on the side of a vast craftsmen-style mansion and worked some magic. Scythe jumped over the fence and tried the rear door. The knob turned easily. *Thank you.*

A fluffy poodle mix met him in the kitchen. She was perfectly delighted to allow Scythe to feed her and shut her in the pantry with an open box of treats. His stomach growled at the plate of gooey cookies on the island as he passed them. Scythe lifted the glass dome with his gloved hand and grabbed a couple.

He ate one on his way up the stairs. The house plan registered with the city showed the master bedroom on the second floor in the east corner. Scythe detected loud snores immediately at the top of the stairs. A wife couldn't sleep through that cacophony. The man of the house had to be alone. After setting the other cookie on the hallway table, he squeezed fast-drying industrial glue into the locks of the other closed bedroom doors.

Scythe walked through the noisy bedroom's door. Quietly keeping an eye on the snoring jerk in the bed, he eased open the bedside table and removed the Glock stored inside. After emptying the bullets out of the slide and the chamber, he replaced the gun and slid the drawer shut. Thank goodness for well-constructed furniture that didn't squeak.

Scythe shook his head at the man who'd snored through all that. He really shouldn't have messed with a Devil Daddies'

Little girl. Finally, he moved a nearby chair close to the bedside and made himself comfortable before switching on the light.

The man stared at him in confusion before panicking and yanking the entire drawer from the nightstand. The contents tumbled to the ground.

"No worries. The gun doesn't work without bullets anyway," Scythe told him, holding up one in his left hand as he aimed his own gun at the disheveled man still half under the covers.

"Ellen! Call the police!" the man yelled.

"Unfortunately, all the signals inside and out are not functioning. Nice of you to endanger your wife's life, however," Scythe observed. "She could have slept blissfully through this without ever realizing she'd had a visitor. Not the protective type, I see. That suits my purposes."

Scythe tilted his head toward the door without taking his eyes off the man in bed as a cacophony of pounding and yells came from down the hall. Thank goodness for the extra noise-cancelling insulation built into these homes. The neighbors wouldn't hear a thing.

Adam didn't answer his wife's calls or seem to care she was frantic. He glared at Scythe. "Your purposes? What do you want?"

"You're going to leave your position as the superintendent of schools. Your daughter will resign simultaneously from her role as the principal of East Elementary."

"Why would I do that?" Adam Young's eyes narrowed, and Scythe watched the fear in his gaze ebb.

Scythe pulled back the hammer on his revolver with a satisfying click that restored the fright on Adam's face.

"Wait! You can't expect me to throw my career away because a stranger demands it."

"A stranger with a gun," Scythe reminded him.

"Why are you doing this?" Adam asked.

"You don't need to know the reason. Before you choose not to follow my instructions, let me tell you what will happen in approximately five hours. The information on this flash drive will be delivered to every news station in the city, as well as each member of the board and the other administrators in your district. The newsies will jump at the juicy story of a criminal who changes her name for a fresh start, only to choose another scandalous path by creating a degree for herself with the help of her superintendent father."

Adam stared at him for several long seconds before arguing, "You can't have proof of anything."

"Oh, but I do. Here, you can see for yourself." He tossed the flash drive to the other man, who bumbled it and dropped it onto the floor.

"Wow. Maybe I should investigate if your degree is actually valid. Didn't you have a baseball scholarship as a catcher for your undergrad studies?"

Adam's pale face lost more color. *Oh, that struck a chord.* Scythe mentally thanked Pirate for expanding his investigation to include the father.

The man straightened his slumped shoulders and went on the offensive. "You're not going to do any of this."

Scythe smiled. "Of course I am."

"You have to be the biker my daughter scoffed about, who visited that worthless second-grade teacher. Her job will be gone tomorrow. The school resource officer ran your license. I can file a police report against you," Adam Young assured him, assuming his superintendent poise.

"Even if your guess is correct, that's not going to happen."

"Why?" Adam seemed confused by Scythe's confidence.

"No one messes with my MC and survives. Now, would you rather I shoot you or knock you out?"

"What! I don't want either of...."

Scythe approved of the superintendent's choice as his fist landed squarely. Adam's eyes rolled back in his head as he slumped sideways on the bed, a lump already rising through his thinning hair.

Scythe shook the sting from his hand. Messing with a man who grew up intimidating two-thousand-pound bulls wasn't smart. Adam hadn't required more than a tap to send him to sleep. Standing, he kicked the flash drive a bit farther under the bed. He'd enjoy the mental picture of Adam struggling to fish it out.

He walked down the hall and slammed the side of his fist against the door Ellen Young still pounded on. She screamed and scurried away from the barrier.

"Convince your husband to do the right thing. You don't want to see what comes next," Scythe growled through the wood.

He turned and picked up the abandoned cookie. No need to leave it. Strolling down the stairs, he munched on the treat as he left through the back door.

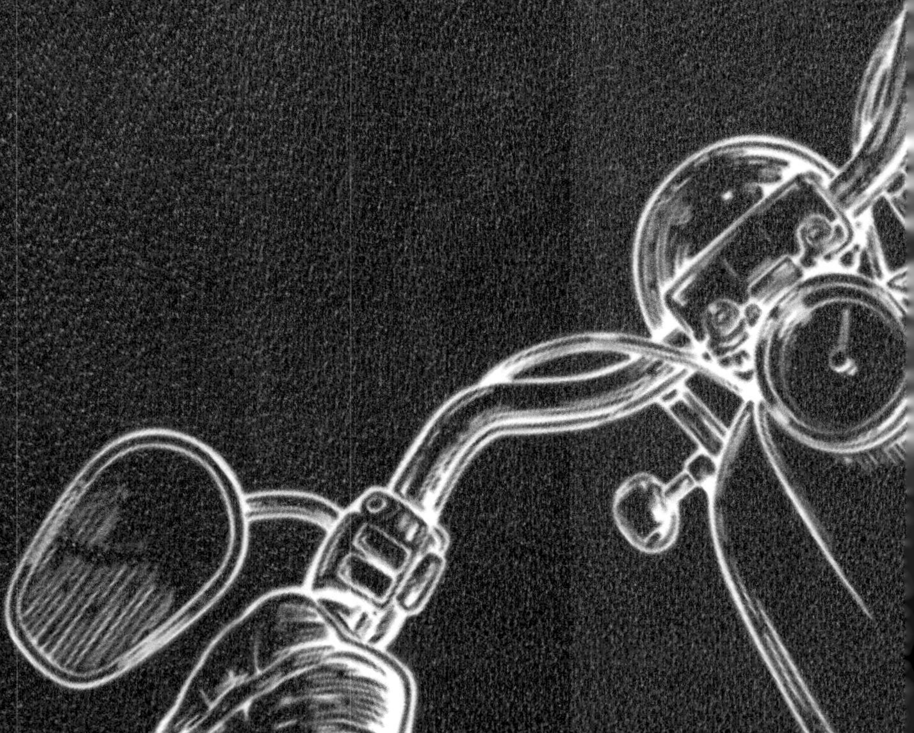

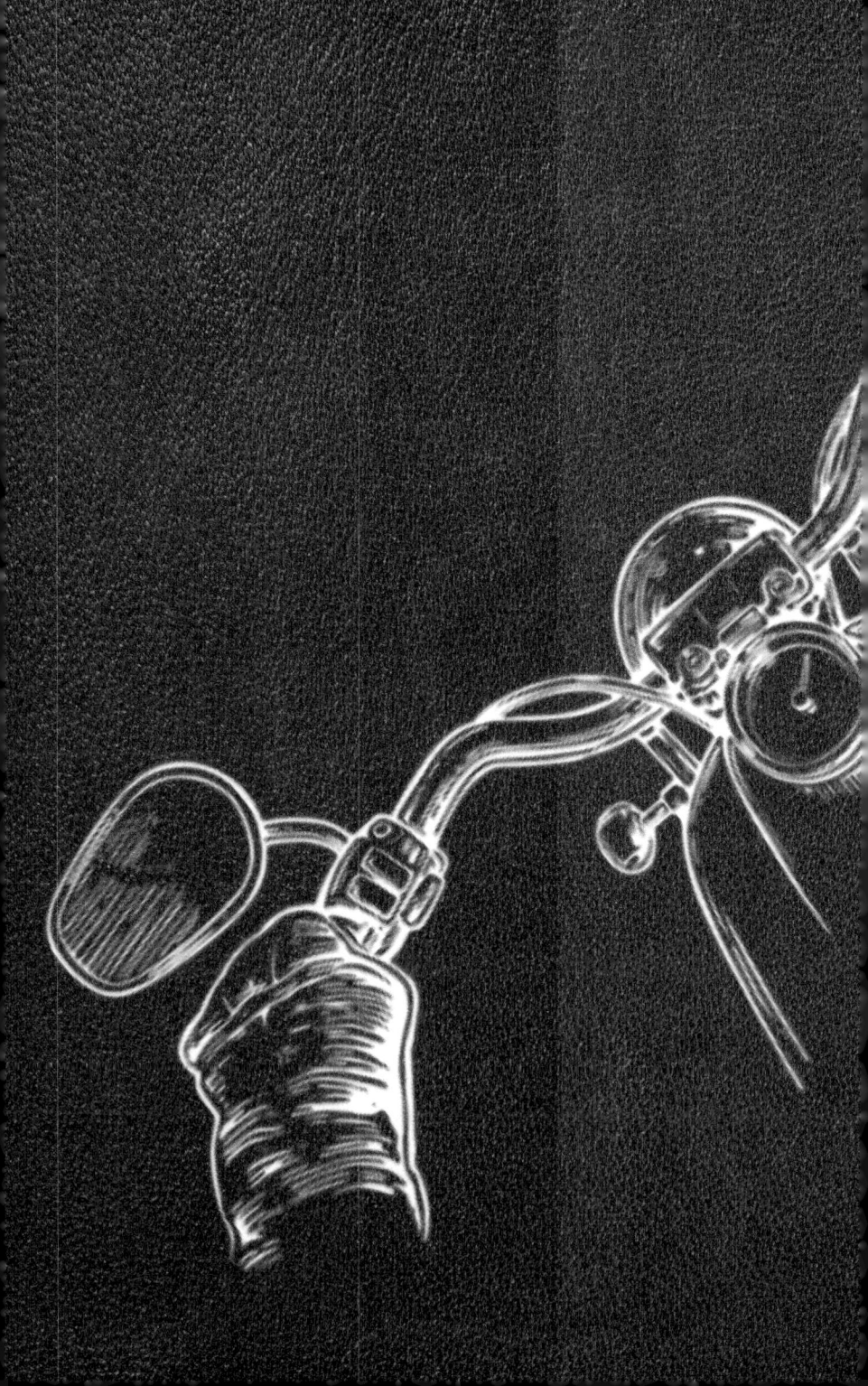

CHAPTER 23

The funeral was lovely and touching. Winnie cried frequently, but Scythe was by her side, lending her strength and handing her tissues. She glanced at the handsome man as they stood outside the small church, accepting condolences and smiling about precious memories that others had stopped to share with her.

He rocked that suit. Watching him get dressed had completely distracted Winnie. She'd barely contained her impulse to jump him. Maybe he'd play billionaire and poor teacher when they got home. She chuckled at that erotic fantasy. Wow, had her life changed.

Winnie hadn't thought it was possible for Scythe to charm Aunt Beatrice more, but one look at him dressed formally had wowed the older woman. Scythe had even handled Belinda's flirting with finesse. All the boys had preferred her stepsister when they'd grown up. Having Scythe devoted to her made the teenage angst fade into oblivion. She'd won the best prize by waiting to find him.

As the crowd thinned, Winnie's phone buzzed with an incoming message. Seeing Abby's name on her screen, Winnie pulled it up. After scanning it quickly, she forced herself to read it a second time. Her mind whirled with the information on the brief note.

"Is everything okay, Winnie?" Scythe asked, his brows coming together in concern.

"You're not going to believe this!"

"What, Chipmunk?"

"The school board has called an emergency meeting for this evening. The gossip is that the superintendent has resigned. I can't believe this is happening! According to Abby, reporters and cameras had swarmed around East Elementary when they took the kids out for recess this morning. The resource officer kept them off school property, but they had lined up on the sidewalk across the street," Winnie said. "I'm going to the meeting this evening."

"I'll go with you," he answered immediately.

"I'd love that. My friends want to meet you. I have to go to lunch with my family. Go check in at Inferno. Shall we meet at the district's head office?"

"That would work best. Are you okay without me joining you at lunch?"

"That's probably best. I think several of my cousins are going to pressure you to introduce them to some hot bikers."

"They aren't ready for a Devil Daddy," Scythe assured her.

"But I am?"

"You are perfect for one specific Devil Daddy named Scythe."

"And he's perfect for me," Winnie pointed out. "Everyone is heading for lunch. Can I drop you off at your bike and steal a kiss with no one watching?"

"You read my mind, Little girl."

A short time later, Scythe disappeared from her view when he walked into the door of her mom's house to change out of his suit. She'd miss him at lunch, but his MC needed him now.

Winnie pressed her fingers to her lips, hoping no one would know how many kisses she'd exchanged with her Daddy. He really was the best at everything.

The loud sound of Scythe's motorcycle drew everyone's attention when he drove into the district office's parking lot. She didn't like how people made assumptions about him because he didn't drive a fancy car and wear a suit. Those tailored jackets could hide a number of flaws.

Scythe stepped off his bike in an athletic move that reminded her of a prowling cat—coordinated strength in a gorgeous wrapper. Once his helmet came off, several ladies gave him repeated looks. To her delight, Scythe didn't notice them.

She walked next to him into the packed school board meeting. Closely watching the entrance behind them, Abby and Becky waved furiously at them. They threaded their way through the crowd and took the empty seats.

"These parents and staff members get pushy when you're saving seats. They're worse than third graders who always make everyone follow the rules," Becky shared with a smile.

Winnie knew she hadn't minded telling people they couldn't sit there. "So, what's going on? Do you know?"

"Only that Dr. Young's name is gone from the website," Abby whispered.

An older woman in front of them obviously overheard and turned around to add, "And the spot for one of the principals at an elementary school is blank as well. It was all over the news tonight. I only caught part of it—something about missing degrees?"

The three teachers exchanged glances and simultaneously grabbed their phones to search. Becky found the listing first. "It's our school! Lorraine is gone."

As Winnie stared at her friends, trying to control her delight from the crowd of employees and parents, the gossiping woman in front of them said, "Yes, that was the name they mentioned. Lorraine Oberson. Do you think they were having an affair too?" the older woman suggested.

"Surely not. He's old enough to be her father," Winnie said aghast. Scythe chuckled next to her. She studied his face. Did he know something or was he laughing at her? "I mean, that happens, but surely not."

"The board is coming in. Let's see what they say," Abby whispered, and they straightened in their seats to listen.

Winnie crossed her fingers. *Please let this be true.* Scythe patted her hand, and she turned her wrist to link her fingers with his. He shifted his thumb over her skin back and forth slightly as if to tell her he was wishing Lorraine was gone as well.

The president of the school board, Edwin Finney, looked around the crowded room as the secretary conducted the roll call. The position of superintendent was announced, and no one answered before she continued. A murmur went through the room, and Mr. Finney called for order. The crowd hushed as she finished the preliminary board opening activities.

Edwin Finney scanned the assembly. "I wish we had this kind of attendance at every board meeting. Thank you for being concerned about the Jefferson School District. As many of you have noted, Dr. Adam Young resigned from his position as the superintendent of our district earlier today. I am limited in how much I can share by the district lawyers."

The crowd reacted with furious whispers, and the sound level rose. Winnie heard a number of guesses why Dr. Young had left. They ranged from the affair theory to wild accusations of illegal acts.

"Did he rob the district?" an angry voice called from the crowd as Mr. Finney attempted to regain control.

"No. There are no allegations or suspicions of financial wrongdoing on the part of the superintendent. Our financial officer can attest to that." He turned to a young man next to him, who stated simply that the books were in order and Dr. Young had taken nothing inappropriate from the accounts.

"Was he having an affair with the principal of East Elementary?" asked the woman in front of them. "She's gone too."

"I'm afraid you've gotten ahead of me. Lorraine Oberson of East Elementary was removed from her position when the board received documentation that she did not meet the mandatory qualifications to be an administrator," Mr. Finney explained.

"What does that mean?" a woman called.

"She did not possess a verifiable college degree." Mr. Finney pulled out his handkerchief and wiped his brow. He appeared extremely uncomfortable. She felt sorry for him.

A familiar figure stood in the front row. Winnie's breath caught in her chest as she recognized her union representative. "What happens to the negative reports she invented about the great teachers at East Elementary?"

"Any reports created by an individual without proper credentials and training background will be removed and destroyed, along with the apologies from the board. I owe you a personal apology, Elizabeth. I did not listen to you when you approached me with serious concerns. That will not happen in the future." Mr. Finney met Elizabeth McGower's gaze directly, and she nodded.

Bless her. Elizabeth had gone all the way to the school board to try to save her. Winnie sent her gratitude and planned to thank her in private.

"Why did these two lose their jobs on the same day? Are they connected in some way?" a woman called, interrupting the silent communication.

"I am not at liberty to discuss that. I can assure you the district has already started the process of locating a new visionary superintendent and a skilled elementary principal," Mr. Finney stated before changing the subject. "We'll move next to the second item on our agenda, the selection of a new library media system. I will recess for five minutes to allow anyone in the audience to leave quietly after hearing the announcements."

Immediately, people streamed out of the gathering area, eager to gossip outside the meeting. A few tried to approach the board, but a security guard prevented them from passing the decorative barrier dividing the board from the on-lookers. When Becky and Abby stood, Winnie joined them. She and Scythe retraced their way out to the parking lot. Pockets of people stood around outside discussing the announcements.

"You need to go home, Chipmunk. You're dead on your feet. It's time for you to rest," Scythe told her.

Scythe took her keys from her hand and unlocked her car. "Are you okay to drive?"

"I'll make it. Can I follow you, so I don't have to stop at the gate?"

"Of course. The guards have treated you well, haven't they?" he asked in a pointed tone.

"Yes. They're wonderful. I'm just peopled out," she explained.

"Gotcha. Climb in and buckle your seat belt. Wait for me."

"Always, Daddy," she whispered.

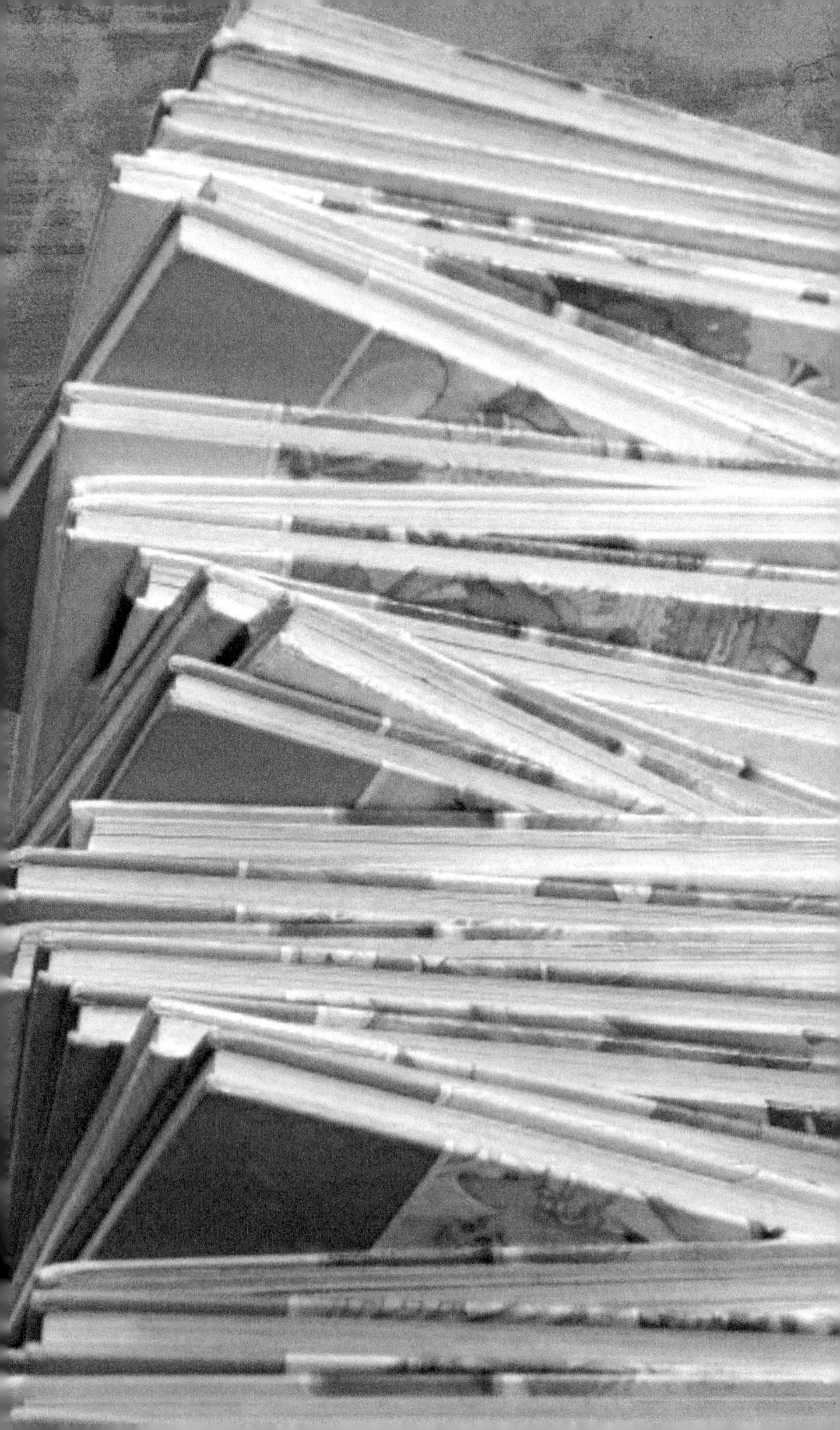

CHAPTER 24

Poor Little girl. She'd exhausted the last of her energy, driving home. He'd helped her shower and brush her teeth before tucking her under the covers. Winnie held out until she had Chippy and her blanket in her arms and he'd read two pages of a bedtime story. Her sniffly snores charmed Scythe.

How did I get so lucky?

Some of her clothing already hung in the closet. They'd go this weekend and pack the rest of her things. She needed to have one place to settle into, and that would be with him.

Tearing himself away, Scythe made the rounds of his home to ensure he'd locked the house for the night. As he reached the front door, his phone buzzed with an incoming message.

In your driveway.

Scythe had heard the motorcycle engine while he was in the kitchen but had dismissed it. Rumbles around here came with the territory. He opened the door and discovered Lucien standing by his bike. Immediately, he joined the MC president. Other members also appeared from their cabins.

"What's up?" Scythe asked when everyone had assembled.

"The Ravagers are threatening vengeance on our club," Lucien shared.

"What's different today than their approach before?" Wraith asked.

"The arrest of three of their members for smuggling seems to be the motivation," Lucien said with a smirk.

"You mean they actually went to the airport, even with the sirens and flashing lights?" Scythe asked, shaking his head in disbelief.

"They had the idea of arriving early as well, it turns out. You must have scattered minutes before they showed up. At least the first three," Lucien guessed.

"Did they get away with any of the ammo?" Razor asked.

"I don't know. It's possible, but the timing would have been incredibly tight for more Ravagers to have arrived, loaded their bikes, and taken off as the cops approached. How long after you left did you hear the sirens?" Lucien asked.

"My group was the last out. Maybe ten minutes?" Scythe guessed.

The entire group shook their heads. Their success could have come with the price of a shootout with the Ravagers. The Devil Daddies didn't shy away from anything. They would have beaten the other MC's ass. The close call made the seizure of the ammo glorious.

"All hail the Devil Daddies," Lucien said with a rare smile of satisfaction.

"Devil Daddies!" the MC replied.

Scythe celebrated with his brothers. They'd just struck a significant blow to the Ravagers. Amidst the backslapping and congratulations exchanged, Scythe caught sight of a sleep-rumpled blonde wrapped in a blanket, standing in the cabin doorway across the street. He nudged Wraith. "Caroline's searching for you."

Scythe turned to check his entrance and spotted gray material poking through his barely open door. Without saying anything to the group, he walked to the cutie who waited for him. Winnie retreated to allow him to enter.

"Daddy? What's the celebration for?"

"Just some good news, Chipmunk. I think you're supposed to be in bed," he said, looking at her sternly.

"Chippy woke me up and told me I was missing a party." Winnie rushed to explain.

"I'm sorry we were loud, Little girl. Let's get you tucked under the covers."

"You never told me why you joined the Devil Daddies," she said.

"It's late and that's a long story."

"I really want to know, Daddy."

He sighed and nodded. Scythe hugged her close and explained, "I've told you that I came to town when my mom lost the family farm. The Ravagers decided to target a young country guy in an old pickup. They beat me badly and only stopped when Lucien and the MC intervened."

"I hate them," Winnie said. Her sweet face hardened with anger.

In all the targeting of her employers, Scythe had never seen his Little girl look ready to kick someone's ass. The fact she reacted in his defense told him how much she cared. He smoothed the hair from Winnie's face and kissed her lightly to soothe her.

"I do too. I healed. The other chickens I had brought with me didn't. It was stupid for me to think they'd be safer with me than with the new owners."

"Sweet. Not stupid. And you still have Patches and Fluff."

"Yes," he confirmed with a smile.

"That's why Lucien offered you a job," she guessed.

"Yes. I didn't join the Devil Daddies until I checked them out," Scythe said. "I didn't want to be part of the MC only because I wanted vengeance on the Ravagers. There needed to be a stronger reason."

"And you found they were Daddies, too."

"Yes. Now it's really time for my Little girl to be in bed."

"Would you join me?" she asked, rubbing her free hand over his chest.

"I don't want to be anywhere else."

Scythe locked the front door and scooped his Little girl up in his arms. Carrying her to the dimly lit bedroom, he set her feet on the floor next to the bed. "Do you need to potty?"

She nodded shyly.

"Go, Chipmunk. I'll get undressed."

"Oh!" she blurted. "Could you wait until I get back?"

"You bet. Go."

Scythe stepped out of his boots and pulled off his socks. As far as he knew, she didn't have a foot fetish and needed him to remove those while she watched. He grinned at the thought that if she did, he'd never wear shoes again.

"Daddy! I'm here," Winnie said, scrambling into bed and propping herself up on the pillows.

Turning to face her, Scythe reached over his shoulder and grabbed a handful of material to draw his T-shirt over his head. Her quick intake of breath made all those bales of hay he'd moved as a kid to create his base of strength totally worthwhile.

Tossing that material away, he reached for his buckle and unfastened it. He slowly drew the leather strip out of the loops of his faded jeans and paused in rolling it up to whack the tail over his palm. Winnie pulled the covers up to her eyes, and he knew she was imagining being spanked with his belt. His cock responded rapidly to the image that appeared in his mind.

"Have you been good, Little girl?" he asked.

She nodded vigorously.

He set the coil on the dresser and walked to the edge of the bed. "Want to help Daddy with his pants, since you've behaved so well?"

"Can I get a good girl sticker on my chart?" she asked as she tossed the covers to the foot of the bed and rose to her knees in front of him.

"I think you'd definitely earn at least one sticker."

She reached eagerly to unbutton his jeans. Her fingers brushed the burgeoning head of his cock as she dipped inside the waistband. "Oh!"

"Careful, baby. Daddy's shaft is sensitive and very eager to play."

Nodding, she tugged the material away from his erection and eased the zipper down. Scythe pushed the material over his hips and down to his feet. He stomped on the material as he stepped out of it.

Her gaze fixed on his dick. He stifled a groan at the almost physical sensation of her devouring him with her eyes. Wrapping a hand around himself, he pulled his grip from base to tip. She leaned forward to taste the small drop of pre-cum that appeared.

"Little girl," he forced himself to say sternly. "Do you have permission to kiss Daddy's cock?"

She shook her head, not moving her focus from his shaft. "Please, Daddy. Can I play with your cock?"

His erection jerked in his hand at the sweet request. He wouldn't miss this for anything. "Yes, Chipmunk. You have Daddy's permission."

Immediately, she settled on her tummy and licked over the head like he was her favorite ice cream cone. Scythe widened his stance to steady himself as sensations flowed over him. Her innocent technique enchanted him.

He wrapped his hand around the back of her head, guiding her gently. Winnie responded immediately and met his gaze, happiness radiating from her eyes. She opened her lips, drawing him inside. The wet heat of her mouth felt like heaven as she swallowed him.

Scythe contained his urge to thrust fully into her mouth and tightened his fingers in her hair to keep her from taking him too deep. He wanted to make this first time easy on her. "Damn, Little girl. Your mouth feels like heaven. Suck me," he suggested and groaned as she followed his instruction.

Time seemed to freeze as she eagerly pleased him. Her small sounds of enjoyment pushed his arousal higher and higher. When Winnie reached a hand out to cup his balls, he moaned at her gentle touch as she brushed her fingers over the sensitive orbs. *Nothing could be better than this.* Then she tugged his sac. His eyes crossed as he struggled to keep himself from filling her throat.

"So good, Winnie. You are making it hard for Daddy to stay in control. When I tell you, pull back. I'm going to come soon."

She released him to shake her head. "I want to taste you, Daddy." Without allowing him to respond, Winnie returned to her tempting caresses. When she gripped the base of his shaft and increased the suction to an irresistible level, Scythe roared his pleasure into the room. His hot cum rushed through his shaft.

Winnie swallowed quickly, and he groaned at the sensation of her muscles contracting around him. Scythe watched her with pride. "You're so beautiful, Winnie. The best Little girl a Daddy could hope for." He wiped away the rivulets of liquid that escaped from the corners of her lips. When he couldn't take any more, Scythe drew his cock from her mouth.

Lifting her, he turned her to rest her head on the pillows. He joined her, forcing his shaky legs to function. Gathering her close, he pulled his Little girl against his chest. Scythe kissed her deeply, tasting himself on her lips.

"So good, Little girl," he whispered, brushing her hair from her face.

"Sticker, Daddy?" she asked with a sleepy wink.

"Yes, Chipmunk. Daddy will get special stickers to go on your chart. Close your eyes, Winnie. It's past your bedtime."

She nodded. Within minutes, she slept in his arms. Scythe studied her sweet face. He'd never imagined he could love anyone as much as he did this adorable woman. Forcing himself to stop planning for the future, Scythe drifted into sleep.

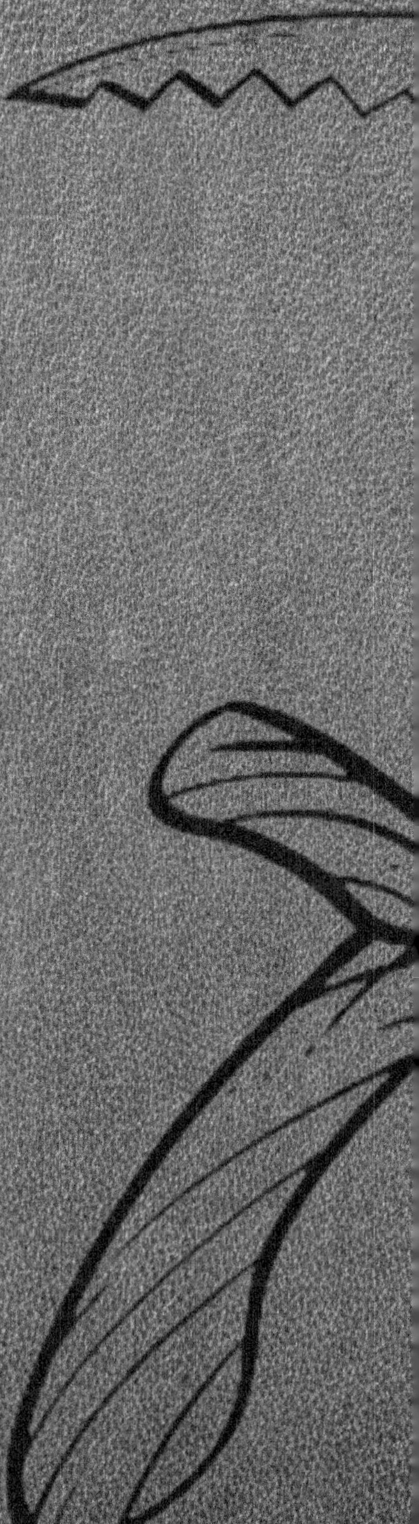

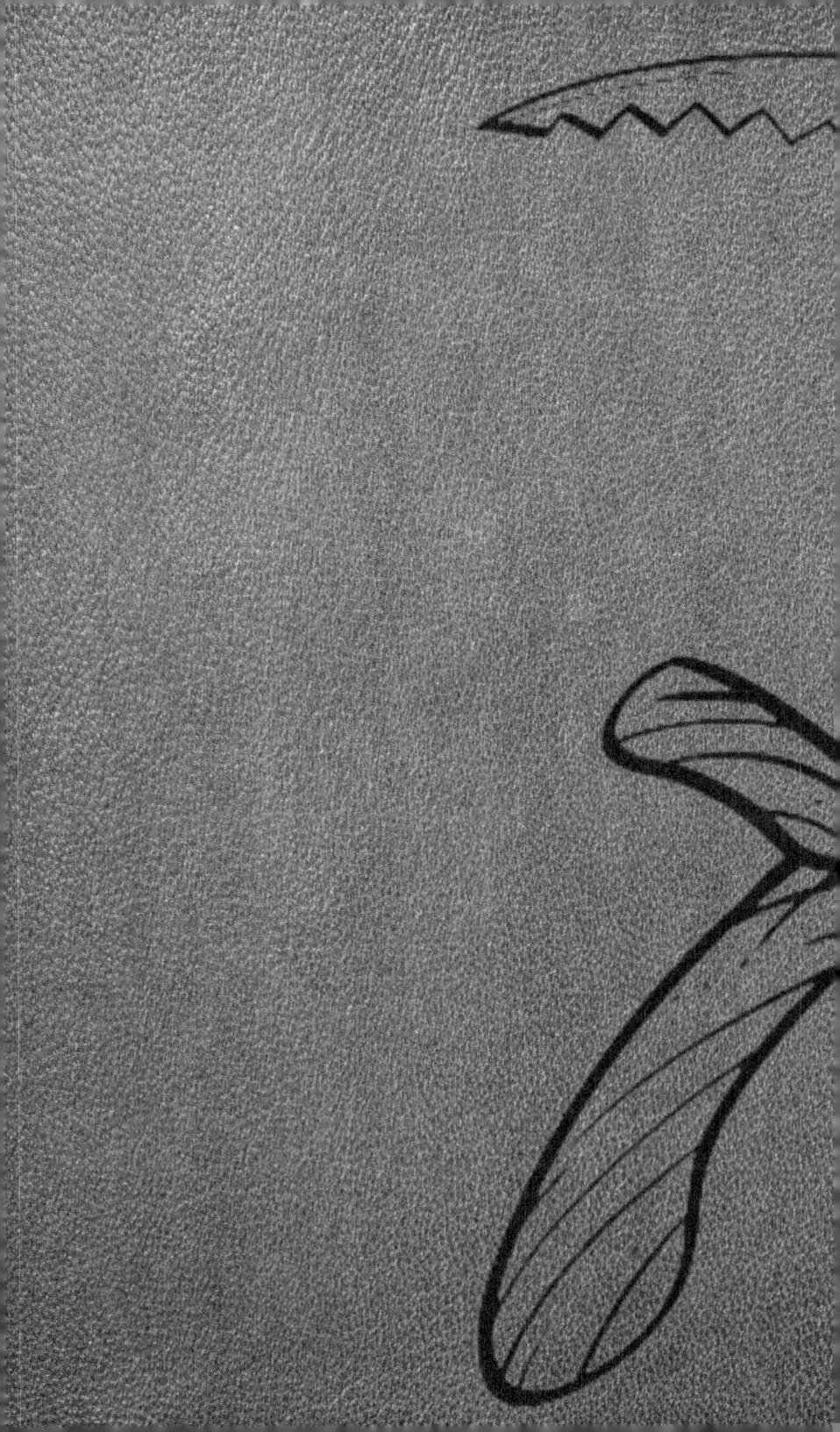

CHAPTER 25

After emptying the last of her things from her mother's house, Scythe shut the truck he'd borrowed from the warehouse. He turned to see Winnie and Belinda talking on the front porch. Scythe waited to see what would come of the exchange. To his surprise, Belinda hugged Winnie, and the two women rocked back and forth together for a long moment.

Winnie bounced down the stairs a few minutes later. "Belinda's ready to put the house up for sale. She's going to move into an apartment closer to work."

"That will make settling your mom's estate easier," Scythe suggested as he guided her into the passenger seat.

"Definitely. I didn't expect her to be so reasonable, but she's realized the house is too big for her alone."

"Good for Belinda." Scythe clicked her seatbelt into place and stepped back to close the door.

A minute later, they were on their way. Winnie didn't turn toward her mother's house but focused on the path in front of her. She was healing. He hoped he'd helped with that.

"I love you, Daddy. Thank you for always being there for me," Winnie told him.

"I love you, Winnie. More than I thought was possible. You know I'm never letting you go." He wrapped his hand around her thigh and gently squeezed.

"I'm counting on that," she assured him, setting her hand over his. "Can we go to Inferno to celebrate?"

"Celebrate your move?" he asked.

"My move, our love, my job being secure, Becky being chosen as the new principal.... After her maternity leave of course! The faculty is so excited. She's such a positive force. We need that after Lorraine."

"East Elementary is going to be a different place, for sure. I think a party at Inferno is definitely in order."

When they pulled into the Devil Daddies' complex, they discovered a crew of men ready to help unload the truck. They finished in a half hour to Winnie's amazement.

"Thank you all so much. We're going to party at Inferno," she said excitedly, going from biker to biker to hug them. Winnie couldn't believe they'd scared her in the beginning. Living with Scythe was like having a bunch of protective older brothers.

Scythe pulled her away from her task and held her hand. "Enough hugs," he told her firmly as the other guys grinned at his possessiveness. Scythe ushered Winnie into the house. One of his brothers would return the truck for him.

"Come on, Daddy. I need to find something to wear that's not too churchy," she said, making air quotes around those last two words as she rushed down the hallway. His incredulous look made her giggle. "Of course I knew what everyone said. That's why I showed up in Belinda's club dress. Maybe if I wore my tightest jeans and cut a T-shirt off halfway. Do you think that would blend in?" she asked as they entered the bedroom.

Winnie's gaze landed on the beautiful dress spread over the comforter. "Is that for me?"

"I probably couldn't fit in that pretty frock. Shall we see if it's your size?" he asked.

"I need to shower first. I can't put that dress on all sweaty from moving!" She pulled her T-shirt over her head and rushed to remove everything else.

Scythe followed her into the shower, but even his hotness couldn't distract her… for long.

Wraith and Caroline manned the door, just like they had when Winnie first made it into Inferno. At her first sight of Winnie, Caroline jumped from the stool, clapping her hands in excitement. "You're beautiful, Winnie. I love your dress!"

"Da… I mean Scythe bought it for me to celebrate! Look how it swirls," Winnie exclaimed and turned in a tight circle, flaring the material out to reveal the shorts Scythe had made her put on when he discovered how high it rose.

"I want a dress like that!" Caroline said, sending a sideway glance at Wraith.

"We could be twinsies!" Winnie said, bouncing up and down in place with her friend. "Da… Darn it. Scythe, could you tell Wraith where you found it?"

"I can do that, Chipmunk. Now, we're clogging the doorway. Let's move out of Wraith and Caroline's way and go get a drink."

"A strawberry margarita?" she suggested.

"If that's what you want," Scythe agreed and wrapped an arm around her waist to steer her away.

Behind them, Caroline shared how good a strawberry margarita sounded. She smiled over her shoulder and mouthed, "I'll bring you one."

Caroline nodded eagerly and answered, "Thank you!"

When Winnie turned back around, she lost her balance and wobbled to the side. She hit a solid mass with a thump. "Whoa! Oh, Razor. I'm sorry."

Scythe had steadied her immediately. "Sorry, Winnie. I didn't think you'd head in that direction."

"I was hoping to run into you," the Devil Daddies' doctor told her. "How are you feeling? Is that medicine working?"

Winnie's face heated four hundred degrees. She had to be blushing furiously. Nodding, she pressed her hands to her cheeks.

Razor leaned close and whispered, "No one else knows what kind of medicine I prescribed."

"Oh! Thank goodness." Winnie recovered quickly.

"Are you going to the bar?" Razor asked.

"A strawberry margarita is calling her name," Scythe answered.

"Two, please," Winnie said quickly.

"Two?" Scythe answered.

"I promised I'd take Caroline one."

"You're a good friend," Razor observed. "Have fun. You look beautiful in that dress, by the way."

"Thank you, Razor." Over his shoulder, Winnie saw a woman stumble and fall to the floor. "Oh, no! She just fell."

Razor turned and headed that direction immediately with Winnie and Scythe on his heels. The doctor knelt by the woman's side.

"Hey, are you okay? I'm a doctor."

"Oh, I'm fine. I've always been a klutz. If you'd help me up, I'd appreciate it," the woman said with smiling lips that trembled slightly.

Something in the back of her mind alerted Winnie the woman hadn't simply tripped accidentally. She seemed shaky. Winnie squeezed her Daddy's hand, making sure he saw it too.

"Of course," Razor told her and lifted her easily to her feet. His hands remained around her waist while she regained her balance. It seemed to take a bit longer than expected. Razor's eyebrows drew together in concern. "How about if you sit and rest for a bit?"

"I was going to that table. The stools are too... high for me to be comfortable," the woman said and noticed another group had settled into that table. "Oh, I missed that one."

Razor glanced at the young men gathered at the closest booth. "Go sit somewhere else."

They spotted his and Scythe's cuts and scurried away with their beers.

"Let's sit here." Razor guided her to the booth and helped her slide onto the bench seat.

When she was settled, Razor sat on the other side. He met Scythe's gaze. "I'll stay with...."

"Honey," the woman supplied with a tired smile. "Sorry. I should have stayed at home tonight and waited until I had more energy."

"Nonsense. Make the most of every day," Razor told her.

Her lips spread into a grin like she was delighted he understood. "That's exactly why I came."

Razor turned to Winnie and Scythe. "Go get those strawberry margaritas. I'll stay here and keep Honey company while she catches her breath."

Scythe immediately nodded and guided Winnie toward the bar. "Let's leave them alone, Chipmunk," he whispered in her ear. "Razor's got this."

Winnie allowed him to steer her toward the bar. What was going on? She got the impression it was important.

The deep pink margarita in her hand distracted her from checking on the couple. "This is yummy!"

The bartender gave her a happy thumbs-up as she handed Scythe another fruity concoction and two bottles of beer. "Enjoy!"

When she remembered to look back at the booth after enjoying the drink with Caroline, a different group sat there. With the slight buzz of tequila in her tummy, Winnie swayed to the music. She glanced at Scythe. Did he dance?

"Do you know how to two-step?" he asked, plucking the empty glass from her hand and setting it on a server's tray.

"Teach me."

"Anything and everything, Little girl. Let's go," Scythe said.

A few minutes later, he swept her around the floor. Her dress turned out to be the perfect two-step garment. His hand on her waist steadied her when she missed a step, or a hundred. The smile on his face enchanted her. Thank goodness she'd borrowed Belinda's dress and had gotten into Inferno.

Walking into Inferno that first time, Winnie had felt like a fish out of water. Now, it welcomed her. Her whole life had changed. She'd gained a skilled lover and the best Daddy ever. She shot Scythe a speculative glance, wondering if he or Lucien had alerted the news and convinced her bosses to leave.

"Stop thinking and enjoy, Chipmunk," Scythe whispered into her ear before lifting her from the ground and whirling in a circle. He kissed her hard.

When he lifted his head, she whispered back, "Yes, Daddy."

Thank you for reading Scythe: Devil Daddies 2!

Don't miss future sweet and steamy Daddy stories by Pepper North? Subscribe to my newsletter!

Get ready for the next story in the Devil Daddies MC series: Razor: Devil Daddies MC 3!

If you think you're teetering on the edge, you haven't met Razor.

Razor knows too much about everything. With all the information rattling around in his brain, it's no wonder he's the MCs doctor and shrink. When he suspects something is wrong with an Inferno regular, he has to intercede. Why is she risking so much by failing to act?

Honey Rhoades loves Inferno. It's the one place she can go to get away from it all. Stress, a crappy car, and the worst job ever can make a woman stumble through life, right? At least here, she can sit pretty and flirt with hot bikers, even if she also gets bossed around by the one with Doctor Daddy vibes.

The members of the Devil Daddies MC will risk all to secure two things: special acquisitions and women with a Little side.

Available from your favorite bookseller!
Preorder yours TODAY!

Read more from Pepper North

Devil Daddies

The members of the Devil Daddies MC will risk all to secure two things: special acquisitions and women with a Little side.ly guard his mate from harm.

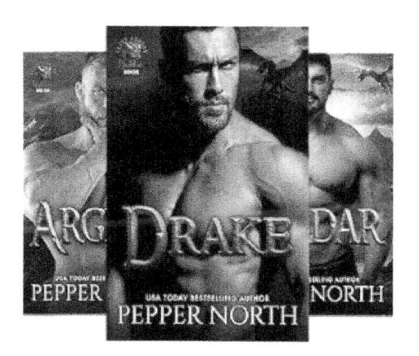

Fated Dragon Daddies

Change is coming to Wyvern.
A centuries-old pact between the founders and their powerful allies could save the inhabitants of the city once again, but only a dragon Daddy can truly guard his mate from harm.

Shadowridge Guardians

Combining the sizzling talents of bestselling authors Pepper North, Kate Oliver, and Becca Jameson, the Shadowridge Guardians are guaranteed to give you a thrill and leave you dreaming of your own throbbing motorcycle joyride.

Are you daring enough to ride with a club of rough, growly, commanding men? The protective Daddies of the Shadowridge Guardians Motorcycle Club will stop at nothing to ensure the safety and protection of everything that belongs to them: their Littles, their club, and their town. Throw in some sassy, naughty, mischievous women who won't hesitate to serve their fair share of attitude even in the face of looming danger, and this brand new MC Romance series is ready to ignite!

Danger Bluff

Welcome to Danger Bluff where a mysterious billionaire brings together a hand-selected team of men at an abandoned resort in New Zealand. They each owe him a marker. And they all have something in common–a dominant shared code to nurture and protect. They will repay their debts one by one, finding love along the way.

A Second Chance For Mr. Right

For some, there is a second chance at having Mr. Right. Coulda, Shoulda, Woulda explores a world of connections that can't exist... until they do. Forbidden love abounds when these Daddy Doms refuse to live with regret and claim the women who own their hearts.

Little Cakes

Welcome to Little Cakes, the bakery that plays Daddy matchmaker! Little Cakes is a sweet and satisfying series, but dare to taste only if you like delicious Daddies, luscious Littles, and guaranteed happily-ever-afters.

Dr. Richards' Littles®

A beloved age play series that features Littles who find their forever Daddies and Mommies. Dr. Richards guides and supports their efforts to keep their Littles happy and healthy.

Note: Zoey; Dr. Richards' Littles® 1 is available FREE on Pepper's website:
4PepperNorth.club

Dr. Richards' Littles®
is a registered trademark of
With A Wink Publishing, LLC.
All rights reserved.

SANCTUM

Pepper North introduces you to an age play community that is isolated from the surrounding world. Here Littles can be Little, and Daddies can care for their Littles and keep them protected from the outside world.

Soldier Daddies

What private mission are these elite soldiers undertaking? They're all searching for their perfect Little girl.

The Keepers

This series from Pepper North is a twist on contemporary age play romances. Here are the stories of humans cared for by specially selected Keepers of an alien race. These are science fiction novels that age play readers will love!

The Magic of Twelve

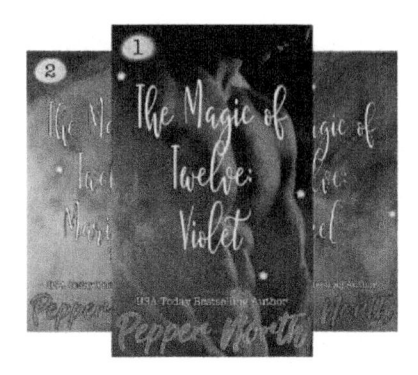

The Magic of Twelve features the stories of twelve women transported on their 22nd birthday to a new life as the droblin (cherished Little one) of a Sorcerer of Bairn. These magic wielders have waited a long time to take complete care of their droblin's needs. They will protect their precious one to their last drop of magic from a growing menace. Each novel is a complete story.

Ever just gone for it? That's what *USA Today* Bestselling Author Pepper North did in 2017 when she posted a book for sale on Amazon without telling anyone. Thanks to her amazing fans, the support of the writing community, Mr. North, and a killer schedule, she has now written more than 180 books!
Enjoy contemporary, paranormal, dark, and erotic romances that are both sweet and steamy? Pepper will convert you into one of her loyal readers. What's coming in the future? A Daddypalooza!

Sign up for Pepper North's newsletter

Like Pepper North on Facebook

Join Pepper's Readers' Group for insider information and giveaways!

Follow Pepper everywhere!

Amazon Author Page
BookBub
FaceBook
GoodReads
Instagram
TikToc
Twitter
YouTube
Visit Pepper's website for a current checklist of books!

Printed in Dunstable, United Kingdom